CODE NAME: WHITE MUSTANG

By

M.L. VERNE

APR / 2003

© 1997, 2002 by M. L. Verne.
All rights reserved.

No part of this book may be reproduced, stored in a retrieval system, or transmitted by any means, electronic, mechanical, photocopying, recording, or otherwise, without written permission from the author.

ISBN: 1-4033-2710-6 (e-book)
ISBN: 1-4033-2711-4 (Paperback)

This book is printed on acid free paper.

1stBooks – rev. 10/10/02

For My Children

"The spirituality of siblings
requires the supreme ability
to live with differences
in forgiveness and trust."

Peter Pitzele
Our Fathers Wells

This novel is loosely based
on actual events.
Some names, places and incidents
are composites,
the rest are by-products
of the author's imagination.

NOT EVEN GOD CAN CHANGE THE PAST
Agathon

There is a military tradition which
speaks of certain individuals
who have advanced from enlisted to
officer rank
with dispatch, in effect
out-distancing their colleagues
in a spectacular manner.
Such persons are called
"Mustangs".

ACKNOWLEDGEMENTS

My gratitude to the United States Navy for allowing me access to information vital in the writing
of some portions of this book.

To the reporters, editors and publishers of the news media quoted herein, thank you.

To my brother Bob for his patience, diligence, professional assistance and encouragement as well as his criticisms,
Merci Beaucoup.

For the times my husband
offered technical suggestions
that worked perfectly,
what a guy!

I am indebted to my friend Dee for her sound advice, insight and integrity.

To my very own "deep throat" without whom this story could not have been told,
I love you!

There are others…Mar, Bud, Bev, Lyle, Verna, Gilbert and the rest of you who have
remained true to your word of honor
and who are, even now,
non-judgmental; you know who you are.
I treasure your friendships.

Finally my Jimmy who was,
and probably always will
be, of inestimable
help. More than he will
ever know. Thank
you for being there!

SYNOPSIS

A Navy Chief Petty Officer (CPO) who has gotten involved with Nigerian nationals, the Turkish government, the Italian Mafia and the drug trade in and around southern Europe will, eventually, say and think *"IF ONLY"*, thus over-working his personal hindsight and his profound regrets.

But meanwhile, because he is on the Admiral's staff, he has a great deal of knowledge concerning classified procedures and top secret information, not to mention problems within his military unit. As senior non-commissioned officer, he tries to warn his superiors with what he has learned about drug trafficking inside the ranks. Initially he is strung along, ultimately ignored.

Due to extenuating circumstances, in time his outstanding Navy career ends. He is court-martialed and imprisoned following a swift and thorough debriefing. All of these events are in motion in conjunction with an investigation that the Naval Criminal Investigation Service (NCIS) has undertaken with the approval of the Chief of Naval Operations.(CNO)

The reports regarding findings being uncovered during the investigation which come across the desk of the CNO are more than he can assimilate or contend with, given his life-long commitment to the Navy and the men and women under his command. When his life ends tragically, the world is told it was a clear case of suicide. The reasons given are unacceptable to clear-thinking Americans. Many wonder if there might be a hidden, more sinister cause behind such a grievous event.

CODE NAME: WHITE MUSTANG

1.

It was one of those effervescent days, the brilliant sun shining on the water, enhancing the zillions of sparkling diamonds that shimmered and danced about like grinning fairies. The salt-laden breeze carried a touch of cool to the sailors' sweaty bodies, fanning their faces gently as they labored at their assignments aboard their ship in the Persian Gulf.

High above the main deck, Mikel J. Steele, always called Chief, was at ease, at home and at work.

"Blue Scorpion Zero-One-Zero? This is Juliet Three tower radio check. Over?"

"Juliet Three tower, this is Blue Scorpion. Aaaahhhh, roger that. Read you loud and clear. Over?"

"Blue Scorpion, this is Juliet Three tower. I have assumed control of safety of flight. Advise when ready to copy numbers. Over?"

Mike was supremely confident in his role as the only enlisted man in the Navy, up to that time, authorized to work as a helicopter control officer aboard a ship at sea in time of war. Or so he'd been told.

"Blue Scorpion, this is Juliet Three tower. I have you visual off my port quarter. Range one-half mile. You have a green deck for a clear deck landing. Over?"

"Aaaahhhh, roger that. Inbound at this time. Out."

As he watched the SH-60 chopper land, Mike was thinking that soon the ship would be homeward bound, having now been underway for the obligatory six month cruise. All hands were joyfully anticipating the warmth and comfort of their homecoming, always a cheery and loving celebration. Mike sighed, blinking a lone tear from his eyes, sensing that time was spinning away from him when, suddenly, he was checking out a huge crowd below on the pier. Quickly, he moved to the 'big eyes' nearby and began scanning the faces, looking for his wife and sons. The shifting, shouting, flag-waving mass of humanity was, as always, the most welcome sight any sailor could ask for, the epitome of love, loyalty and courage.

"Oh, my lord, there they are!" Mike was beside himself, smiling like a fool, not caring who saw him. There she stood, his Althea, who he called Teea, her long black hair with the deep red high- lights waving about in the wind as if to signal him how much she had missed him, how happy she was that he was home again. He ran his fingers through that hair at every opportunity. It was a sensual experience for him, the feel of its texture, the fragrance like freshly picked, sweetly scented spring flowers. Standing next to her and jumping up and down, punching each other playfully, were their twin sons Jason and Joel. Ten years old and already so handsome it made Mike's heart swell with pride. They had been told the boys were fraternal. Actually, their parents believed they were a phenomenon. One had dark brown eyes like Teea, the other dark blue eyes like Mike. Otherwise, they looked identical.

"I must get down to them as quickly as I can" he told himself as he began descending the gang-plank, reaching for them as he went. He almost tumbled to his knees in his haste, grabbing for support while managing to keep his eyes glued on their faces when, in a flash, he realized they were receding from his sight. He felt a cold rush of anxiety as he propelled his body forward, racing at top speed, trying to reach them before they vanished.

"Wait!" he was screaming. "Wait! It's me! Wait!"

They ignored him as though some unknown force held them captive in a net. He continued to race toward them, beginning to panic.

'It must be the noise of the crowd keeping them from hearing me,' he told his anxious mind. He hyperventilated, was sweating profusely, then reluctantly admitted, 'It ain't gonna' happen.'

It took all of his waning strength to keep from falling under the press of the mob where, he knew, he could be trampled underfoot.

Then, without warning, up on deck sailors began shouting, bells began clanging and Mike heard "GENERAL QUARTERS!" over and over again. He jumped, ran, felt as if he were swimming through a sea of karo syrup, was getting nowhere and thought, 'I must get to my G.Q. station. There's no time to lose.' Abruptly, he fell on his face and pain shot through his lower back when he tried to stand. He opened his eyes wide and saw that he was on the floor of his bedroom just beyond the foot of his bed.

Stunned, gathering his thoughts, orienting himself, he came to realize, to understand, he had been having a hideous nightmare. Before reality could take hold of him he fought it off, not wanting to deal with the pain he instinctively knew was waiting. His mind closed down and out. He drifted into a kind of limbo where it was dark, warm, comforting and free of any thoughts.

2.

The dark corridors of his mind were reverberating with unrelenting noises originating in an unseen, echoing void. It was a throbbing that was both frightening and painful. Inevitably, it intruded into his subconscious state. As he began to merge with wakefulness, to acknowledge the racket, to question what it might be, it stopped. He was left with a heavy silence into which a sense of pulsing undulated like the winds of an approaching storm. He opted for oblivion, dragging his bedclothes with him, becoming cocoon-like within the softness of his surroundings. As he drifted away he thought 'Will these grotesque dreams ever stop? What is to become of me?'

He reached for nothingness to envelop him, to release him, to give him a small measure of peace.

Time slid by. Again the noise violated his rest. This time, he was closer to an awakened, alert condition. Thus, he was able to identify a ringing telephone. Knowing at last what it was did not relieve the banging in his head. As he struggled, throwing sheets and blankets aside, trying to get his aching body upright, he heard himself groan. It startled him fully awake.

'Where did that come from?' he asked himself.

He had a fleeting vision of having been deposited on some foreign, forgotten, mist-shrouded island, a fog horn vibrating in the shadowy gloom.

'Ridiculous idea,' he admitted, knowing full well he had made the noise himself. He tried to open his eyes but they were sticky and he had no luck. Still, somehow, he was able to grab for the offending instrument, yanking it with such force that the table, the phone and some books went crashing to the floor. The ensuing clatter caused his eyes to fly open after all. He uttered another torturous moan and in that instant spied the bottle lying at the edge of his desk across the room. The label was visible, the neck seeming to point an accusing finger at him saying 'Oh yes! You *DID* drink the whole thing!'

Peach vodka. Unbelievable. His mind refused to remember.

Carefully, he put the listening end of the phone against his ear and mumbled "Hello...."

Nothing. No one. All he discerned was the vulgar, buzzing sound of a uniquely European dial tone. He sent a silent thanks heavenward and got to his feet slowly, carefully, desperately needing to get to the 'head' and relieve himself. Hopefully, he would find something for his physical pain while he was in there. His skull felt as if it were ready to tumble off his shoulders.

Once he was up and moving, he imagined he felt a little better. Five seconds ago, he wouldn't have given himself a chance in hell of ever again taking a single step. Staggering, leaning on the wall as he went, blinking to keep his eyes in focus, he got to the toilet, peed and turned to the sink. His intention was to grab hold, stabilize his tremors, then check himself out in the mirror to be sure he really *was* awake this time. He'd had enough of nightmares.

On any ordinary day, his mirrored image would be that of a well-proportioned, muscular sailor who was average in height and weight, proud of his clean-cut American looks, his physique acquired and kept through hard work with barbells, exercising and good eating habits. In a movie star sense, he wasn't handsome but there was a look, an aura about him that caused women to turn, in passing, for a second glance, perhaps a wishful thought. His eyes, a clear, sparkling deep blue, were usually full of humor and amusement. His hair had been graying prematurely for years, since he was a teenager. He kept it cut short not only to conform to military regulations but also to try and hide the color, having long since become saturated with the gibes. As much as anything else, it was his easy going attitude that had carried him on an escalated ride to early promotions, respect from his peers, his subordinates and the senior officers he worked for and with. His Navy career was on the move, had been from the beginning.

Some months back, at the insistence of his previous Captain, he had applied for acceptance into the program the Navy had created for the advancement of enlisted personnel into officer ranks. This program, called Limited Duty Officer (LDO), would allow Mike to ultimately reach the rank of Captain, all other things being equal.

No one was prouder of his accomplishments than he. His career and his future looked more promising every day.

But on this day, for better or worse, he was in trouble and knew it. Digging deep for courage, he dared to peek into the mirror.

And wished he hadn't!

What a ghastly sight! Hair matted down, eyes red-rimmed and barely focusing, scraggly-looking whiskers of at least two days growth, blotchy, yellow-looking skin, teeth crusted over both on top of and under the braces he was wearing to correct his bite, his smile, the tendency of his jaws to lock up unexpectedly.

"Mike Steele" he snarled at the outrageous image staring back at him, "you've screwed up big time, getting drunk, passing out, losing track of time." For all he knew he was, essentially, AWOL. He had no clue what day it was.

Then, with no warning, it all came back and hit him square in the gut. He doubled over and had to sit down on the rim of the tub. For a moment, he was unable to breathe and wanted to vomit.

They were gone, his wife and boys! They'd left him high and dry. They'd climbed onto a plane and had flown back to the states, leaving him alone in this foreign country. His grief was over- whelming.

Unbidden, the entire scenario replayed itself in his mind's eye. The trip to the airport with Teea staring stonily out the side window saying nothing. The boys in the back seat crying, begging: 'Dad, let us stay. Please Dad, please let us stay, or come with us. Dad?'

It had torn his heart to shreds, listening to them. The unending wait at the airport for the boarding call made him crazy and then, when it finally came, the twins hanging onto his legs for dear life with all of their ten year old strength. Teea had, quite literally, dragged them off of him and across the tarmac. They had disappeared into the belly of the plane as he stood in a fugue, watching them take off, climb, then vanish into the western sky.

It was a cold, hard fact. He'd been abandoned and he didn't know why. Teea hadn't been honest, of that he was certain. But, she had clung to her story and he'd been unable to budge her. Not for one minute did he buy her excuses of the boys being picked on at the playground and the gossipy women in the neighborhood ruining her life. Those were petty things that could have been resolved with a minimal amount of effort. No! There was some- thing else. Would he *ever* be told?

They'd been in Italy only seven months and had arrived there full of happiness and joy because they were going to have three whole years together as a family. It was a rare gift in a Navy career.

Remembering, he lost it. He sat with his head in his hands, elbows on his knees, a few tears dripping through his fingers onto the cold, hard tiles of the floor. He sobbed once, twice, gulped and wept his heart out.

Finally, when he had no more tears, he stumbled blindly back to his bed, fell face down onto the mattress and vowed he would never rise. It was, quite simply, too much for a man to endure.

3.

Again? Yes, again. The damn telephone! Would it *never* stop? He relented and said to himself, 'This time, by God, if no one is there, I'm having it disconnected.' Then, on second thought, he was *absolutely positive* that his boys were calling him. He lifted the receiver, convinced he would hear their cherished voices yelling 'Hi, Dad!'

Instead, across the wires came "Yo, man! What the fuck's goin' on? Been tryin' to reach you all weekend. I was just about to come over there to see if your corpse is stinkin' up the place or some such thing."

Mike was instantly pissed. This was the very last person he needed to be hearing from right now. But, he bit his tongue, held his temper.

"Lenny? Hey, man, I gotta' get some decent sack time. Give me a break, will ya'? I'm feeling like shit. Call me later, man."

"No way, my man. I'm coming over there *now.* You have got to get your act together, man. Tomorrow's a work day. I know what your problem is and it's nothing we can't work out together. No sweat, man. That's what friends are for. I'll see ya' in a few...." and he was gone.

Mike groaned and bitched silently about the rotten turn of events. Lenny was annoying, bothersome, a genuine fourteen carat pest. Quite often, Mike asked himself why he tolerated the guy. Frankly speaking, there was absolutely nothing to be gained by continuing the relationship. So what was the deal? Mike had been unable, so far, to come up with an answer to his own question. Unless he became downright rude. But *that* sort of behavior was beyond Mike's normal practice of decent, courteous conduct.

He lay back down and covered himself with a light throw that his Mom had sent for a Christmas gift. Teea had neglected to take it home with her and Mike was glad. It seemed to give him an extra measure of comfort, something he sorely needed. It sort of warmed both his body and his soul. He tried to fall back to sleep but it wasn't working.

He kept thinking of his family. The longer this continued, the more emotionally painful it became. Finally, he forced himself to think, instead, about Lenny.

Lieutenant Commander Lennard D. Jones was a Navy officer with enormous, ongoing potential. From their earliest days together, Mike was convinced Lenny would be an Admiral before his Navy days ran their normal course. He was a military genius, at the top of every promotion list and destined for immortality. His climb had, so far, excelled even Mike's, which, in and of itself, was spectacular. Both of them, inside their individual spheres of influence, were high achievers.

An image of Lenny's face materialized in Mike's head. Round and smooth, with wide set eyes that appeared to be sleepy but, Mike knew, were well aware of everything going on around him. His nose appeared wider than it really was because of unusually large nostrils. His ears were small and close to his skull and his head was covered with an abundance of coal black, tightly curled hair. He seemed to have a perpetual aura of negativity and cynicism about him which caused people, in general, to keep their distance.

Mike often wondered if Lenny had a personal problem with the fact his skin was the color and gloss of highly polished combat boots.

Lenny was average in size, but inclined to gain weight if he wasn't careful. He'd complained often that he couldn't eat his favorite foods if he expected to look sharp and trim in his uniform. He sported a pencil-thin mustache which he kept groomed to perfection. He strode when he was on the move, rather than walking, and his personal ambiance was full of arrogance that seemed to exude insolence.

He did not tolerate foolish behavior from his subordinates or his equals and readily displayed distaste if such conduct became evident among his superiors. Long since, Mike was convinced that Lenny lacked a sense of humor. Truly, he had not been an easy person to be around and this truism only confused Mike even more.

'Why do I tolerate him?' was a constant question in Mike's mind.

Still, as he thought more about it, he knew if he needed a friend, Lenny was there! As a matter of fact, Lenny and his wife, Cate, had been there for the entire Steele family from the very first day they met. Both families had arrived in Gaeta, Italy during the same week and had all stayed in the same hotel while awaiting the chance to move into more or less permanent homes for the duration of their tours of duty. Mike and his family were without a vehicle, their car somewhere on the Atlantic Ocean in a boat on its way to them, so Cate had made a very generous offer. All of them would drive around the area together, discovering what was available.

Lenny had purchased a wonderful big, black, shiny BMW which had enough room for everyone to ride comfortably when they went on their jaunts.

Almost from the moment they had learned of Lenny's senior rank, Teea had been warning Mike the relationship was to be avoided.

"It's fraternization, Mike," she'd repeated over and over. "It will, in the end, cause more trouble than the companionship is worth. We need to find friends in the enlisted ranks!"

But he had ignored her. Although he knew she was right and he was walking a tight rope, he continued to be drawn by Lenny's magnetism. Rationalizing, he told himself, 'After all, if everything goes the way it should, I'll be an officer myself before too much longer. Then, it will be okay.'

As he lay on his couch thinking all those thoughts, he decided once and for all that he would break off the friendship. There was certainly no substantial reason to continue. Teea had been right all along! How he wished she was there, at his side, so he could tell her. She would grin her dimpled smile, feel justified in having harped loud and long about Lenny, his shortcomings, his Navy rank.

"Maybe" he nodded, "I will mention that the next time we're on the phone together."

He lay back on his pillows, closed his eyes, crossed his fingers in hopes there wasn't another nightmare lurking, and dozed off.

4.

Mike's belly began to rumble. It woke him up. He couldn't remember when he'd eaten last. It had to be at least a day ago, probably longer. He wandered into the kitchen and poked about in the fridge. He found some pickles and cheese, noticed a couple of tomatoes on the window sill that were ripe and juicy looking and decided to build a sandwich. His saliva glands started working overtime. He began to feel giddy and couldn't wait to take the first bite. As he chewed, he got some good strong black coffee going in his tiny *caffettiera*.

He'd always been the chief cook in his household and it suited him to a 'T'. He enjoyed trying new recipes out on his little family and they, in turn, ate whatever he prepared. Now that he was alone his culinary hobby would serve him well.

As he puttered about, his thoughts returned to Lenny. Mike knew all about his opinion of 'he-men who did women's work'. He'd told Mike many times that it was an insult to the male gender. Sometimes, Mike went into mental orbit over Lenny's machismo.

Long since, Lenny had shared his early years with Mike, telling him he'd grown up in rural Mississippi where he'd learned about the seamy side of life almost from the time he began to walk. 'You know, man, I could be one sorry black dude right about now considering where I come from. My old man was gone all the time, playing jazz on his beat up old horn, spending his life with his musician cronies, in and out of joints day after week after month after year. He didn't support us in any sense of the word, including financially. He just lusted after 'the big break, due any day now.' You know what, man? He's old now. I mean *old*. And he's still doing and saying the same things. Go figure.'

He'd gone on to tell Mike his mother had worked, like, forever. She had scrubbed the toilets of the wealthy white folks in town And, occasionally, she'd be asked to help serve at one of their dinner or cocktail parties. In the telling, Lenny's face would crinkle up and the veins in his neck would bulge out. 'Man,' he'd said, 'sometimes all me and my brothers got to eat for days was the leftovers from those gigs. My Mom would hand stuff out the back door of whatever house she was at and we would cram the food down our throats right on the spot. You think that kinda' shit didn't motivate me to get the hell out of there? Of course, my brothers found another way to escape. Both are in prison. It like to kill my Mom when they fucked up. Well, I send her a check every month and now she doesn't have to kiss white asses any more. And I'm out of that stinking black ghetto forever.'

He'd studied hard, ending up with a scholarship to the Air Force Academy in Colorado. Except for the winter weather, which he'd never before experienced and didn't like, he'd loved every moment of it, graduating near the top of his class and immediately opting for a commission in the Navy. When Mike asked why he'd made that choice, he skillfully avoided a direct answer. He'd yet to tell Mike the rest of the story…how, early on, he'd learned all about drugs; dealing, using, all of the consequences. He watched the activities late at night, easily concealing himself behind fences, buildings, cars, any sort of cover. He'd been late maturing and was small in stature well into his teens. That had been a big plus in one way, but in school a huge minus. He was never able to play sports, being so small. He replaced that early disappointment by earning big money. He had started up his own little drug business and was able to get away with the entire scheme because his elders thought so highly of him. No one would have *ever* suspected that the highly intelligent, well-behaved little black son of their housemaid could even *think* of being involved in such scurrilous activities.

Once his dealing was established, he'd only catered to kids and not once did his conscience bother him. After all, *someone* was gonna' supply them…it might just as well be him. All he wanted was to amass enough money to get *out*!

In the doing, he kept track of who bought what. How much, when, where and so forth. He kept the data in his head. This early discipline eventually surfaced when he made the military his career. His superiors were amazed at his 'photographic memory'.

He'd witnessed overdosing so many times it wasn't long before he was immune to the horror of it. One night, as he peeked through a knot hole in a fence, he saw a woman shoot something into her arm and assumed it was heroin. Almost immediately, she had toppled over, falling into the middle of the dusty, unpaved street. It had been an ugly sight, the shuddering and writhing of her body as it lay there dying. He'd had bad dreams for a while afterward and because of that experience plus many more similar ones, he'd vowed he would never use drugs. He thought too much of himself. He had kept that promise and when he'd been appointed to the Academy, he'd put his nefarious activities on hold for the duration of his undergraduate years.

In Colorado he'd been a star, a son any mother would be proud of. By the time he graduated his brothers were in prison, so his moms' attendance at his ceremonies was a special source of pleasure for both of them.

His reason for choosing the Navy was shameful. He knew he'd get to more places around the world, thus giving him a 'rare opportunity' to contact drug dealers in most of the major foreign ports. His intention was to build his own drug cartel in the military, big money being the prime motivater.

By the time he and his family landed in Italy, he had all of his ducks in order and was ready to make his fortune. He planned to be a millionaire many times over by the end of his tour of duty. And, in short order, he had chosen Mike to be his right arm.

The deciding factor in his choice had been his wife Cate's opinion. She had been on the lookout for a personality that was easily manipulated and had pointed Mike out to Lenny after only a few days into their newly formed friendship.

'Not only is he naïve', she'd told her husband, 'but he is easily persuaded to change his mind, his plans, his priorities and so on. In other words, he has a large tendency to be wishy-washy.' She had assured Lenny it would be a cinch to lead Mike around by his nose.

If Mike had known of these evil plans, if he'd been more alert, a little less gullible and unsuspecting, less trusting, perhaps things would have turned out differently. In the end, none of it mattered.

5.

While Mike was enjoying his meal, Lenny was loading up his Beemer to make the short trip to Mike's place. His car was, for him, an important status symbol, a source of tremendous pride.

"Come on, Whitey boy" he told his dog, "jump in here. We're off to Mike's to help him with his dilemma, try and get him out of his funk." Except for Mike, Lenny considered Whitey to be his best friend, the shaggy animal who had shown up at his door one cold, blustery evening, whining and scratching to get into the house. True, he was a mutt without one single special thing going for him but, Lenny had been lonely that night, so he'd let Whitey in. He had dried him off, fed him and eventually gotten too fond of him to chase him away. He'd hoped for a pal and a watch dog. He needed both, especially a dog to patrol his area. He was living in a heavily wooded, secluded part of town in a house he had leased from a colleague, Commander Irene "Irish" Kelly. She'd gotten unexpected orders to report to the Pentagon on some sort of secret assignment that she wasn't able to talk about to anyone. Even Lenny, with all of his official connections, couldn't dig the information out. She'd had to leave immediately and Lenny, who had just shipped his wife and son off to the states, had needed somewhere to live. It had worked out for both of them.

Because the place was so remote, it was perfect for what he needed in order to conduct his 'business'.

Whitey seemed to be a gift from the gods. As it turned out, he'd gotten a pal but the animal was no kind of protector. Lenny became disgusted in a big hurry, too often watching Whitey run toward the house, his tail between his legs, if anything even as small as a field mouse or a squirrel happened to cross his path.

He kept the dog because he enjoyed the company. Also, he had a racial secret which kept him amused. 'How many black dudes had a Whitey who could be harassed at will, with no repercussions?' and he would grin wickedly.

Driving around in his BMW took a great deal of TLC because Italian drivers, notorious for their bad driving habits, would be delighted to ram into him, give him the finger and drive off in a cloud of smoke, laughing uproariously. All U.S. vehicles had license tabs that read 'AFI', meaning Armed Forces Italy. The locals knew there would be no after effects for them, should an 'accident' take place. Better still, the usual upshot was a complete inability for an American to get restitution for damages. This was another source of amusement for the local people. The bottom line was that Lenny drove cautiously and very defensively in his beloved Beemer.

Whitey rode in the front seat which Lenny had, long since, covered with a towel. Whitey drooled copiously. As they drove along, Lenny told his pet "Good god, boy, you are an *ugly* bastard. The only creature on the planet that's ugly and lovable all at once." Whitey then looked adoringly at Lenny, smiling a wet, slobbery smile. Lenny snorted and then couldn't help himself. He had to chuckle. 'Who'd believe it?' As they drove along, Lenny kept up his one-sided conversation.

CODE NAME: WHITE MUSTANG

"That wife of mine is a piece of work, man. The only reason we married was because of her education. God knows she's no beauty. But, she majored in business with a minor in psychology, so you have to know that comes in handy in the drug business. Right? She went to Oxford. That's in England, man. That's what attracted me to her. The first time I was in Italy, years ago, we met at a social function. I was underwhelmed until a guy stopped at my table and gave me a little information about her. I guess he noticed I'd been watching her. He told me about her college background first. That got my attention. Then, he filled me in on an interesting story about her family history. Seems her Dad was an early POW during World War II. He'd been a foot soldier in the Italian army. After he was captured, he was sent to England where he spent the major part of the war. He, along with the rest of the prisoners, were treated better than they'd ever expected and this made a lasting impression on Cate's dad. After the war he returned to Italy, married his childhood sweetheart and they went back to England. They lived there for quite some time while he 'made his fortune.' They had several children, one of whom was Cate. She loved England too, never forgotting it even after the family moved back to Italy where, eventually, they got wealthy growing olive trees. Wealthy by Italian standards, that is. By the time Cate was ready for college, they could afford to send her back to England which was what she'd always wanted to do. So now you know the rest of *that* story."

Whitey woofed and drooled some more. Lenny continued his rambling narration, telling Whitey how Cate had almost literally fallen at his feet when they were eventually introduced at that party. "I was still a young stud then, man, but it was time for me to get serious about marriage because, though I hate to admit it, a wife is essential for climbing the promotion ladder in the military. That is, a wife like Cate with an awesome education and a personality that enhances mine. You know, I'd had women all over the planet by that time so it was no big deal if Cate was lacking in the looks department. She had a great body back then, could socialize with the best of them and make a favorable impression. Since our marriage, she's done lots of good for my career but, even more important, for my 'business.' Why the fuck she took Lonzo and left is a mystery to me, but she'll come back on hands and knees. They always do!"

Whitey growled low in his throat as if to say, 'Right on. She never should have left you.'

Lenny checked himself in the rear view mirror. He admired his image whenever he had the chance. He was vain about his smooth, unblemished skin. In fact, he felt he was too good looking for words. He stared at his reflection, his eyes staring back at him, so black he couldn't discern the pupils. Best of all was the mustache. He stroked it gently as he continued on his way, feeling erotic at the touch. He was secure, believing no one in the military services looked sharper in a uniform than he did. Especially when he was in his full dress whites, a stark and surreal contrast to his ebony skin.

Often he would bypass social events to avoid the rich booze and canape's so his body would keep its 'sexy shape'. He was obsessed with his teeth, believing them to be his most alluring asset. This tended to cause him to smile a great deal though the smiles seldom, if ever, reached his eyes. It would never have occurred to him that all of his smiling, many times inappropriately, might be causing onlookers to become suspicious of him, a kind of 'I wonder what he's up to?' attitude. His peers didn't trust him, his superiors persistently avoided him and his subordinates feared him. Yet, he was certain everyone respected and admired him.

As for the relationship with Mike, he had taken Cate's advice. He trusted her ability to pinpoint Mike's character flaws. He was ready to begin his manipulation of the guy, get him involved in 'the business'. He'd need to approach carefully, be subtle and devious. At least, in the beginning. After all, Mike was no dummy. But he, the 'macho man', could handle it, no sweat.

Although Mike was unaware of the pitfalls awaiting him, Teea had sensed from the start there was trouble brewing. Well he, Lenny, had gotten rid of that barrier. It had been a piece of cake, turning out better than he could have imagined. She was gone and that was that!

After getting to Mike's, Lenny intended helping his best friend to survive the absence of his family. He anticipated an easy time of it because he had some terrific news which would end Mike's depression immediately, cheer him up, brighten his future considerably.

6.

Mike was striving not to think about Lenny's imminent arrival. Just who did the guy think he was anyhow, announcing he'd be coming right over, not even waiting to hear if it would be okay. The whole idea irritated him so much he had to get off the couch and pace around. He picked a pillow off his bed and banged the wall several times, gritting his teeth. Not a good idea. Sometimes, he forgot he was wearing a full set of braces.

Teea had told him a hundred times that Lenny made her skin crawl. But he persistently ignored her, euphoric because he had his family with him, the only important consideration in his life.

Now, waiting for Lenny, Mike asked himself if *that* could be the reason Teea had gone home.

'Naw,' he reassured himself, 'she'd have told me, or I'd have pried it out of her. It's gotta' be more than my having turned a deaf ear to her warnings.'

Unexpectedly, he recalled an incident involving the four of them that had taken place a few months back and which still had the power to make the hair on his arms stand up. They'd been sitting in the sun enjoying a pitcher of iced tea and cookies that Cate had baked, lazily talking of trivial matters. Then, someone suggested they ought to treat themselves, have a night out on the town some evening soon. They'd discussed it and agreed 'the sooner the better. We deserve a break.'

Teea had been assigned the task of finding a 'boy sitter' which she was happy to do. She was fluent in

CODE NAME: WHITE MUSTANG

Spanish and had easily picked up basic Italian, telling Mike there were 'tons of similarities' in the two languages.

"I've already spoken to a couple of the maids in case we'd need someone and there's one who's available most of the time."

It was a date then, for the following Wednesday evening. The girls had gone to the beauty salon for hairdo's, facials and manicures. After getting all prettied up, they put on cocktail dresses, heels and jewelry. Rhinestones. 'Wait a minute'. Mike's memory was clicking in. 'Those stones around Cate's neck and hanging from her ears had to have been the real thing. I was too distracted at the time to realize it.'

His heart speeded up as he pictured the two women. Cate's gems may have been real and they may have outshone Teea's costume pieces, but Teea had outshone Cate in every other department...

'God, how I miss her. I'm so proud of her...the way she looks, the way she carries herself, the proud toss of her head, her athletic prowess, the way she cares for our boys...' he had said to himself, over and over. Damn! He had to stop thinking such things or he'd start weeping again.

Lenny had assured all of them that he knew 'just the right place' for their evening out. "The best Gaeta has to offer for dinner, drinks and dancing.' Wonder of wonders, he did know! Mike was impressed at the time, he recalled. By then, he had gotten used to Lenny's bullshit. The *ristorante* had been marvelous. The waiters, dressed in tuxedo's, were superb. They went about their business quietly and efficiently, linen towels draped over their forearms, speaking English with pleasing accents. The setting was imposing, subtly European, the sound of voices and service muted. Sparkling crystal chandeliers shed soft, subdued light onto the tables which were arranged with snowy linens, centerpieces of slim vases, each holding one multicolored, long stemmed rose and fern, the glassware and silver glittering, the china obviously of a very high quality, starkly white with silver edging.

They had been seated just off-center in the dining room, but close enough to the ballroom to enjoy the dance music, a delicate background to their conversation. They enjoyed before-dinner cocktails, chatted comfortably together and when the entrée was served, they were delighted; the food was delectable. They'd ordered identical meals of fresh, homemade pasta, a scintillating marinara sauce and an enormous portion of *gambretto,* the tastiest shrimp they had ever bitten into.

"The secret to the awesome sauce is the use of freshly picked tomatoes that have been vine-ripened and are full of warm, Italian sunshine", Cate told them, then added, "the *basillico* must also be freshly picked. It has to be dark green and sweetly herbal. It is the only way to do the sauce properly."

They pigged out. The fresh, warm, crusty Italian bread, with butter melting all through it, was almost sensuous to the palate. The green salad, served lastly, was crisp and cleansing in their mouths. All throughout their meal, they savored an obscure, local Lambrusco which their waiter had recommended. It was unanimously agreed to be the 'nectar of the gods.' Even Mike nodded a vigorous 'yes' and drank several glasses. His preference was usually beer, so Teea was happy for him.

They had been eating for over an hour when the dessert was served. They hadn't ordered anything, but the waiter knew American habits and brought them each a small dish of the famous Italian *gelatto*, vanilla flavor, with espresso. They welcomed his idea, as he'd known they would, and ate the ice cream leisurely while sipping their little cups of pure caffeine, what espresso in Italy is meant to be.

"Forget the dancing", Lenny announced. "I couldn't move a muscle at this point in time. It's no wonder the ancient Romans ended their meals by throwing up their food if they ate like this. They built and routinely used vomitoriums you know."

'Leave it to him.' Teea was disgusted and thought he was just too gross for words.

But Mike insisted they would need to get up and dance in order to start the food moving in the right direction. "Otherwise, we'll end up feeling like turkeys. You know, stuffed." He grinned and so did Teea. Cate didn't get it and Lenny glowered.

Finally finished, Lenny beckoned to their waiter who pulled the ladies' chairs back and then escorted the four of them into the ballroom where they had a table reserved for them. They were seated at the edge of the dance floor but far enough from the music so they could talk without the tunes drowning them out.

There were several other couples scattered around the room. Everyone appeared to be enjoying their evening.

A huge round globe of multicolored glass spun slowly in the middle of the ceiling casting soft, pastel colors over the faces of the dancers. It was romantic, classy and a balm to the senses.

In spite of his earlier protests, Lenny got up almost at once and led Cate out onto the floor declaring "This is our song."

Teea noticed a questioning look and raised eyebrows on Cate's face, but Mike saw only his lovely wife.

He leaned across the corner of the table and took one of Teea's hands into both of his. He stroked her arm and told her with his eyes how much he cared for her. "I have this great sense of anticipation, Teea. I believe the next three years will be the best yet for us. It's been so long since we've been able to have a normal family life. I think it'll take a little while to get settled in but I, for one, am looking forward to every moment we're going to spend together."

Teea smiled, her brown eyes sparkling, her jewelry reflecting the colors of the spinning globe overhead. Mike was overcome with his emotions and tears welled up in his eyes.

She leaned over and kissed him softly, telling him, "I love you too, Mike. And I share your excitement. This is going to be a great tour of duty. Once you get settled into your new job, we can make plans to travel around and the boys can learn about the ancient history of this country first hand. Later, we can go to other countries too and all of us can learn stuff."

Mike felt his heart swell with love and pride for the girl he had married. He gazed at her mouth and saw the tiny dimple that appeared in one corner when she was pleased about something.

CODE NAME: WHITE MUSTANG

His own mouth opened and he was about to share more of his feelings when suddenly a loud commotion broke out on the dance floor. Looking over Mike said, "Good god Teea, it's Lenny and Cate. They're having an argument. I can't believe this. Shouting in public about how and when they should have sex? It's horrific!"

His instinct was to grab Teea and get the hell out of the place. 'Who needs this humiliation?' he asked himself.

As if reading his mind, Teea urged, "Let's go, Mike. This is too much. We can get a cab out front and go home. Come on!"

Now, as he recalled the scenario, Mike thought he ought to have done exactly as Teea had wanted. Perhaps their lives wouldn't be all torn apart if he had done what even his own good sense had been nudging him to do. Instead, he had ignored Teea, had walked onto the dance floor and had taken Cate's arm, steering her away from Lenny. With every step, he was aware of at least a dozen pairs of eyes following his every move. At the corner of his vision he even thought he saw their waiter leaning against the wall, his arms folded, a smarmy grin on his face.

His intention had been to take Cate back to the table, but as they turned in that direction, Mike saw Teea hurriedly leaving the room. Mike had no choice but to follow her. They headed to the exit, leaving Lenny behind to deal with the situation.

As they left the room, Mike glanced back and saw that Lenny at least had the presence of mind to look sheepish. He was walking toward the waiter, pulling a wad of bills from his pocket as he went.

M. L. Verne

'Good' Mike thought, 'he can pay up for causing this horribly embarrassing predicament.'

Outside, none of them were in a mood to wait for the valet. With a sneer, Lenny stomped off toward the parking lot to find his car, leaving the rest of them standing on the stairs, shivering in the cold breeze that occasionally blew in off the ocean.

Lenny screeched up to the curb, the others climbed in and even before they had closed their doors, he was burning rubber, pulling away, careening around the corner, heading for the expressway.

Many weeks later, Mike recalled that nightmarish ride and marveled that none of them had been killed. He could still feel the jolt as Lenny had pulled up to the hotel and slammed on the brakes.

The car had shuddered and lurched to a stop. If they hadn't had seat belts on, they'd have been hurtled through the windshield.

As Mike climbed out of the car, he'd begun to speak, later wondering where it had come from. "Lenny, why don't you and Cate take the weekend, go off somewhere, try and work out your problems. Teea and I will take care of Lonzo for you."

Instantly, he knew he was in big trouble with Teea but, he also knew that she was fond of Lonzo and pleased that the twins got along so well with him. He really was a great kid, in spite of the way Lenny treated him, exploiting the boy to enhance his fatherly image. Lonzo was extremely bright, handsome and charming. The verbal abuse he lived with seemed to strengthen his character. Cate, Mike was sure, was responsible for keeping him on an even keel.

No sooner were the words out of Mike's mouth and Lenny accepted the offer without giving it a second thought. No thanks were proffered either. His attitude seemed to be, 'You owe me'.

Teea was provoked beyond speech. She got out of the car and literally stomped into the hotel without a backward look.

Mike geared up for the storm he knew was coming as Lenny peeled away. 'The fool can't even let his wife out first. Poor girl will have to walk in heels from the parking lot now.' Mike was totally disgusted. Inside their rooms, he paid and thanked the sitter, ushering her out the door. She lived someplace nearby and was driving her own car. The urgency to have her gone was almost palpable.

Once the door closed behind her, Teea erupted. "How dare you! You didn't even *ask* me first. What*ever* are you thinking about? You *know* I despise that creep. Oh sure, Cate is my friend and oh, sure, Lonzo is good company for the boys. Mike! The bottom line here is, he's taking advantage of us, using us. *WHY* can't you get it through that thick head of yours that he is *no good* for us. For some reason that I can't figure out, he is intent upon creating chaos between you and me. You need a heads up on this Mike. Trust me!"

She had run out of breath. Infuriated, she clenched her jaws and stormed into the bedroom, wanting badly to slam the door, barely restraining herself knowing it would wake up the boys. They didn't need to be exposed to this quarrel.

She got out of her party clothes and threw them carelessly over a chair. Her anger needed to subside.

As she allowed that to happen, breathing deeply, she felt a sense of sadness creep over her. It had begun as such a lovely evening. Both she and Mike had felt a renewal of their earlier passions and she knew that he had been looking forward to some long postponed intimacies, just as she had.

'Well, it's not gonna' happen tonight!' she told herself. No way. So when Mike came down the hallway, she turned over and feigned sleep.

For his part, Mike didn't think climbing into bed with his wife right then was such a wonderful idea so he went on into his son's room to check on them. Standing there, looking at their handsome faces in the dim glow of their night light, love and pride overtook him. 'Come what may,' he promised himself silently, 'they will always be my top priority.' For him, they were the one perfect thing he had done in his life. 'Rather, two perfect things,' he corrected himself. He fully intended being their best friend, their best buddy, for as long as he might live. There was nothing he wouldn't do for them, within reason of course. This tour would cement their family ties for all time. If only he and Teea could get their combined act together and stop the petty bickering, theirs would be the ultimate perfect marriage.

He sighed and shook his head sadly as he walked into their bedroom. Immediately he noted she had her back turned. 'Don't dare bother me.' He knew *that* body language all right. Sighing again, he got out of his clothes, the best 'civvies' he owned actually, and let them drop to the floor. He slid carefully onto his side of the mattress and instantly felt Teea's anger. It pulsed in the darkness like a living, breathing, vicious animal.

Meanwhile, she was biting her cheeks in an effort not to shake, still breathing deeply, as silently as she could manage. With sheer will power she got herself under control.

In moments the chaos of the night caught up with both of them and they drifted off to sleep thinking the same thought; 'We must get the matter of the Jones's taken care of, once and for all.'

It was an ignominious end to an evening that had begun with such bright promise. It was also the last time that Mike and Teea would share 'a dressed up, social occasion.'

7.

"What I need is some more strong, black coffee." Mike talked to himself frequently. Out loud. He'd gotten into the habit a few years before, during a tour at sea, working alone for hours at a stretch. He had craved some kinds of noises other than blips, bips, beeps and the commotion that his communication equipment spewed out continuously. It got to be nerve-wracking when it went on without let-up. In time, the sound of his voice was a consolation to him. Lately though, he'd begun to wonder if he should try to stop doing it. There was a good possibility it was irritating his co- workers. He'd noticed a few strange glances his way now and then.

As he busied himself brewing more caffeine, he faced up to the reality of the situation. He needed to get on the ball, find a less expensive place to live. He didn't need a three bedroom villa all to himself. And Teea needed the furniture shipped back to her. She and the boys were bunking with her parents. No matter the kinship, two adult women in the same house inevitably made for trouble. She'd be wanting her own space, sooner than soon.

What a mess. Why, why hadn't she stayed where she belonged? Here. In Italy. With him… Then, he would need to find a moonlighting job. Teea would be working, too. When they were living apart, maintaining two separate households, it was the only way they could survive financially.

All these thoughts dumped him into another funk. He poured and sipped his coffee, burning his tongue.

CODE NAME: WHITE MUSTANG

"Shit!" he swore, hoping his braces weren't melting. "If that doesn't give me a jump start, nothing will."

He waited for his coffee to cool off and got to remembering how quickly Teea had picked up the local language, adapting to the lifestyle almost overnight. When he'd told her how proud he was, she'd just smiled and told him it was 'a piece of cake.' Her dimply grin assured him that she'd been pleased with his compliment.

They'd been very lucky finding the villa they moved into. Initially, they were told it would take at least six months to find accommodations. But one afternoon they were driving around, just looking at things in general, when Teea had spied a 'For Rent' sign, in Italian. She had Mike stop the car, they had peered into the front door of the house, liked what little they could see and copied down the phone number. They looked at each other and silently wondered, 'Think it'll be ours?'

Once back in the hotel, Teea called and asked a few questions. When she hung up she told Mike, "It's available right away. It's more than we planned on spending, almost more than we can afford. I told the woman we'd come over now and have a look."

They climbed back into their car, which had finally arrived in Italy, and returned to the house. The woman was waiting for them and cheerfully escorted them around, pointing out the virtues of the 'villa'. It wasn't fancy, but it was clean and roomy. They paid many thousands of lira, on the spot, to secure the deal.

"Somehow, we'll manage," Mike assured her when they were back in the car. They drove to the transportation offices and Mike made out the paperwork to have their furniture delivered. Their household goods had come on the same ship with their car.

When they told the Jones's about their good fortune, mentioning in passing that it was a bit more than their budget would normally allow, Lenny offered to lend them as much money as they might need to make ends meet.

That did it! Later, Teea admitted she'd been unnecessarily rude. "No thank you. We can support ourselves. We do *not* need any help from the likes of you." Her stomach had flipped over and she had rushed out, leaving the others agape.

"God, how I detest that man," she mumbled as she walked back to their rooms. All of them were coming down with severe cases of cabin fever and hers was the worst.

In four days time, they were in, settled and content. On the fifth day, Teea went out to find a part time job. It was an absolute necessity if they were going to afford living in the place.

Again, they got lucky. She found a position as a waitress at one of the many service clubs in the area. It was convenient for them in several ways, the most important being the hours. With Mike in his new office all day, she needed and had found an evening job. She would not have to leave until Mike was home. So the boys were covered.

After settling in, they began to look around the area. Across the cobblestone alley-way lived an elderly couple, the Bernini's, Vince and Anna. They spoke understandable English and Teea's bilingual talents filled the gaps. The Italians welcomed the Steele family into the neighborhood and had them for dinner after just a week.

Their home was rather sumptuous, on the second floor of their building, surrounded on the outside by a balcony which Anna occupied for long stretches every day. She watched the local activity, gossiped with the other women, who also hung out, and all of them yelled shrilly at the children when they were at play.

It took Teea exactly two weeks to become wary. And angry.

Meanwhile, they accepted the dinner invitation and were charmed as they climbed the stairs toward the wonderful odors emanating from above; charmed by the two beautiful pieces of sculpture displayed on the landing, by the glass cabinet in the hallway at the top of the stairs displaying a marvelous collection of porcelain figurines and by the etched glass mirrors placed at random on the walls. The kitchen, obviously, was the center of activity. The TV was perched on a table in one corner, volume turned up full blast. Several pots were bubbling merrily on the stove. An enormous bottle of red wine sat in the middle of the table which was the size and shape of a picnic table back home, only wider, and it was covered by a white tablecloth. Dinner plates were stacked at one end and silverware was piled into a big glass container on the counter by the sink.

"Have wine! Sit! Be comfortable!" Orders from Anna. Already, Teea was uncomfortable. However, Vince was grinning, almost toothlessly, and looked so cute Teea had to smile back at him.

M. L. Verne

The boys were all eyes, watching the TV but not understanding a word. Anna teased them and they giggled.

Mike poured wine all around, toasted the host and hostess and drained his glass. Teea took a sip and was delighted. It was home made, delicate and unbelievably delicious.

Anna continued talking non-stop as she finished the last of her preparations so no one else was able to get a word in.

'Pretty soon I'm gonna' get nervous if she doesn't let up.' Teea was thinking, struggling to remain calm.

Luckily, Anna started the pasta just in time and, as with all homemade food in Italy, it was awesome. Descriptive words in English couldn't begin to explain the marvelous flavors.

Heavenly tastes, delectable smells, pure delight.

The meal lasted through several courses with much wine drinking. After each course, Anna would do up the dishes; washing them, rinsing them, placing them on an open rack in the cupboard over the sink where they drip-dried.

Mike and Teea had never seen that particular way of 'doing the dishes'. They glanced at each other with amusement in their eyes as if to say 'Well. How peculiar.'

When it was over and they'd returned home, they had to agree that it was probably one of the most wonderful meals they had ever eaten and that it would remain in their memories for a long, long time.

They were invited again and again, sometimes accepting, other times, for one reason or another, taking a 'rain check'.

Eventually however, Teea had to stop accepting. Anna began to bug her to distraction. The woman had some habits that Teea simply could not abide. Not only was her voice perpetually set to high, an ear-splitting range, as she constantly ordered folks about, but she was involved in other people's business, thereby making a nuisance of herself. And, she had the most annoying habit of poking a listener's shoulder or arm, in a most painful way, with her index finger.

Most days at almost any hour, she would be hanging over her railing yelling at the children who were at play down below.

"She's a bossy, nosy, meddlesome busybody, Mike," Teea carped.

But he felt it was important for his family to maintain a friendly, neighborly attitude. "After all, we are visitors in their country" he would argue.

Teea, at last, was having none of it. Eventually, this small rift in the Steele household would grow into a major problem.

Gradually breaking away from the Bernini's was occurring, simultaneously, with the boys coming home for days on end telling their mom that the kids at the neighborhood playground were spitting at them, trying to pick fist fights and calling them bad names like *bastardo* and *stupido*.

Each time she would caution them, "Don't tell Dad. He'll get mad. Let me see what I can do about it."

She investigated quietly and discovered that the bullies were several years older than her twins, nearly full grown teens. This was an acute source of anxiety for her, but she tried to remain calm while she spent time figuring out what to do.

Several weeks went by and, finally, the situation was such that she could no longer tolerate it.

By then, even the smaller boys in the area were tormenting Jason and Joel. Teea opened her mouth umpteen times to ask Mike for his help. But each time, some inner voice told her to wait.

One day it all came to a head. When Mike got home from work, Teea was waiting. "We're out of here, Mike. The local kids have been abusing our sons until I can't tolerate it any longer. I'm taking them back to the states where they'll be able to grow up decently and not have to be afraid to go outside the house."

He was stunned. "Why haven't I heard about this before now? And where is this 'going home' coming from? This playground problem is a kid thing, Teea. We can handle that, even if it means moving some place else. What the hell is going on here?"

She told him she hadn't wanted to worry him while he was getting settled into the routine of his new job, but that the whole situation was now out of hand and going home was the only solution.

He didn't buy it. Not then. Not any time later. He knew in his gut it was a cop-out, a concocted excuse, but she stuck to her story, in spite of every argument he threw her way. When she became belligerent he knew, for sure, there was something else behind the whole thing. But, it was clear she had definitely decided she was leaving.

He admitted to himself that he was helpless to change her mind. She'd gone all right, and now he sat in the kitchen of the house where they had talked of all the fun things the four of them were going to do in the next three years. And for the first time since they'd left, he got angry.

"She had *NO* right to do that to me" he raged. His pulse began to pound and he felt the beginnings of a migraine coming on with the usual brilliant, colorful aura filling his visual field.

"Hell and damn it" he mumbled as he half fell into the 'head' to look for his medication. If he didn't get a couple of pills swallowed right away, he might as well cross the next few days off the calendar. The pills went down, and he was on his way to the couch when the door burst open and Lenny walked in, Whitey trotting along behind him.

Mike groaned silently, closed his eyes to gain some mental stability, then said "Lenny listen, man, I'm getting a migraine. Can't we do this another time?"

"No way, man. You're not getting off that easy. You need to get your little white ass in gear and quit your sniveling. Tomorrow is a workday, man. Here's a beer. In five minutes you'll be feeling great. Trust me. And hey, man, I know you don't care much for Whitey. But, you know what? He's warm and fuzzy, a good pal that never talks back. And look, he likes you or he wouldn't be thumping his tail on your floor."

"I like dogs, man. Don't give me any shit. As far as I'm concerned, Whitey is just stupid but hell, you can't hold that against him. He's just an animal. He can't help it."

"Glad to hear it, man. 'Cuz I gotta' be out of the country on an errand for a couple of days, and I was hoping you'd take this creature in while I'm gone. He's great company for a guy who lives alone."

Mike felt so lousy he didn't even answer. And Lenny took his silence to mean 'yes'. If Mike could have taken a look into Lenny's mind just then, he would have seen a satisfied grin and the thought that 'Cate knew what she was talking about. Mike is so easily manipulated it isn't even fun. This guy is gonna' be a *huge* asset for my business.'

But Mike was paying no heed to Lenny as he tried to think his headache away. Lenny was droning on and on in a numbing monotone. Mike dozed off.

"Mike. Hey, man, hey. Wake up! Are you listening to me?" Lenny's voice woke Mike up with a jerk.

"I'm trying to get this message into your head, man. Listen to me. I know you're missing your family and you feel rotten. Hell, man, me too. You gotta' face the fuckin'music."

Mike doubted Lenny would ever miss anyone for more than two minutes, as long as he had his inflated ego to keep him company. The guy slept with any woman who looked his way twice. Poor Cate. She'd seemed unaware of her husband's infidelities. He'd never mentioned to Teea what he knew about Lenny's habits, knowing she'd run right out and tell Cate. He'd had no intention of getting mixed up in a mess like that.

Lenny was still prattling away. "I've gotten used to her being gone, man. I sure as hell ain't lettin' *that* get me down and that's the attitude you need to be adopting if you're ever gonna' get straightened out and get on with your life. The bitches *always* come running back, begging to be taken in again. You just gotta' wait a while and be patient. Watch and see if I'm not right. The minute I get to Pensacola, she'll be pounding on my door. Oh! I forgot to tell you...I'm transferring back there by the end of the year. Gotta' get a little training and then I'm assigned as Executive Officer aboard a destroyer."

Mike remained silent. But he thought, 'XO! More fodder for that overbearing ego of his.' His mind wandered again and he recalled the events that had transpired during the days following the weekend he and Teea had taken Lonzo in while Lenny and Cate had gone away to 'work out their problems.'

When Cate had picked Lonzo up she'd been acting very strange, Teea told him. "She wouldn't look into my eyes and barely responded when I asked her if they'd had a productive two days. She just grabbed her son and dragged him down the sidewalk, mumbling under her breath and sort of stumbling on the sidewalk. I was really worried about her strange behavior, so, I finally went over to see what could possibly be wrong. When she answered the door and saw it was me, she started to cry. She pulled me inside, closed the door and we both went into her kitchen and sat down at the table. The whole time, she was sobbing uncontrollably."

As Teea related her tale to Mike, she'd shake her head, as if she couldn't believe what she was saying. She went on to relate that eventually Cate had apologized for her rudeness and had asked her, Teea, to help her come to some important decisions. She'd told Teea that Lenny had gotten roaring drunk and had ended up beating her.

"He's no fool, Teea. He never hits me where it might show. I suppose I contributed in some way to this latest abuse, but I've had lots of counseling and I know I'm not supposed to make excuses for his evil behavior."

At that point, Teea said Cate showed her the bruises. It had made her nauseous. Black and blue, turning purple and green, all up and down her back, her buttocks and, worst of all, her breasts.

"It was just horrible! Mike, I wanted to put my arms around her, try to comfort her, but I was afraid I'd hurt her even more."

Thinking and remembering, Mike could still feel Teea's loathing for Lenny. He got angry again as he looked across his living room at the man who had been so brutal to his wife, saying he could not for the life of him understand 'why the bitch left me.'

Mike prayed that Cate would find the strength to divorce the bastard and put the whole ugly situation behind her.

But Lenny was blissfully unaware of Mike's dark thoughts and was talking on and on, non-stop. Mike's eyes opened wide in another moment when he heard "and Mike, that's why I've been trying to reach you all weekend. Your paper work for LDO came across my desk on Friday. All the prelim requirements have been met."

Mike sat bolt upright, his headache at least forgotten, if not gone. With all of the trauma and turmoil of the past few days, his commissioning had been the farthest thing from his mind.

"You've been highly recommended for the program, Mike. Everything needs to be reviewed one more time before it all goes to the Pentagon. I've been asked to sit as the senior officer chairing the committee for this final go-round. This should have been taken care of on Friday, but I couldn't reach you. I've taken the liberty, meanwhile, of setting up the panel that will meet with you on this coming Wednesday. You are to be in the conference room of my building at thirteen hundred hours in full dress uniform."

Now he'd have the best possible news to tell his family, if only this guy would stop talking and get out of his house!

"But" Lenny went on, "with me in charge, you're a shoo-in for the whole enchilada, man. You'll be going to Florida first, to what we call 'fork and knife' school. It's like where you learn how to act like an officer and a gentleman. A lotta' silly shit, as far as I'm concerned. A waste of time and the taxpayers money if you ask me. But, of course, no one ever has."

Mike willed Lenny to leave. He needed to call Teea. His paper work would never have gotten submitted for LDO in the first place, if it hadn't been for Teea's help. He had to call and tell her, again, how much her encouragement meant to him as well as their life together. They'd be getting a pay raise, too. *THAT* was always good news, in and of itself.

"Let's have a beer and celebrate," Lenny was urging. There was no way to stop him, Mike supposed. He'd leave only when he was good and ready. Lenny continued running off at the mouth while Mike began making plans for the immediate future. He would need to find that smaller, less expensive place and the moonlighting job. Right away. He also needed to call the transportation offices first thing in the morning, get the arrangements made to have the house- hold things sent to Teea so she could get out on her own. What a shame she'd left when she did. Now it would take two extra moves to catch up.

'Nothing to be done about that at this point. Wonder when the orders will come. No use worrying about that either. The wheels of military re-assignments turn slowly.'

All of those disjointed thoughts were spinning in Mike's head while he waited for Lenny to go home. Then, just as he thought he couldn't tolerate another second of the b.s., the guy finally stood up. Mike was right behind him, opening the door so there'd be no mistaken ideas about getting more beer out of the fridge.

As Lenny left he said, "Man, I'll be in touch about bringing Whitey over before I have to leave town. Meanwhile, I'll see you Wednesday afternoon, if not sooner."

And he was gone, just in time to save Mike from blowing his cork.

It took a while to get his call through to Teea. It was Sunday evening in Italy, time for morning church services in Colorado. But finally, they were home. The moment he told 'JnJ', their shouts of joy overwhelmed him. "Dad, Dad, come home now!"

Teea was subdued. She knew all about how slow things went in the Navy. Even though she was happy for Mike, his career, their future together, she couldn't find the enthusiasm to reassure him which, she sensed, seemed to be what he needed.

"You do understand what I'm telling you? he asked her.

"Yes, I assure you I do, Mike." But he thought she sounded as if she was going to cry. He thanked her again, profusely, for all her help. They hung up because neither one of them had anything else to say. The entire incident made Mike apprehensive. Troubled, he wondered what might be going on.

On the following Wednesday afternoon, Mike showed up in the conference room as Lenny had instructed. He was calm, collected, amazed at himself. He felt very comfortable through the whole thing, almost cozy. It was probably due to Lenny being in charge. After all, they did have a personal relationship but he didn't think anyone on the panel was aware of that fact. They seemed rigidly disciplined, each taking a pre-arranged turn to ask Mike questions. It was apparent that Lenny ran a tight ship, had given the members a specific amount of time and expected them to adhere to their written notes.

Someone asked him what his extended plans were with regard to his military career. He looked each one of them in the eye as he assured them his intention was to make the most of the coming years in his effort to serve his country, the Navy, his family, and that he expected to excel in all of his undertakings. At the proper moment, he proudly ticked off his outstanding achievements, his numerous honors, his hard earned medals, his many tours of sea duty and closed by telling them how important the hoped-for promotions would be. As he left the room, Mike was confident, pleased and proud.

It was unfortunate Mike had no way of knowing how Lenny happened to chair the interview, unaware of the fact that he had ferreted out all available information about Mike from every source he could dredge up. In so doing, he concocted his plan. Mike had applied for LDO. Fine! He, Lenny, would use it. For all it was worth.

First step, he'd gotten selected to head up the board. That had been a cinch. One phone call and it was done.

The Nigerians working for him were securely in his pocket. They had needed a leader and he fit the bill. He had used his charisma, his military expertise and his black skin to woo them. All he needed to complete the endeavor was Mike.

It was a 'give and take' situation. You want to be an officer? Cross international borders for me and my drug business, you got it.

Had Mike known of this despicable plan, it might have made a difference. But for now he was euphoric, envisioning himself as the kind of Naval officer who just might end up in the history books.

8.

Teea found herself with more than enough time on her hands, sufficient to enable her to do a great deal of thinking about the 'situation', as she called it. Although she had found a part time job after filling out only one application during her short search, her days were just not full enough. She worked a few hours in the afternoons at the local ice cream parlor while her Mother watched the boys after school for her. She'd been athletic since grade school and still kept herself in excellent condition. She was hoping, as she ran each morning, that she'd get a call soon to play softball. The game was her first love. She was MVP material. She was confident and felt that, once the word got out that she was back home, the anxiously awaited call would come.

Meantime, when she ran, her thoughts automatically returned to Italy, to the events that had taken place there. She was trying desperately to deal with her demons, not having much luck. She had been able to admit that all the trouble started from the very moment they set foot in the hotel after landing in Gaeta. She and Mike had been completely jet-lagged, bone weary, out of patience with the boys who were full of energy, questions and too much excitement. During the oceanic flight, the crew had taken them under their collective wing and spoiled them. The flight attendants had even taken them into the cockpit several times. 'One would think,' Teea told herself, 'a person could get plenty of sleep under those circumstances.' No way. Neither one of them had and she had no logical answer for that.

Once they'd landed, they had been met by an Air Force man who had been assigned as their family sponsor. He was more than helpful, offering his services for anything they might need while he tended to their immediate necessities. He collected all of their luggage and got them settled into their hotel rooms expeditiously.

After he left, they lectured the boys, telling them they could check out the building but only if they were very quiet and stayed indoors. Luckily, they'd had the foresight to pack some Nintendo stuff because there was a VCR in the room and, 'if you're very careful, you can play your games,' they were advised.

"Okay, okay, Mom, Dad, we know, we know, geez, we aren't babies any more. We know how to behave."

"Right," the parents nodded, too tired to quibble about it. They went into their bedroom, fell onto the bed and were asleep before their heads leveled out on the pillows.

Much later, Teea discovered that she and Mike had no sooner retired and the twins had left the suite, escaped into the hallway and had immediately bumped into Lonzo, who was also bored and tired of being cooped up. All three boys were delighted and became friends instantly. Lonzo had never known twins, so he was totally intrigued when he saw the two faces that were mirror images.

"You guys are really cool looking," he told them with a big grin on his own face. "Come on, I'll show you this place, 'cuz I already checked out all the corners."

They roamed the entire building and found no trouble to get into so Lonzo finally told them, "We can play some of my games. My parents are having a nap too, but if we're quiet it will be okay. Come on, let's go up there. This is boring."

Soon enough, their laughter and chatter woke up Cate and she was thrilled that Lonzo had found some buddies. She'd known how humdrum the days were for him.

"Hey, guys, here's my Mom. Will you fix us a snack, Mom?" Lonzo asked. "These are my new friends, Jason and Joel. They just got here and their parents are catching some sleep right now. We're having a really cool time together."

She was happy to feed the kids. As she began getting some food together for them, she asked about the boys' family. "Oh, they're Mike and Teea Steele. Dad just got off of sea duty, so we can stay here for three years. Anyhow, thanks for letting us hang out here so they can sleep."

As was their habit, one would start a sentence and the other one would finish it. Cate was enchanted. Since her minor in college had been psychology, she had more than a passing interest in their behavior.

When the parents finally met, it was not the best of conditions. Teea had awakened first, probably because there was total silence when there should have been some commotion from her boys. She'd shaken Mike awake frantically and they'd started to panic after going up and down the halls looking in every nook and cranny, finding no one. They were on their way back to their rooms to call security but, as they passed the Jones' suite, they heard the unmistakable laughter of their sons. Cate opened the door to their knocking and invited them in, but Teea immediately, and as politely as possible through her combined relief and anger, asked for a 'raincheck.'

"Hey, Mom," the boys yelled, "we already ate here! Can't we stay and finish this game?"

Mike looked at her with his eyebrows raised as if to ask 'Why not?' But she was having none of it. "Come on, boys. Say your thank-you's and you can visit again some other time."

They pouted, obeying reluctantly. Their Dad grinned to himself because he loved them so much. He considered their existence to be a very special blessing.

Teea had already gotten a gut reaction as she glanced behind her and saw Lenny when they turned to leave. He was just emerging from the bedroom, a satanic scowl on his face directed at Cate.

Teea quickly looked at Cate and shivered. She saw fear, mistrust, apprehension. 'Not good. Not good. Gotta' steer clear of this….'

She did not yet know she was destined to battle with Mike over the Jones's and would not win.

9.

Far removed from Italy, safe and snug in Colorado, Teea recalled how fond of Cate she had become. She'd been grateful for Cate's having taken the boys in, initially, and seen to their comforts while she and Mike got a little sleep. Without that, their recovery from jet lag would have lasted a whole lot longer. Not only that, Cate had offered her time and transportation for the purpose of getting all of them acquainted with the area. Shopping centers, military facilities, neighborhoods with potential for living quarters and so on. Her generosity had been overwhelming and greatly appreciated.

As she thought about it, Teea tried to remain objective. They had accepted Cate's offer, of course. Their own transportation hadn't been available for several weeks, and she could still recall how her belly had twisted and lurched when she'd gotten her first look at the Jones' automobile. She and Mike had shared an incredulous glance and Mike had asked, "What rank is Lenny that you can afford a buggy like this?"

Her answer had been nonchalant and she'd shrugged her shoulders. "Oh, no big deal. He's a Lieutenant Commander, but that shouldn't have any impact on our little trip, should it?"

If only she'd paid attention to her instincts. If only she could have convinced Mike at the outset that they ought not get involved. If. If. If. Too late now to change history... must move ahead to the future.

So went her thoughts and she knew, for sure, that Mike needed now, more than ever before, to be adhering to the Navy's strict guidelines in all things if he expected to be commissioned. His stature, his reputation, his attitude, his behavior; all of those things and a whole lot more were on the line. She felt another twinge of guilt for having left him alone at such a critical time in his career.

Well, it was the past. She strove not to get caught up in 'what might have been.' Still, she *had* lived it. The entire scenario was kind of like delayed stress syndrome, she thought.

She'd gotten the job at the club and had to ride the bus to work. No problem. Mike did, too. Their car was supposed to arrive soon. If they needed her for a weekend shift, also no problem. Mike was home with the boys.

On one particular evening, as she scurried around getting busier by the minute, running herself ragged filling order after order, she gradually became aware that something unusual was taking place. The clientele, military persons and their spouses, were all riled up, yelling across the room to each other about something she thought sounded like 'Tailhook'. At one point, she overheard someone saying that all Naval officers had to submit a formal letter to their individual commands stating, in no uncertain terms, that they had been nowhere near the Las Vegas Hilton Hotel when whatever happened had happened.

From that, she deduced that the Navy was having another public relations problem. She was much too busy to ask questions as she took orders, served drinks consisting mostly of sambuca with beer chasers, the drink of choice, and snacks, trying not to get jumpy.

The atmosphere was tense and argumentative. She was glad she wasn't working the bar because the lines were three, four deep over there and customers were shouting their orders, cussing, smoking, causing the air to become so heavy with cigarette smoke the exhaust system could not handle it. The room, as big as it was, had started to resemble a Los Angeles freeway covered in a thick brown haze on a hot summer day.

Then, almost abruptly, she noticed that the place was emptying out. She glanced at the clock on the wall and was instantly uplifted. It was closing time. Incredible. Where had the time gone? Now that she could slow down, she began to notice how sore her feet were and how much her back was aching. Sighing, she stopped to collect glasses from yet another table and felt a hand on her shoulder. She turned slowly so her tray wouldn't tip over and there stood Lenny!

"Teea, let me take you out for coffee when you get finished up here. You look positively beat. Then I'll drive you home and you won't need to wait for the bus."

Her skin began to crawl. Lecherous Lenny! What a creep. Still, she knew if she got as verbally rude as she felt inside, and told him off, he would reciprocate in kind and nothing would be gained

"Thanks, Lenny, but I still have several chores to take care of before I can call it a night. It's already quite late and I'm sure Cate is wondering where you are."

"Teea," he insisted, "let's not beat around the bush here. I've seen the way you look at me with desire. I

M. L. Verne

can tell you want my body, know you can't wait to get it on with me, and I'm more than willing, so why waste time?"

Even months later and an ocean plus a continent away, she could feel the revulsion. It had been insufferable. The man was evil and absolutely repulsive. She recalled she had literally reeled at the absurdity of his claims. Her knowledge of his abuse of Cate and his bestial treatment of Lonzo was horrifying enough. But now *this*? Whatever was she going to do?

One time, Cate had confided to her that he was always on the lookout for a woman, *any* woman who would go to bed with him. Had she, Teea, said or done something that would lead him to think she was 'any woman'? Not a chance. She'd always shown only a cool, barely concealed contempt for him and she was sure he had long since known exactly how she felt. So what? Was he thinking he'd screw her and 'show her?'

But no, he was already revealing what he had in mind. He was right in her face, telling her if she didn't go to bed with him, he'd see to it that Mike's career went down the tubes. "And I can do that you know. Do not, for one second, think I can't. I have enormous pull and connections in the Navy, clear to the Pentagon. No one would ever doubt what I have to say about an obscure Navy Chief. So give it some serious thought, bitch! I'll be getting back to you."

He turned and strutted out of the place while she stood staring after him in a kind of stupor. 'Have I lost my mind? Did I hear that right? Is he threatening us? I cannot believe this!'

One of the girls stopped and asked her if she was getting sick. "You look like you saw a ghost or something."

That helped her to snap out of it, both in Italy a while back and now in Colorado, as she was remembering. She made up her mind, on the spot, to get the professional help she knew she needed. 'I could never get this dilemma resolved alone.'

Before the day was out, she called several people she knew, got the name of a counselor and made an appointment for two days later.

10.

Beginning on the first day of his new assignment with NATO, Mike had been enthralled, enthused, caught up in the excitement of the day to day challenges that came across his desk. His was a high security position and he worked closely with the Admiral many times throughout each work week.

When he had time to think about the Admiral as a person, Mike was awed. He'd never worked for, or with, another human being quite like this new boss. The man was funny, self-effacing, and a very warm individual who regarded the men and women under his command as the most important components of his beloved Navy.

He was an inspiration to Mike, who often heard him say things like "...adhere to the buddy system, look out for each other." It seemed as if that were his personal code.

Mike found, within himself, an enormous on-going respect for the man, a feeling that encompassed not simply the stars on his epaulettes but his earthy humanness as well. He was not alone in his admiration. There were few sailors in the command who didn't share the same appreciation for Admiral Kingston.

Put another way, this was going to be the ultimate assignment in Mike's career thus far, the stepping-off point into skyrocketing advancement in rank and responsibilities. He felt it almost from the moment he had reported in for duty. Once again, he was 'button-busting proud' to be a member of the greatest military force on the planet.

It was no wonder, then, that he had failed to notice the subtle changes occurring at home. More specifically in his wife who, ordinarily, was happy, out-going, talkative. There were storm clouds gathering, but he was oblivious. He took for granted her loving care of himself and their sons. Ever since his marriage, he'd had the attitude 'I will take care of the Navy and the Navy will take care of my family.'

The time would come when he would deeply regret his apathy, his negligence, but that time was not yet. Meanwhile, he recalled how sickly she'd looked the day he took them to the airport. It was amazing he hadn't noticed until she was leaving. Now he could see her clearly as she had slumped over, walking to the plane. Like she was carrying the weight of the world on top of her head. She'd been pale and drawn, had lost weight, had not talked to him when ordinarily she was bubbly and enthusiastic about everything. He was horrified at himself. Where had his head been? He vowed to make it up to her beginning at once.

Even as he faced up to his personal problems, Mike was performing superbly on the job. It was imperative that he do his best, not just to enhance his career but because he worked so closely with the Admiral. His immediate superior was Commander Gus Keef, the only man between himself and the Admiral.

The nature of his duties was such that he could not make a mistake. What he was doing was highly sensitive. Sometimes, when Teea and the boys encroached on his reserve, his inability to share his work, he would wish he didn't know all the things he'd been entrusted with. Still, his own self rule was to take

M. L. Verne

pride in a job well done and, in spite of everything, he wasn't going to make any exceptions to that policy.

Almost from the first day on duty, Mike had been catching bits and pieces of conversations regarding the presence of drugs in the command. As the senior noncommissioned officer in charge, he would need to investigate, get to the bottom of the scuttlebutt and do what had to be done.

He began by carefully maneuvering himself into the company of his subordinates. In such a situation, he was thankful the guys respected him or he'd never have gotten to first base. As it was, several weeks went by before the first invitation to 'have a beer together after work' was extended to him.

He then proceeded cautiously, learning next to nothing the first time. He had asked one or two non-provoking questions, displayed nonchalant curiosity and did not probe. Before he left them, he proposed that they 'get together to shoot the bull' and maybe get rid of some of their gripes 'every Friday after work.'

"Right on, Chief! Cool suggestion!" All of them were enthusiastic. As he left the bar, he paid for two more rounds of beer for them. 'That should put me in solid,' he thought.

A couple more weeks went by and it was during their fourth Friday get-together that Mike sensed the time had come. He dropped a large hint.

It worked. Two of the guys began to point fingers, their attitude such that Mike was aware they needed to get it out of their systems. They insisted they did not want to be narcs, but what they knew to be facts was too explosive to keep inside any longer.

"Chief, we're relieved to let you take over with this. It needs to be brought to the attention of the brass, and soon. Things are getting out of control, we think. The last thing the Navy needs right now is another fiasco."

He assured them he would get the information to Commander Keef the first thing Monday morning but then was surprised.

"And Chief, this isn't personal but we all agree we shouldn't be meeting with you any more. Once the word gets out that there's an impending investigation, all hands are gonna' be sensitive to every spoken word."

He assured them he took no umbrage and that he understood fully their feelings for discretion. He left them after thanking them, feeling secure with the list of names they had confided to him, certain that he'd get everything taken care of so the Navy *didn't* get another smear on its reputation.

Much to his surprise he bumped into Lenny as he neared the exit.

'What's a Lieutenant Commander doing in a beer joint frequented by the lower ranks?' he was wondering but, as he opened his mouth to ask Lenny that very thing, the sailors he'd been meeting with rushed past him and out the door.

'How odd,' he thought. 'And they left their beers unfinished. On Friday night. Must be they know Lenny's rank. Why wouldn't they? Everybody knows everything in this command.' It didn't occur to him there might be racism involved. Or worse, a drug connection.

M. L. Verne

"Hey, man, how's it going?" Mike asked. "What's happening? Funny you should show up in a second class joint like this. I thought you had more class!"

"Look who's talking, man. What are *YOU* doing here? This isn't your kind of place either!"

'*Touche*', man. No, it's not. But then, once in a while I like to get together with my troops, find out what's going on behind my back in the command. Turns out there's a slight problem they wanted to talk about outside of the office. How about a beer? On me, man. I think this is the first time we've been in a bar together since the girls left. Let's have a toast to happier times ahead."

"Yeah, man, I'll take you up on the beer. Thanks."

"Grab a table, man, and I'll get the beers at the bar." Mike needed a couple of minutes to gather his thoughts together. He'd have to stall Lenny's questions. There was no doubt there'd be a bunch of them. The guy would never pass up a chance to meddle in something that didn't concern him.

The waitress was picking up an order as he reached the bar and she told Mike she would be happy to serve their table. He walked through the smoky room, reaching for his pack of cigarettes on the way. He'd been trying to quit, again, but with all of the turmoil, he wasn't having any luck. Once, he'd quit for several years. He couldn't remember why he'd started up again, but, his other self kept telling him 'Gimme a break. I need something to calm my nerves.' And he kept on smoking.

As Mike pulled out a chair to sit down, the waitress came with their order. Lenny grabbed his glass, took one gulp and exploded.

"Hey, bitch!" he shouted, "don'tcha know Americans like their suds served ice cold? What the hell is your problem? You don't care if you don't get some good old greenbacks for a tip or what?"

With that, he turned his glass upside down and poured its contents on the floor. The liquid splashed onto her legs, Mike's legs, Lenny's legs and, in the process, enraged Lenny even more. He raved like a maniac.

Mike was rendered speechless. He got up, threw a handful of lira on the table and walked out thinking 'If I stay, it'll end up in a melee, something I don't need right now.' He had a flashback to the night they were in the nightclub and it motivated him to move even faster.

Driving home, he kept shaking his head in disbelief. Why was Lenny in that particular bar? Why had he totally lost it over something so trivial? Why had his men gotten up and left the moment they saw Lenny?

Too many unusual things, bizarre behavior, unanswered questions. It would all come back to haunt him but not until long after he'd lost his naivete'.

11.

Mike spent a restless night, tossing and turning, trying to figure out just exactly how to handle the information he now possessed. How was he going to present it to Commander Keef in such a way that the man would understand there was a huge problem. When he got up, much earlier than usual, he still didn't have a solution. He got ready for work, drove off and stopped on his way for a large cup of espresso to jump-start the day.

As soon as he got to his desk, he dialed the commander's office. He could come over in half an hour, he was told.

While he waited he fidgeted, unable to start work on his own agenda. Finally, when it was time, he made up his mind. "No detours, no embellishments, no hemming and hawing. I will simply state the facts." As far as he was concerned, he couldn't get it done fast enough. He needed to pass the responsibility on to someone who had a lot more clout than he did.

As he walked the corridor, the question of what Lenny had been doing in that bar came back to bug him. 'Why am I thinking about that now?' he wondered. 'The guy has a right to be there as much as anyone else.' Still, the idea made him nervous. 'Could Lenny be an undercover NCIS agent? Does he know about the drug dealing and is he investigating me and my office personnel?'

He sighed deeply, knocked on the commander's door, was told to 'come in' and, after wishing 'the boss' a good morning, he closed the door, took a chair and began talking. "Sir, I have been struggling with the information I want to share with you for several weeks now. I feel it can't go unheeded any longer. It's been brought to my attention that there is serious drug dealing going on here in the command. It involves both men and women in every group, as far as I can discern. I regret I've waited this long to come to you."

"Chief, I appreciate your candor, your willingness to come forward. It can't have been an easy decision for you to make. What we need to do is contact Admiral Williams. He is the appropriate person to handle this kind of problem. I'll just dial him up, see if we get lucky, see if he's in his office this morning. Down there in Naples at NATO where he is, things seem to be a whole lot busier, more involved, than what we up here are accustomed to."

* * *

Mike could have no way of knowing about the personal relationship between the commander and the admiral. The two men had been room-mates as undergraduates at the Naval Academy, had been commissioned together, had shared assignments on several occasions and had virtually identical careers until, one morning, Gus woke up to find that his best friend had been promoted while he, Gus, had been passed over for advancement. Jealousy had reared its ugly face and Gus had to literally fight himself to keep a mountain of hatred from obscuring his logical reasoning. In time, it happened again. Now, his best buddy since they were teenagers was an Admiral while he, Gus, remained stagnated in rank. It was a huge, ongoing, personal problem for him.

In the meantime, Admiral Williams had sensed his pal's reaction. He had made it his business to call in some markers which kept Gus's name at the top of each possible promotion list. He had also seen to it that Gus was assigned to Italy when he, Greg Williams, was so they could continue their close companionship.

Gus Keef felt comfortable calling the admiral any time and had access to a private number which reached only the admiral. He dialed quickly and as he waited for Greg to answer, he was forming his remarks carefully. He had to alert Greg to the necessity of discretion somehow. For, the truth of the matter was, he was involved in the drug deals himself. And his old friend the admiral knew it. It may have been true that he was on the far-flung fringes, but it *was* involvement.

When the admiral answered, Gus repeated almost verbatim what Mike had told him. He mentioned, in what he hoped was a veiled way, that Mike was sitting in the room with him.

The Admiral heard him through to the end without interrupting and then stated, "Gus, you tell the Chief I will get right on this, alert the NCIS at once. Assure him that I will be getting back to you both with a progress report as soon as I hear something. Tell Chief Steele that his conscientious action in coming forward with this will not go unnoticed."

After thanking the admiral for taking his call, Commander Keef hung up the phone, turned to Mike and smiled, placed his clasped hands together behind his head, then leaned back in his swivel chair.

CODE NAME: WHITE MUSTANG

"Chief, the Admiral would appreciate it if we treat this predicament in a confidential manner for the time being. He feels certain that you understand the reasons behind his request. He will be contacting us the moment he has any information to pass along."

Mike assured the commander that he'd treat the situation properly, then thanked him for his time, walked out the door and felt as if he'd been resurrected from a tomb filled with evil omens.

Once Gus was sure Mike had gone on his way, he re-dialed the admiral who, he knew, was waiting for him to call back.

"Greg, it's me, Gus. Let's go secure, right?" He waited a moment until Greg gave him the word to go ahead and talk. He assured his friend, "We won't be overheard, monitored or taped now, Gus."

"Hopefully, you got my hint that the Chief was sitting here, Greg? I hated to spoil your day, but I couldn't think of any other way to handle it with him right here in the room."

"No problem, Gus. But now, I'm forced to reiterate what I've been saying to you all along. You need to get out of that situation. I may not be able to protect you much longer. The money *can't* be that important to you. I strongly urge you to come to your senses, Gus. Now that the word is out, I *MUST* act. You are more at risk now than ever before. I have no idea how deep this drug thing goes or what will be involved. You are my oldest and dearest friend but you *know* that I have to protect myself. If it ever comes to choices, a highly likely circumstance, I will have to sacrifice you in the interest of myself, my family and my own career. Trust me, Gus. As my kids would say, 'Get your act together'." And the admiral broke the connection without further ado.

After having listened to Greg, Gus felt an overwhelming sense of embarrassment. He had just been chewed out by an admiral who also happened to be his best pal. Not to mention, Greg was absolutely correct in advising him to straighten up. He would definitely take the advice into consideration.

Meanwhile, he would continue to accept the unmarked envelopes that turned up on his desk. He was a gambler at heart for one thing. *Surely* he would never be found out. Then too, the money was very welcome. The only thing required of him was to close his eyes and his mouth. *Someone* was gonna' do it…it might as well be him!

He leaned back in his creaky swivel chair, steepled his fingers, shut his eyes, and thought about the things he was accumulating thanks to the extra money that was his for doing nothing. A smile crossed his lips as he nodded off, taking a short, unscheduled nap in the middle of a morning filled with hustle and bustle.

12.

Teea, increasingly amazed, was finding each day a little easier to get through. Her Mother's willingness to take care of the twins when she had to work was a huge help. Her workplace was getting busier all the time. Word was spreading through the community that the ice cream parlor was *the* place to hang out.

The owner, a middle-aged lady, had designed the interior to replicate a World War II hangout. The long counter was fitted with wrought iron stools, several tables scattered about had matching chairs and all of the seats were covered in red and white striped fabric. She wanted the place to look patriotic. There were four booths lining one wall, the seats upholstered in faux, navy blue leather. Every other booth had a miniature juke box on the wall and the music available, for a nickel a pop, was vintage nineteen thirties and forties. Miller, the Dorsey's, Goodman, Shaw, Woody; the 'swing' bands.

The waitresses wore white 'snoods', a heavy hair net that was in fashion during the same era.

The uniforms were red, white and blue striped and so many compliments were given out that the girls soon began to relish their positions. The store was often crowded with senior citizens who basically came to listen to the music, tap their feet to the rhythms and enjoy a reasonably priced ice cream treat.

Cones were five cents, sodas and sundaes fifteen. Malts? A dime! Unheard of by the younger group, a fond memory for the oldsters. Best deal, banana splits a quarter!

M. L. Verne

The thing that surprised Teea was the number of teens who began frequenting the place. Even stranger, it appeared it was the music that was attracting them! Her Mom had told her, 'In my day, it was called a jump beat.' And jump they did. The older customers had a good time watching the kids try to jitterbug. Every so often, a grandfather type would help a couple of the kids out, show them steps.

It had become a fun place to work and Teea found she looked forward to her shifts. Meanwhile, she'd gone for her first session with the therapist. It had been a Thursday and they'd agreed on a standing appointment for however long it might be necessary.

Evelyna Kendrick, the therapist, was a fiftyish woman with an impressive array of professional accomplishments, the proof framed and hanging on her office walls. She was also pleased to show off her 'hobby', a virtual showcase of paintings. Quite beautiful, seeming to emit a sense of peace, rest, quiet. They were mostly ethereal land and seascapes.

Teea had been to three sessions before she found the courage to begin speaking about her wretched experiences in Italy.

"I'm a runner, Ev, an athlete with fairly good credentials. It's something I've always thoroughly enjoyed and worked hard at. I did my share of running over there, too. It wasn't an ideal situation, but I persevered. Running is the only way I know to stay in good condition between softball seasons. The running surfaces where we lived were basically cobblestone. You can imagine then why it was necessary for me to branch out to a paved area where it was smoother."

At that point, she'd had to pause, close her eyes, take a deep breath and gulp some water. Her agitation was showing. Ev waited quietly, giving Teea a chance to get herself composed. She stared fixedly at the items on Ev's desk to keep herself oriented to time and place. Seeing things like a writing pad, a telephone, a small reading lamp and a tape recorder sustained her.

After a few moments, she continued her narrative. "As it turned out, the choices I had made were all wrong. How was I to know, without a crystal ball and a fortune teller? The old women in the neighborhood were forever hanging over their balconies, sitting on their porches, sticking their noses into everything, gossiping like there was no tomorrow. I couldn't imagine *why* I would run past them and chance their snide remarks. None of *them* cared how they looked, how fat they were. That plus the bumpy terrain is why I ran outside of the area. With hindsight, I should have taken on the old bags and run around the school playground instead. Well, I opted for traffic and figured I would be relatively safe from getting killed by a crazy Italian driver if I kept as far as possible from the highway, close in to the fences along the sidewalks. Anyhow, this one particular day..." and she stopped, took another several swallows of water, emptied the glass, asked for more.

Ev obliged, checking the time surreptitiously.

The hour was up but no way was Ev going to interrupt. She sensed the entire story was about to burst forth, the cause of all her clients' distress. It was a vitally important moment.

Teea was seated in a lounge chair, stretched out, her head supposedly relaxed against a cushion.

Actually, she was so tense her head was suspended, inches from available ease and comfort.

Ev broke one of her strict, self-imposed rules. She walked behind Teea and massaged her neck and shoulders until she felt Teea start to relax, felt the tension seem to abate, her shoulders feeling more flexible. Then, she returned to her chair and raised her eyebrows, signaling Teea to continue. She reached over and turned the tape recorder back on as Teea resumed after folding her hands, hoping they wouldn't start shaking.

"On that particular day the weather was perfection. Fairly cool, a slight breeze, minimum pollution, for a change, because it had rained the night before. I hurried through my morning chores so I could get out there and enjoy exercising in a fairly pleasant atmosphere. I have to tell you, if you think this country has a pollution problem, you haven't seen anything until you visit the southern half of Italy! And, as far as I could tell, no one cares. The general attitude is, 'the old woman is gonna' blow again any day now and we're all gonna' get buried, so why bother?' Vesuvius of course. Cars on the highways slow down, huge sacks of garbage get tossed out the windows into the ditches alongside or just to the edge of the pavement. The stench gets overwhelming and a person has to drive with the car windows shut in order to breathe. You can imagine how awful that is on a hot summer day. But, I digress."

She got up and started pacing, having gotten worked up again. As she moved about the room she continued, "I began running the moment I stepped out of the house, and picked up speed quickly because I was feeling good and the weather was lovely. I was wearing my Walkman, listening to some good sounds, thinking about the problems Mike and I were trying to resolve, the things I would never be able to tell him about Lenny's harassment of me, his personal threats and so forth. It would never do to reveal all that stuff because there was no telling what Mike might do. He's usually pretty easy going, but under those black clouds of intimidation, there was no guarantee he wouldn't go off the edge."

Again, she slowed her steps and breathed deeply, wringing her hands. Then, she picked up her water glass and gulped until it was empty. And she whispered, "I ran faster and faster. I suppose it was the thoughts going through my head, the anger building up inside me. I was thinking 'How dare he do this to us...' and about then I got a stitch in my side, needed to slow down, try to catch my breath, get past the discomfort."

"Excuse me, Teea. I'm sorry to interrupt, but you'll need to speak a little louder in order for the tape to pick up your voice. Please, go on." Ev hated to stop the flow, but she had to have the scenario on record so she could go over it later.

"Sorry. It's so painful. So traumatic." Teea paused one more time for a last deep, cleansing breath, then continued, determined to get it all out into the open.

"As I stopped then to catch my breath, I leaned against the fence that bordered the sidewalk, needing a bit of support. I happened to glance toward the street where the traffic was dense, speeding by in a blur. Oh, my God! There he was! Lenny! He'd been there right along! I was certain of it! He was stalking me, from the comfort of his BMW. Just as I spied him, he slowed his car to a crawl. With him at the edge of the highway and me on the sidewalk, it flashed through my mind that I could outrun him, get home before he could park and come after me. In that moment, I knew how an animal must feel when it's being hunted. I straightened up, preparing to run. I will always believe if I had first seen him at some intersection, I would have made it. However, I was in about the middle of the block, with six lanes of traffic on my left, a high fence on my right and Lenny in-between. As I neared the corner, he pulled his car across the sidewalk, butted it up against the fence and I was trapped. I had been running again and I was going too fast to get stopped in time. So naturally, I ran right smack into the side of that car. It literally knocked the wind out of me. I had to grab at the door handle for support while I got my bearings.

Then I tried to ease my way around the car, thinking I still might have a chance of getting away. He stuck his face out the window and leered at me, the s.o.b. I cannot tell you how loathsome he was. He could see on my face that I hated him and was planning to keep running. So he nudged the car up as tight against the fence as it would go and left me with only one way out, alongside the car to the rear and then away. There was a thin gap there so I knelt down, planning to turn backwards. Lenny was calling, "Hey, baby, come to daddy. It's just you and me. Today's your lucky day. Climb in the car, girlfriend. We'll go on over to your place and get it on." At the same time, he was climbing out of the car. My nervous system was pretty well shot by then. Still, I had my wits about me. I sort of knelt down at the side of the car.

Thankfully, it was the passenger side. I watched under the car to see where he would go, feeling like I was frozen in time, everything moving in slow motion. I determined he was walking to the front of the car. That gave me extra seconds to make my move. Even though my heart was pounding like a jack hammer, I got into a sprinting position, took an enormous deep breath, stood up and ran. I mean, I ran like I had never run before! If I made it, I would have manipulated a manipulator and that thought, along with my hatred for him, carried me on winged feet. I was sure, by that time, that I had outmaneuvered him. He'd been acting strangely, and later I learned that he was high on crack and alcohol. But right then, I had no clue. I think it was a good thing I didn't or I'd have probably been too terrorized to go anywhere."

Teea stopped talking then and realized that, contrary to the tension she'd felt when she began her narration, she was now feeling relaxed, at least to some degree, and it came to her that her time was up.

"Ev, I'm sure the clock has run out so I'll finish this up next week. Obviously, I made it home safely that terrible day. There's more, but it will keep. Thank you for listening."

As Teea drove home, she thought about the end of her tale of terror. She'd run into her house, slammed and locked the door, ran to every ground floor window to be sure they were locked, was thankful she hadn't opened the window coverings before she'd left for her run and then she'd collapsed on the couch, exhausted. Wiped out. Panting for air. Covered in sweat. Miserable.

M. L. Verne

As the time passed she wondered, once or twice, what had become of Lenny. She also thought 'What's he doing way out here in the middle of a duty day?' Then, just as she was getting adjusted to breathing normally, preparing to take a shower, he was pounding on her door.

"Teea, you bitch, open up. I know you're in there. Open up or I'll break this fuckin' door down!"

The only thing she could think about was Anna across the street. If she was home and hearing that, oh lord what would happen? The entire neighborhood would know about it in a matter of seconds, that's what. 'I can only hope she went to the market.' It was a prayer.

As Lenny continued with his bizarre behavior at her front door, she sat numbly on the couch, shivering and trembling. 'Nerves' she told herself. 'Just calm down. This can't last much longer.'

Eventually it had stopped and, after a few seconds she had dared to tiptoe to the window and peek out. It was then that she knew Lenny was at least drunk, but probably was using some kind of drugs, too. It came as no surprise…she'd been suspecting it for quite a while. He was reeling his way down her front walk toward his car, seeming barely able to stay upright. She hoped he wouldn't pass out in the car in front of her house. She also hoped he wouldn't kill some innocent person as he drove drunkenly down the highway to wherever he was going.

The fool had driven away while Teea stood there thinking he was an abomination. She remembered how he'd ogled her at a couple of social functions everyone had been required to attend recently, how nervous it had made her, afraid Mike would notice and start something. Right then and there, she made up her mind to take her boys and go home to the safety of Colorado, U.S. of A. 'I can't tell Mike, I can't live with the stress, and I can't tolerate the abuse my boys are being subjected to. Even if I did tell Mike, he'd never believe me, he's so military. He'd find some kind of excuse for the Lieutenant Commander.'

After showering and scrubbing extra hard to rid herself of the creepy feelings, she'd gotten dressed and gone at once to the phone. The reservations were non-refundable. Mike would never cancel them and forfeit all that money. Then she packed. By that time, the boys were home from school so she told them they were going back to see their cousins for a visit. Then, they sat down to wait for Mike.

M. L. Verne

13.

Admiral Kingston stopped Mike in the corridor outside of his office, they spoke briefly and, as always, straight to the point.

"Chief, as you know, the situation in Bosnia is becoming more crucial with each passing day. NATO is going to beef up the forces there and we've been asked to send along a few key personnel to help out. Commander Keef suggested that you might appreciate the opportunity, the challenge. His reasoning is that the experience would look good in your service jacket now that the final phase of your application for LDO is almost ready for Washington. Think about it and get back to me in a couple of days, Chief."

As he watched the Admiral walk away toward his office, Mike thought, 'His job is so awesome, so filled with world affairs. Where does he find the time and space to include all 'his sailors',' as Mike knew he thought of everyone in his 'huge bundle of responsibilities?'

The more he considered his own questions, the more he realized that the Admiral, having risen to lofty heights from his beginning as a raw, basic recruit, would naturally know what life was like 'within the ranks.' Somewhere along the way, he'd managed to acquire a college degree and the rest was an amazing success story.

Suddenly, Mike found he was uptight and angry about the fact that neither Commander Keef nor Admiral Williams had gotten back to him about the drug problem. It had been long enough, his wait, and he decided to call, see what was holding up the NCIS investigation. 'I owe that much to Admiral Kingston,' he thought. 'The man has enough on his plate without adding an indigestible meal to his daily menu.'

Returning to his office, he sat down at his desk and immediately dialed the commander's office. As luck would have it, his Yeoman put Mike straight through to Commander Keef. Could this be a positive sign? He was hopeful.

"Sir, I'm calling with regard to that problem we were discussing a couple of weeks ago? I was wondering if you have any recent news to pass along to me?"

"Chief," Commander Keef answered him, "I'm glad you called. You know, with this Bosnia thing escalating, I've had to shelve most of my other matters temporarily, but let me relieve your mind by telling you Admiral Williams has taken full control of that situation you brought to our attention. He asked me to relay that message to you and tell you that as soon as he had something concrete to share, he would be contacting you personally. Meanwhile, if you want to call his office at some point, I assure you that would be acceptable. But, give yourself some slack. Incidentally, I'd like to encourage you to accept that offer to go to Bosnia. It would be a big plus for your career."

Mike hung up the phone with a frown on his face. He didn't know anything more than he had before he'd made the call. Plus now, he had two dilemmas to solve. Should he go to Bosnia? Should he call Admiral Williams? He hoped his phone would stay silent for a while so he could think without getting interrupted.

M. L. Verne

Luckily, he'd gotten the inside number to Admiral Williams' office so, all things being equal, that ought to put him right into the admiral's ear. Pro's and con's see-sawed back and forth in his head. Finally, tired of his own uncertainty, he dialed the number. The admiral's aide answered and said the admiral was not available. Mike asked if he would have the admiral return his call at his earliest convenience. The aide assured him he would be glad to oblige. "I'm sure you'll hear from him sometime today, Chief."

Mike then turned his thoughts to the offer of duty in Bosnia. It was a weighty matter and, when his phone rang, he had to admit he was grateful to have some distractions. His day got busier and it wasn't until after the lunch hour that he was able to think about Bosnia again. He turned it over in his mind, looked at the positive and negative aspects of it and finally was pretty much convinced that he wasn't going to avail himself of the opportunity. Why? He just seemed to have a 'gut feeling' that it wouldn't be in his best interests in the long run.

'Somehow, it doesn't feel right.' Even so, he would take it home and sleep on it.

'Should I? Shouldn't I?' crept in and out of his restless dreams. Even though the Admiral had assured him it would be his own decision, he couldn't help wondering if it would disappoint the man if he declined. It was a sack of worms.

Arriving in his office the next morning, he looked tousled and tired. His eyes were red and feeling scratchy. He hesitated a few moments, then lifted his phone, dialed Admiral Kingston's office and left him the message that 'I am honored to have been considered for the assignment to Bosnia but I feel I must respectfully decline the offer.' He gave no reason. He didn't really have anything plausible to excuse himself.

While he was at it, he made another call to Admiral Williams' office where only a messaging service answered. He repeated his request for the Admiral to return his call at his earliest convenience and then got busy with his own ever-increasing pressures.

Later that day, as Admiral Williams rifled through his messages, he saw that Mike had called twice in the past twenty four hours. He'd been in touch with the NCIS but, thus far, had heard nothing from them. He considered his options, then decided he would wait until he had some concrete information to relay before he touched base with Chief Steele. He called to his aide, asking that he be reminded he needed to call the NCIS offices in the next day or two.

Mike's messages went into the admiral's shredder. During the week, the admiral's aide reminded the admiral, two or three times, to call the NCIS. Admiral Williams was buried under paper work, all of it regarding the escalating hostilities in Bosnia. By Friday, Mike's request was history.

Over the next several weeks, Mike attempted to reach Admiral Williams a few more times, but had no success. Eventually, and also due to Bosnia, his own work-load grew into monumental piles of paper. Everyone was inundated. Admiral Kingston had gone to Washington on official business, Commander Keef had made two trips to Bosnia, some of the enlisted personnel had left Italy for one reason or another connected to the hostilities and Mike forgot about the drug dealing, the NCIS and all related subjects.

Almost everything that did, and did not, happen during that period of time was to have grotesque consequences in the coming months. Quite literally, world-wide.

14.

Not only was Mike up to his eyeballs at the office, but he'd been trying to find a smaller place to move into, and a part time job. He was about to become discouraged when one day he got lucky. He solved both dilemma's within hours of each other.

He got hired at a Navy mini-mart in an area where he also found a suitable apartment. The complex was gated and close enough so he could walk back and forth to the mart. There, he'd be stocking shelves along with various other duties.

Some of the guys from the office helped him move over the following weekend. Two of them had pickups, so it was all done in one trip. Then, they bar-b-q'd hamburgers, drank beer and had a helluva good time. So good, in fact, that they crashed on the floor and stayed the night. The next morning there were some aching heads, but all agreed it was worth the fun, an easy job since Mike had already sent most of the household goods home to Teea.

The apartment had enough furniture to suit his temporary needs; there was one bedroom, a 'head', a combination kitchen-living room, a closet, a stove and a fridge. A couch, a bed, a small dresser, a kitchen table and two benches, dishes, pots and pans, an extra fouton-like apparatus in case of company. The cook stove was something out of the dark ages, powered half by gas, half by electricity. Most unusual, to say the least. The fridge was quite definitely not self-defrosting.

M. L. Verne

He'd kept towels out of his shipment home, his stereo and one TV set. The shows were all in Italian, but he didn't watch much so he didn't mind. It was the sound of voices that he needed once in a while. He definitely wasn't planning on high volume like his old neighbors, Anna and Vince, preferred. He remembered how that had driven Teea buggy.

He still intended visiting the two old folks when he got a chance. He, unlike Teea, was fond of them and they enjoyed his company since their own sons were no longer residents of Italy.

When it was all said and done, he felt comfortable in his new 'pad', though lonely. The cooking arrangements in his weird kitchen were a humorous challenge for him and he was glad he enjoyed cooking. It saved him time and money.

One negative aspect to the place was the hot water system. It was totally foreign to him. He'd had to get a non-English speaking neighbor in to try and find out how to use it. What an experience!

They ended up laughing uproariously because it was such a 'trip', neither one of them understanding what the other was saying. Eventually, the neighbor went through the steps, one by one, while Mike watched carefully. Finally, he thought he could manage it and profusely thanked the guy. "*Grazie. Grazie.*" He repeated it over and over. He *had* learned the basics, after all.

And he hated the system. One of his favorite things was to get into a nice hot shower and just stand there letting the water pound down around him. Occasionally, he even sang some tunes while he soaked. Now? First of all, there was no *tank.* He discovered that the water ran through a series of small pipes and the connection to a gas outlet was of minimal help in heating the water. Therefore, he had to light the gas, wait a few moments, quickly get into the shower, wash, rinse and get out in the time it took to say a Hail Mary. There was no storage tank for the water; it only heated to a tepid degree and it was very frustrating. As soon as he was through he was obliged to turn the gas back off; the neighbor had strongly emphasized that.

'Not for long,' he promised himself. 'Come on LDO orders!'

The gates to the complex were manned by security guards who worked in shifts around the clock. They were friendly, outgoing, Italian, bilingual, speaking good English when Mike was around. He became friendly with all of them in a short time and they had smiles and jokes for each other. Very soon, they opened the gates for Mike when they saw or heard him coming.

When they learned that Mike had been walking to and from the mart at night, they were horrified. They pulled him aside and cautioned him. "This is not a safe area at any time, day or night. Why do you think the complex is secured? Murdered people get found in and among those trees over there on a regular basis. You must *always* drive your car, *never* walk again. Especially at night!"

Sheepishly, Mike agreed, thanking them for their concern. 'Well hell, how was I supposed to know?' he wondered. The business about the murders piqued his curiosity, so every now and then he'd ask a question or two when he slowed to drive through the gates. Soon, he pieced the information together to form a picture of the situation.

It seemed that the real estate in the entire area was owned jointly by two brothers who were members of the local Mafia. Occasionally, a dispute would erupt among some of them and their underlings, usually concerning the sale of some of the land. Inevitably then, someone would be found dead in the surrounding woods which were almost forest-like in their density.

No one was ever arrested, accused or brought to justice. It was 'a family matter' and did not concern anyone else. Blood ties were the bottom line. For Mike, it was an interesting story but also scary. Certainly, he never walked to work again.

There were times when he needed to remain in his office overtime which inevitably caused him to be tardy at the mart. His boss would get irritated with him, nasty about keeping him on under the circumstances and threaten to fire him. Mike would shrug and go about his duties, always catching up, getting ahead of schedule. His attitude was, 'I was looking for a menial sort of job when I came here. No big deal. Do what you must.' And the boss got the message because he never did anything other than threaten. He knew he had a good deal with Mike running things. Which was how it turned out almost right away. The boss needed a manager he could trust and Mike filled the bill.

The scenario was a source of amusing, droll humor for Mike. Here he was with a brain-dead job at the mart on the one hand and a boss who had the idea he was doing Mike a favor by keeping him working. On the other hand, he spent the days in his office dealing with world-shaking events which his Navy boss trusted him to do without interference. It was a window into the complexities of human behavior.

One evening, as he was hauling the trash outside, getting ready to close, a pretty young woman stopped to chat with him. He'd noticed her a couple of times in the mart visiting with Jill, one of the cashiers. Jill was also a sailor, stationed in Italy with her family, working the second job to help supplement her income. Her husband, a Navy Chief, was underway aboard a ship with the fleet in the Mediterranean.

"Hello there. My name is Margo Conway and you're Mike, right? I've seen you around some, here at the mart and at the Exchange. I work there, in the fine china department. I think you are really cute. Do you suppose we could get to know each other?"

"Thanks for the compliment, Margo, but I'm a long time married guy and it would probably be best if we just had a passing acquaintance, like, say 'hi' when we see one another?"

"You're being married isn't a problem for me, Mike. Think about it. Jill told me your family went to the states, so I bet you get lonely now and then. What's the harm in having a cup of espresso together, trading stories? Well. You know now where you can find me. If you change your mind." And she was gone. Just like that.

'Weird,' Mike thought. 'What was *that* all about?' In a short minute, he'd completely forgotten it. In the meantime, his social life *had* picked up a little, much to his delight. He admitted to himself that Lenny deserved the major portion of credit for it. He had absolutely insisted, wouldn't take 'no' for an answer, that he "get out of that dump you live in, man. Get your little white ass out, have a couple of beers with the guys. It'll do you a world of good."

Admittedly, he'd balked at first. Then he thought, 'Why am I making such a big deal of it? Because of Teea, that's why.' Well, she wasn't around to monitor him now so, what the hell….

Whether together drinking beers, talking on the phone or bumping into each other 'unexpectedly', Lenny was cleverly manipulating Mike, who didn't have an inkling. The 'social' aspect was a shrewd move. It was an easy maneuver, getting Mike dependent upon him for good times. In Lenny's lust for power, his greed for money, he *needed* Mike to make everything work. And for more than one reason. In spite of his promise to himself long ago, he had eventually succumbed and was now addicted to crack, worried that he might screw up on the job, afraid he would get caught and have to pay the ultimate price, but much too filled with his enormous ego to get any help. Except for Mike, who was going to help him all right. He was going to be the drug courier.

Lenny had made a trip into Turkey recently to check out the scene first hand. He needed to know every angle so, when the time was right, he could brief Mike. This new aspect, crossing international borders, was a little scary, a new concept for him. He'd had a close call returning to Italy on that trip. Only quick thinking and his lucky star saved him. He got through customs convinced they had stopped him, threatening his freedom, because of his black skin. It was a wake-up call. He needed to speed up his courtship of Mike who, as a lily-white American member of the armed forces, would have no trouble crossing borders all over Europe if it eventually came to that. His management of Mike's lifestyle was working wonderfully. Mike, depending on Lenny, unaware of the calamity in store, went about his two jobs, his nights 'out on the town' and his joyful anticipation of a family reunion buoying his spirits. He was one happy guy.

M. L. Verne

15.

The evening breeze brought with it a feeling that fall was just around the corner. It had been a wonderful summer with bright flowers and warm Italian sunshine, now and then a refreshing rain. Mike felt the cooler air as he was finishing up his evening chores at the mart. He'd stepped outside with the trash and paused to savor the crisper smells that were wafting in from the beach nearby. As he stood with his eyes closed, breathing deeply, he thought he heard a tapping somewhere. It was insistent, so he followed the sound into the mart and toward the front door. He saw a silhouette in the window of the door and approached slowly. He'd never forgotten the warnings from the guards at his apartment complex about the neighborhood at night.

There was a small light bulb shining from above the doorway and he was able to make out the face of the young woman who had introduced herself to him a while back, there at the mart. Damned if he could recall her name though.

She tapped on the window again and waved her fingers at him, smiling through the dirty window. Still he hesitated, thinking she might have someone out there with her, standing in the shadows, waiting to pounce on him. He couldn't imagine why anyone would want to do that though, since there was next to no money in the place. The boss always went to the bank at the end of his day.

He shrugged and went up to the window, noticing again how cute the girl was. She stood there grinning

CODE NAME: WHITE MUSTANG

at him, her eyebrows raised in a question mark. He couldn't resist. He opened the door, took her arm, pulled her inside quickly, closed and locked the door instantly. Then he felt foolish. She was quite obviously all by herself.

"Hey there," he said, smiling, "what can I do for you?"

"Hi. It's Mike, right? Thanks for letting me in. I was afraid. I am so relieved that you're still here. It was very creepy out there in the dark. Can you believe it? My car has broken down."

As she was speaking, Mike was checking her out, trying to be subtle. She was well-dressed, tastefully well-dressed. Her makeup was applied carefully, flawlessly. She had silky-looking, shoulder length blonde hair that Mike just knew was her natural color. Well, maybe a slight rinse. He'd learned those little female tricks from Teea. Her eyes were wide, round and a brilliant green, the lids edged with incredibly black lashes which were daintily touched with mascara. 'A little Barbie doll,' Mike thought at first, but then, 'no, she definitely resembles Jodie Foster. But even cuter.'

And she had been saying "...so I just had no other recourse but to cross my fingers and hope you would still be here. Mike, would you consider taking me home? It's kind of a long way, actually the other side of the city, but at this hour there won't be much, if any, traffic so we can make good time. I would be so very appreciative and will gladly fill your gas tank."

"You got lucky, Margo, in spite of whatever is wrong with your car. In five more minutes, I'd have been out of here for the night. Sit down there on the counter and I'll be right back."

He had a couple more things to tend to. It did not enter his mind to take a look at her car. He was a fairly competent mechanic, having learned lots of skills from his Dad over the years. If the problem was minor, didn't require any parts, he probably could have fixed it.

Instead of thinking about that, he was crowding his mind with questions about her showing up as she had, just at that hour, so soon after her other visit when she'd been hitting on him, telling him his marital status wasn't a problem for her. She was trolling and *he* was her prey!

As he emerged from behind the shelves, he started to ask her just how far it would be to her place but, instead, stopped dead in his tracks, stunned. She was sitting on the counter with her back arched, her breasts thrust forward, her head tipped back, her long, slim neck encircled by pearls. She was looking at him from the corner of one eye, her ears also holding small pearls in their lobes. Her 'lbd', little black dress as his brother called such a frock, clung to her body seductively and her shapely legs were crossed, the dress at, or just above, mid-thigh. 'What a picture', he sighed to himself as he felt a stirring in his groin that he'd not experienced in one heck of a long time. He didn't know it yet, but he was hooked!

She knew it and was grinning inside her brain as she thought 'piece of cake. I was *right* about him being easy.'

Just a few minutes before, Mike had been ready to go home, fall exhausted into his bed. Now? He'd already forgotten his weariness he was so eager to get going with her in the car next to him. He was anticipating her cheerful, smiling companionship.

He helped her down from the counter and they walked toward the front door together. He opened it, they exited and he locked it securely for the night. His car was parked out in the lot, and he didn't even glance around to see where her car might be. He opened the passenger door for her and it squealed like a witch on Halloween. She slid in and fell to the seat, which was flat on the floor, laughing as she dropped.

Her laughter was contagious. The sight of her sitting below the level of the window was hilarious. They both had to stop and catch their breaths after a moment.

He took the opportunity to apologize for the broken seat which he'd totally forgotten he'd dislocated, making it easier to take his laundry in and out of the car when he went to the laundromat.

He'd gotten only one or two words out when Margo said, "Mike, don't mention it. I have always wondered why you military guys go for these wrecks and I must say, yours is one of the worst I've ever seen." And again she began laughing.

By then, he was helping her back out of the car so he could fix the seat. He had some supports in the back so all he needed to do was take the front seat out, put the supports in place, put the seat on top of them and that would be that. It wasn't very safe except that the seat belt was available, in spite of everything else being wrong. He didn't think she'd be in any danger riding that way. They discussed it briefly and she assured him she had no qualms about it.

The entire episode had turned into a cozy, intimate moment for the two of them. As they drove along Mike said "You'd best not say any more negative things about this buggy of mine. Just listen to that motor. It purrs like a kitten. The way it looks is of no consequence. In fact, it's a plus. Anyone looking at it doesn't bother to try and get me into a crash…not worth their effort, they think. Meanwhile, it gets me where I need to go, with no problem, like, on greased wheels you might say."

She smiled at him, her sparkling white teeth gleaming in the light from the dashboard. Her complexion was as clear as the skin of a blemish-free peach. She started to giggle as he looked at her.

"What?" he asked. But she shook her head and didn't respond. She settled more snugly into the seat, pulling the seat belt tighter, sighing quietly.

"Margo, I thought I detected a slight accent to your speech. What's that all about?"

"My Dad is a retired Navy Chief, Mike. He and my Mom were married here in Italy where they met. Mom is a Neopolitan. He was on shore leave at the time and he told me he was smitten by her beauty. In a little while, they had me. Then Dad had to go back on sea duty and they really never got back together. Mom isn't about to leave her beloved Naples and Dad had to finish his time so he could retire. Then he decided he didn't want to live in Italy although, to give them both the credit they have coming, they did try to make a go of it. Anyhow, he now lives in New England, Mom is in Naples and I am bilingual. That's the long way around telling you about my slight accent."

Mike told her about his twins, how proud he was of them.

"They are so handsome, Margo. And so smart." He explained that they were in the states with their mother but went no further, thinking it was really not any of her business. Besides, he didn't want to spoil their time together by getting sad. She was already aware of his family problems, but was smart enough not to hammer the subject. Some of Mike's buddies had mentioned his troubles to her when she'd asked them questions about him. Truth be told, she was on a mission, Mike was her goal and he didn't have a chance.

It seemed like only five minutes had flown by when Margo was directing him into an apartment building parking lot. "Here we are, Mike. That wasn't so bad, huh? The time went quickly. Will you come up for some coffee before you drive back home? You probably need some so you can stay awake."

Just for an instant, he stalled. What would he be putting himself into? Jeopardy? A vision of Teea flashed through his mind's eye. In another instant he'd convinced himself he was 'a big boy now', could conduct himself properly. 'If I can't handle this, I need to go back to square one.' Then he smiled and accepted her invitation for some coffee. They crossed the parking lot after locking the car doors.

Margo told him they would need to refrain from speaking until they got into her apartment.

"It's probably the most important reason I moved here. Peace and quiet. Many of the other tenants are elderly and they're in bed so early it makes my head ache. But I like their style. Am I making sense?"

M. L. Verne

They entered the building, climbed one flight of stairs and walked silently down the carpeted hallway. At the end of the corridor, she held up her hand, put her key into the lock of the corner doorway and they went into her place, closing the door without a sound. Then they looked at each other as if they'd been involved in a conspiracy and again they busted out in laughter.

She was so charming and Mike was so charmed, it felt as if he'd known her forever. It had been a long time since he'd felt good inside for no special reason.

"Mike, have a seat and I'll get us something to drink. Do you still want coffee? I have beer, wine, liquor, whatever you'd like."

"Surprise me," he answered her as he sank into the most comfortable looking chair in the room. It had an accompanying ottoman. He rested his legs on it and before two minutes had passed, he was dozing.

Margo returned with a tray, glasses and a bottle of chilled wine. She was reluctant to disturb him, placing everything on the coffee table as quietly as she could manage. But the glasses clinked together slightly and it woke him up with a start.

"I don't ever remember feeling so relaxed and cozy," he told her.

"I'm glad," she said, smiling at him. "You don't need to move an inch. Here, try some of this local wine. It's a favorite of mine and I think you'll enjoy it."

Then she lifted her glass and offered a toast. "To you, Mike. It feels right to have you here in my home. As a matter of fact, I've often day-dreamed of this very thing. Now you see, you *are* here. So as I said, to you and also to dreams that come true."

She had changed into 'something more comfortable'. He admired the difference without putting his thoughts into words.

Mike had been married a long time and had forgotten about the male/female sexual rituals. He did, however, recognize that he was bewitched by this lovely girl.

She had planned this tryst with great care, up to and including what she was going to 'change into.' The gown was a pale, lustrous peach in color, just barely hinting at transparency. It was floor length, tied under her breasts with a sash of varied colors of pink, peach and ivory which were all braided together to make a delightful splash of gently vibrating colors. The neckline was scooped just low enough to reveal a hint of cleavage, the sleeves gathered at her wrists in graceful folds.

Mike sat admiring her and thinking, 'What a sexy creature. Good lord, I hope I don't screw this all up. It's been a long, long time.'

Any thoughts of his family had vanished. He was totally focused on Margo, her petite young body, her silky hair, her shining eyes that were daring him to 'do something…' He was painfully aroused and knew she could see his erection. His scalp was itching under her scrutiny. For her part, she had a small grin on her lips but it was accompanied by an overall look of sweetness, not irony.

They were sipping their wine in unison, the room pulsing with unleashed pheremones, the atmosphere thick with their wants and desires. As they raised their

M. L. Verne

glasses again Margo said, "Mike, you need to stay for the night. I have what you'll be needing."

He began to chuckle, rose from the chair and started across the room toward her. He did not care if she 'had what he'd be needing' or not. He'd go to the office naked if he had to!

Margo felt a shiver of satisfaction ripple down her spine. She'd planned this since the very first time she'd set eyes on him and was determined to make their time together safe, tender, full of joy and laughter, for however long it lasted.

16.

He could not believe his good fortune. For the first time since Teea and the boys left him, he was whistling as he worked. The guys in the office were snickering behind his back. It didn't take a brain surgeon to figure out that their Chief had 'gotten laid'.

Eventually, they'd discover who she was. Meanwhile, they were happy for him. They had a great deal of respect for and confidence in him. All agreed he deserved a break; he'd been very lonely and miserable lately. Besides, if the Chief was in high spirits, life would be easier for them!

Mike sat at his desk in a pink cloud of euphoria. The girl was a marvel of tenderness, greed and unrestrained appetites. In just one incredible night she'd taken him from despondency to ecstasy, shaken him to the core of his being. He knew it was partly due to his having had no sex at all for a long, long time. He and Teea had just not been able to continue the intimate part of their life together. It had begun even before his last six month cruise.

Way more than that though, Margo was an accomplished lover. Grinning internally, he was thinking, 'She knows just which buttons to push and, oh, brother, did she ever push mine!'

She was so young. If he added only a couple of years to his own age, it would make him old enough to be her father. Incredible!

He couldn't help wondering where she'd learned all of her tricks and decided that some day he was going to ask her.

M. L. Verne

Gazing out of his office window, reliving the whole experience in his mind, he felt himself getting aroused again.

They had quite literally crashed into each other in the middle of her living room. She'd thrown her legs around his waist, clinging to his neck, he grabbing her smooth, round, solid backside in both of his hands. They had hung there, embracing.

He'd tried to kiss her mouth but she was kissing his face so he couldn't make contact. She'd torn his shirt open, buried her face in his neck, then in his chest hair. She had begun moaning, pointing toward the bedroom behind them, whispering to him that he could back up and she would guide him to the bed without mishap.

He backed up slowly, trusting her, hoping they wouldn't bang into walls or furniture along the way. She didn't fail them. He felt the mattress pressing against the backs of his legs in a moment. He lowered them together onto the bed, ending up with her on her back looking up at him, giggling with delight. Again, it was a scenario which caused them both to burst into shared laughter.

Later, he was unable to recall how it came about but in an instant, they were naked. First, they were clothed, then they were not. Astonishing!

She had rolled aside, nudged him under her and was on top of him before he could blink an eye. He could not take his gaze from her breasts which were surprisingly full for such a petite, small girl. She was certainly proud of them, the way she thrust her chest forward, arching her back to make them appear larger.

He reached up and stroked the nipples which became erect with a simple touch. Pinkish tan areola's surrounded them, smooth and enticing. Her breasts fit comfortably in his hands and he sighed with satisfaction as he cupped them tenderly.

Her eyes were glistening in the soft light coming from the pink bedside lampshade, the color complimenting her face on one side, casting the opposite side in seductive shadow. He sensed, rather than saw, a tear trickling down each of her cheeks. But everything was happening so quickly he had no chance to speculate on any possible reasons for the unexplained emotion.

Then, she was grinning again as she reached behind her and took hold of his erection in one hand while maneuvering into a position which made it simple for her to slide slowly down his belly, leaving a trail of her lubricating juices along the way.

She'd mounted him slowly, erotically, encompassing his organ into the moist warmth of her innermost self.

Sitting in his office, mentally savoring the experience, he saw again the bursting stars, the streaking comets, all the colors of a rainbow swirling around their heads. It was sheer bliss. Again, he experienced the rapture of their shared orgasm in his memory.

He felt anew the breathless contentment they had shared after reaching orgasm. Their hearts had been pounding in sync, their bodies shining with sweat. They'd lain in an easy embrace, breathing slowly, returning to normal, devoid of any strength to move. In moments, they fell asleep.

By their reckoning, it wasn't much later when they'd awakened, looked at each other, smiled and it had all begun again. Only the second time, it was slow and deliberate instead of frantic. Mike took charge, exploring every nook, cranny and crevice of her delicious body, bringing her to such arousal she had begged him for release. She'd been breathless from panting and only then did he enter her. They had soared to dazzling pinnacles of eroticism that left both of them deliriously exhausted.

"I *knew* it would be like this," she whispered. "The first time I saw you I knew. We are going to have the most wonderful, memorable relationship you could ever imagine, Mike!"

He'd been wordless, had lain there staring at her as if he'd found Shangri-la. His thoughts had swirled around in his head like mini-tornadoes. Finally, he'd swallowed, cleared his throat, hoping his voice wouldn't fail him, praying he wouldn't flounder.

He said to her, "Margo, I don't quite know how to express my feelings. I'm not very good at romantic talk. Holy matrimony! I've never known anything like this. I guess it all comes down to a simple thank you for finding me. For caring enough to make this happen. For putting joy back into my life. For reminding me that there *is* a life outside of my self pity."

She'd shown her pleasure at his words by caressing his face and smiling sweetly. No more words were needed. They fell deeply asleep then, with her head on his shoulder, his cheek atop her head. He'd been hoping, as he drifted off, that the sunrise would be magic, one he would always equate with the fantastic experience they had shared.

No luck! He'd forgotten this was southern Italy with all its smog, smoke, soot, reeking odors and debris in the atmosphere. He opened his eyes slowly at dawn and found himself looking directly out the slightly opened window. He expected to see the early rays of a brilliant sun coming through the leaves of the tree. It was just within arm's reach. As the light turned from gray to early sunlight, he saw only the tree. Beyond that? Brown smog. Even the birds, if there were any, weren't singing.

It was a disappointment following close upon the marvelous night he'd just spent with Margo. Even so, it wasn't a daybreak he wished disappointments into, so he turned to look at Margo. Which was actually not only *not* disappointing but was memorable. She looked as innocent as a new born babe as she slept, her pearly shoulders gleaming faintly in the early morning light. Her hands were tucked under her chin infant-like and she had a slight smile on her lips. 'Even in sleep she's heartrendingly lovely', he thought. Momentarily he was saddened, wishing he could spend the day with her. But he knew he had to get up, get moving.

As carefully and quietly as possible, so she wouldn't be disturbed, he got out of bed and went into the 'head' to take care of his urgent necessities. She'd thoughtfully laid out everything he'd need in the way of toiletries, true to her promise of the night before. Soap, shaving cream and lotion, tooth brush and paste, comb, razor, mouth wash, deodorant…He showered quickly because he was already behind schedule. But, he relished every second nonetheless. It was the first time he'd had adequate hot water since moving into his place. It was a gift! Once he'd dried off, he crept through the bedroom, grabbing his clothes, dressing swiftly as he went.

M. L. Verne

He wandered into the kitchen looking for a note pad and a pencil. Hastily he scribbled, 'Margo, you are a doll, absolutely beautiful in your contented sleep. Thank you for the joy of this new day. I will call you later.'

In his office, remembering all of it, he continued smiling and whistling a little tune.

Then his phone rang. It was the signal for him to begin another busy day serving his country.

17.

Now that he had a *life*, Mike was in a perpetual state of satisfaction with everyone and everything. Margo was 'a keeper' and he intended keeping her! After only a few days, he asked her if she would think about moving in with him. "Consider it done," she'd laughingly replied. He didn't know she'd had her belongings packed by mid-morning after their first night together. The girl knew what she was about and had wasted no time going after her objective.

The same guys who had moved Mike into his apartment were gathered together to move Margo. *Now* they knew. And they most definitely approved.

Behind his back they said, 'He's a lucky son of a bitch.' They high-fived, grinning like fools, while they each confessed they'd lusted after her too. She was the gorgeous one who worked in the Navy Exchange.

They got her settled into Mike's apartment and declined the invitation to bar-b-q again. Hey! If they had a girl like that in *their* place, they wouldn't want a bunch of idiots hanging out, waiting to be fed.

As the days went by they got around to talking over mundane things, like, Mike had installed an answering machine. But he told her, "Under no circumstances," was she to answer the ringing phone until the machine clicked on and she found out who was calling.

"I do *not* need to share you with my family, Margo!"

"No problem, Mike. No big deal. Relax...I may be young but I wasn't born this morning...."

He had also re-affirmed with her, one night after making exquisite love, that their arrangement was temporary. He thought of their relationship as having fallen in lust. Again, she reassured him. "Mike, I know you'll have to go back to the states eventually. Don't worry about it. Your family comes first. So does mine!"

Then she told him she had a two year old son who lived with her mother in Naples.

"His Father is the nephew of one of the Mafia Dons around here. He doesn't take any responsibility for the child we have. The boy has never seen the man. I doubt if it will ever happen. I have to work to support my son, but I go to Naples whenever I have time off to relieve my Mom and also to spend time with Joey. I named him after my Dad, Jonah. You would love him, Mike. He's just starting to talk and he's *so* cute! Maybe one day you can come with me to Naples."

She had stopped talking then and Mike, sensing there was more to the story, decided to give her some space.

'She'll tell me the rest one of these days,' he assured himself.

Eventually she did and it was a long, involved narrative about the Mafia families in the area.

"You have to understand, Mike, it's an entirely different culture from what you know about in the U.S. Family blood lines are the absolute top priority. My son is an inroad for me personally so then you by extension. You just never know when a connection like that will come in very handy. The guys at your security gate? Nephews, cousins. They've told me they respect and admire you. That makes you extremely lucky, locally."

The only thing he knew about the Mafia was what he'd seen in American movies, the Hollywood version. He thought her tale was interesting. However, it certainly had nothing to do with him

She sensed his disinterest but wanted him to know where she was coming from if they were to have a completely open and honest relationship. So she continued. "He, the Don, wants me to marry the father of my baby, his nephew. It's that old fashioned idea; birth out of wedlock is a sin. It's against '*Chiesa santo madre*', they keep telling me. Yet they murder, cheat, run whores in circles and want me to get married because it's against Holy Mother Church to have an illegitimate son? Give me a break!"

She'd gotten herself all worked up. Mike saw there was a need to change the subject so he started to tell her about Lenny.

"The guy has been a friend to me, but you know what? I really need to try and get him out of my life. There's something there that I can't put my finger on. It gives me a funny feeling in the pit of my stomach. Besides, he's much too controlling."

Margo had met Lenny once. She had disliked him instantly.

"You got that right! He comes on way too strong to suit me. I haven't yet figured out why you stay tied up with him."

He'd rushed to Lenny's defense immediately but as Margo continued talking, he'd come to see what the guy looked like through someone else's eyes. More or less.

M. L. Verne

Teea's face flashed through his thoughts, there and gone. She'd said almost the same, identical things. Ignoring her at the time, he had told himself, 'It must be a wife thing.'

"It's a difficult situation for me, Margo. Forgetting everything else, he *is* in charge of my final acceptance into the LDO program. So the very last thing I should be doing right now, in the interest of my military career, is alienating him. It's kind of a 'Catch 22', you could say."

She wasn't sure what that meant, but if it eventually led to his shedding the guy, she was all for it. Like her talk of the Mafia to Mike, his talk of Lenny to her was a bore. They spoke of other things then, getting their thoughts back on the track of their own personal involvement with each other.

As for Lenny during that period of time, he knew all about Mike and Margo. Eventually, he knew, he could use the situation for extra leverage. Everything was falling into line. He was elated! With the two of them living together, Mike would be that much more easily controlled. It might take a bit of blackmail but he, Lenny, was very good at what he was doing. Everything was going to come up smelling like roses.

CODE NAME: WHITE MUSTANG

18.

Bosnia was getting hotter by the day. NATO was in control. Mike's work place was a flurry of activity. Occasionally, when he had a minute to reflect, he regretted he hadn't taken the opportunity to go there on the mission the Admiral had suggested. Then he and Margo would climb into bed and he'd thank his lucky stars he'd turned down the assignment. 'Oh, boy. If I'd gone, we may not have met. That would have been a loss.'

He was so immersed in his ever mounting responsibilities he almost didn't see Admiral Kingston walk into his office.

Belatedly, he scrambled to his feet, nearly knocking his chair over in his haste.

"Don't worry about it, Chief," the Admiral said, grinning. "I know you weren't expecting me. Let's sit down for a few minutes. I have some news that will be affecting you. The Pentagon has ordered us to close up these facilities. The word just came through. I know it's an unexpected shock and I have no answers for your questions. Just like you, I'm subject to higher authority and must jump when the word comes down. Your immediate job will be to secure everything you're in charge of and to begin dismantling at once. It'll be your show. I'll leave all of that up to your discretion knowing you'll do your usual outstanding job. Meanwhile, I've already made arrangements for your temporary duties while you wait for your LDO orders. Commander Keef will be remaining here, in the compound, until it's all buttoned up and will then move across town while he awaits his new orders. You will be following him. As for me, confidentially for now, I've been ordered to the Pentagon to assume the duties of the Chief of Naval Operations, God help us all! Summing up; I want you to know I've taken care of you. Now, let me wish you good luck as you take on more rank and responsibility."

Mike was taken aback, stunned, speechless. He stared at the Admiral who continued speaking, perhaps to allay Mike's shock.

"You will be an outstanding officer and I'll be keeping my eye on your progress. We'll meet again one day. Count on it!"

Mike was able to regain his speech well enough to half-stutter, "If I may Sir, I'd like to wish you the very best too. It looks as if both of us are about to shove off into unknown seas that will be loaded with serious challenges. It's been an honor to work with and for you, Sir. And thank you for your kind words."

They shook hands and the Admiral left the office without saying more. Mike stood rooted to the floor, his mind in turmoil.

'Close the compound? It's a very important part of allied defenses in Europe.' He could not comprehend it! Unbelievable! Then, when he thought about the things the Admiral had said to him on a personal level, he felt a lump forming in his throat. He had been privileged to have the man come to *his* office. The compliments and good wishes were an added bonus.

As his day wore on and he started 'undoing' everything he was responsible for, he thought about all the changes that were about to occur. Closure of the area, a move to another office across town.

CODE NAME: WHITE MUSTANG

As if that weren't enough, a new job which he didn't yet have a clue about, the Admiral to be the new CNO. No longer working for the Admiral....Holy Matrimony!

He needed to *talk* to someone. Margo had the late shift. Then, she was going to Naples after work. Anyhow, she wouldn't understand the fallout from all of it. Besides, the Admiral had asked him to keep things confidential for the time being.

He called Lenny, who probably knew everything already anyhow. It was his job to be on top of such things.

"Wanna go for a beer after work, man?"

"Fuck yeah, man. How about 'The Place?' Sixteen hundred hours? That good for you?"

Mike agreed and they disconnected. Lenny could not believe his good fortune. He knew Margo would be out of town, he knew Mike was shook up over the changes, he knew *this* was the time to move. 'Yahoo' his brain was yelling. Before the night was over, he'd have Mike in his back pocket. He was sure of it.

19.

Lenny got to the tav a few minutes before Mike and had two foamy beers ordered up, sitting on the bar. He was sure he had all his ducks in order and was impatient to get the show on the road. Glancing toward the door, he saw two men come in who he'd been expecting, two Air Force guys who were on his drug payroll, contacts to other 'fly boys'. He nodded as they passed him, headed for the rear of the room. It had all been pre-arranged. He was glad they'd shown up before Mike.

When Mike arrived, Lenny rejoiced inwardly. He'd been right. He could tell by Mike's body language, the look on his face, that he was in a funk. It would make his devious approach that much easier. Mike was gonna' be a push over.

As he neared the bar, Lenny yelled "Hey, my man, I could not believe it when you called. I was thinking about you, off and on, all day. Great timing. What's happenin'?"

Mike slid onto the stool next to Lenny, took up the glass of beer, gulped half of it, lit a cigarette, inhaled, sniffed, wiped the foam from his upper lip and swirled the icy glass around on the counter top.

Then he told Lenny, "Bad day for me, man. Could not be worse. I need to vent. Hope you're up to hearing me?" He didn't wait for an answer but kept right on, spilling it all out.

"I thought nothing could be worse than having my family go away. I was wrong. Have you heard? Our compound has been ordered closed. That place has

CODE NAME: WHITE MUSTANG

been in operation since the second world war. What the hell are they doing, man?"

"Yeah, I heard. Bummer. Got the word this morning in my mail pouch. That's prob'ly why I've had you on my mind all day. But hey! It's like good news, too. You're gonna' be up front in Kingston's mind."

"So?" Mike scowled at Lenny, wondering what *that* meant.

"Well hell, man, he's gonna' be the new CNO and you've been on his staff here and you're gonna' be an officer and he's not about to forget any of that. He's got a soft spot for you. Oh yeah, I know what I'm talking about. He called me up to chat about you before he came by to give you the bad news you're all shook up about. See, we had already spoken together before your review by the LDO panel in my office, so he knows we communicate. I suggested that he find you a temporary job in my building until your orders come through. That's the other good news, man! You're gonna' be right down the hall from me. A pissy job, as far as I can tell but fuck, man, it's just for a little while."

He paused to drink some of his beer, watched Mike out of one eye, then lit another cigarette off the butt of the one he'd already been smoking. It gave Mike a chance to try and get all the news in order inside his brain. He didn't realize he was shaking his head from side to side while mulling it over, but Lenny noticed and it made him giddy.

'The guy is struggling. It couldn't be a better time. I gotta' *move!*'

M. L. Verne

Out loud he said, "What else is new, man? How's Margo?"

He knew Mike wasn't listening, but he kept on talking, allowing Mike a chance to get his thoughts in order.

"Whaddaya hear from your boys? Cate and Lonzo are all settled in a condo in Pensacola. She's got a job in an art gallery. Assistant Curator or something. She's into that kinda' shit. I think it's a waste of time myself. Culture? She can have it all. Still, that's why I married her. Good for my career, you know. Culture and a great education. Her parents live down in the 'boot' and they grow olives. One of these days, we're gonna' take a trip down to visit them. They're *always* glad to see me."

'Whatever,' Mike thought. He was already wishing he hadn't called the guy to get together. Mentally, he shrugged. 'Guess I'll never learn,' and he wondered if Lenny had ever heard the old adage 'When you're talking, you don't learn anything.' Plus, he already knew the bullshit the guy had to offer. He could not, for the life of him, understand how Cate continued to stay married to the jerk. He abused her physically and their son emotionally, if not psychologically. "Go figure," he mumbled into his chin.

At last, Lenny began to wind down. It gave Mike a chance to speak. "Man, I've been thinking about getting a motorcycle." Instantly, he knew he'd screwed up. Again!

"OoooooEeeeeee!" Lenny screeched. "What a cool idea, man. What kind? When? I wanna' get one, too!"

CODE NAME: WHITE MUSTANG

Mike had no alternative. The cat was out of the proverbial bag. So now, he had to finish what he'd started.

"A Harley, man. It's the only way to go. Do you happen to know any of the guys in the biker's club on base? I was thinking I'd get in touch there, see what they have for suggestions."

"Let's do it, man. We can go tearing around this friggin' country in leather and shades lookin' like 'easy riders'."

Mike's heart went kerplunk. 'Shit,' he groaned to himself. 'He's a *CLING ON*! Now I'll *never* get away from him.'

Lenny was shouting in his exuberance. Eventually, he got around to pointing to the table at the back of the room by the pool table and said to Mike, "See those guys? They're fly boys. They belong to the bikers club. Let's go sit with them and we can find out the best kinda' bikes to get."

'I do not want to go riding around Italy with this guy', Mike was thinking. 'In fact, I do not want to ride *anywhere* with him. It can only lead to some kind of mishap.'

But instead of speaking out, telling Lenny exactly how he felt, he succumbed again to the overpowering personality of the man, following him to the table in back just like a child after the pied piper. Lenny was waving his arms wildly, yelling across the smoky room

"Hey you guys, we're comin' over. Make room. You ready for another beer?" He gestured to the waitress for a new round.

Mike asked himself, 'What the hell? This is no way for a senior officer to be acting in public. I don't care if he *is* off duty. It's a disgrace!' He frequently asked himself how come Lenny chose to hang out with lower ranked enlisted guys in a run-down beer joint. So far, no answers.

He could not possibly know that Lenny was high on crack and the three beers he'd already consumed only exacerbated the shape he was in. All his raucous behavior wasn't lost on the Air Force guys either. What a way to represent the Navy. They knew he was into drug dealing, of course. He'd hired them to be on his team. But though they suspected, they hadn't been able to prove that he also *used*. They knew, for sure, that he hung out in 'The Place' because that was where most Gaeta drug deals went down.

Lenny introduced Mike to the fly boys as Craig and Bill. Nothing more. In an attempt to divert their attention away from Lenny's manic behavior, which was embarrassing him, Mike poked fun at them, bantering over the fact they'd chosen the Air Force above the Navy. It was all in good humor, the way of military people who belong to different branches of the armed forces. All throughout their verbal fun, Lenny continued to rant and rave. No one was paying him any attention, but he didn't seem to notice such a minor detail.

The more beer the four of them consumed, the more fun they thought they were having. They told dirty jokes, swilled more beers and laughed uproariously. They were getting very drunk but at least, at one point, had enough sense to order food. Big, fat, juicy hamburgers, fries and slaw. If not for that, they would have fallen off their chairs.

CODE NAME: WHITE MUSTANG

Soon, Lenny steered the conversation around to drugs. He related how he was making mountains of money the 'easy way', explaining to them that they could do the same thing with no negative consequences. Bill and Craig asked a few direct questions which Lenny had equipped them with, earlier in the day, as bait.

It was all a ruse to hook Mike. Lenny answered the questions, directing his words straight at Mike. He elaborated on his comments about trips to other countries, taking money in and out, bringing drugs back, foreign people involved, everything so fascinating to his three listeners they stopped swilling beer for a little while. Finally, when he was sure he had their absolute, undivided attention, he unloaded his secret. He couldn't keep his ego under control any longer. He shared the fact that he was a user, then asked, "Mike, have you ever done a line? Cocaine, that is."

"Hell no, man. I don't get into that kind of shit. There's no place in my life for it. Teea would kill me. Dead." His words were slurred, his eyes unfocused. He needed to pee. His bladder was overflowing. He got up, almost fell, grabbed the edge of the table until his head stopped whirling and reeled through the tables on his way to the 'head'. He was giggling, thinking what a good deal it was not being able to focus his eyes, especially on Lenny's ugly face. He banged into the corner of a table once and yelled "Shit" because it hurt like hell. When he got to the 'head', he stood relieving himself and suddenly had a sobering thought, one he'd had before but had forgotten. 'Could Lenny be undercover NCIS? Could that be why Admiral

M. L. Verne

Williams didn't call me back? Is he lying about dealing, using it as a cover for a covert investigation?'

Finishing up and washing his hands, he happened to glance into the cracked, filthy mirror over the sink. The image he saw was no one he recognized. He shook his head, left through the creaking door and walked straight out the exit to the parking lot. He was intent upon getting home and never gave Lenny or the other two a thought. Had he glanced at the table where they had all been sitting, he might have wondered where the guys were. The table was empty.

While he'd been in the head, Lenny had spoken quickly to Bill and Craig.

"This is the chance I've been waiting for. I need your help now. We're going out to the parking lot and when Mike shows up, I'm gonna' convince him he's too drunk to drive. I'll insist that I take him to my place for the night and I'll bring him back here in the morning to pick up his car. You two keep out of sight and if it looks as if I'm gonna' have a problem with him, then you come over and we'll manage to get him into my car. No rough stuff, of course. He's drunk and I don't think there'll be any trouble. If I can manage alone, then you guys can go on home and thanks for being available."

As Mike came out of the bar, trying to recall where he'd left his car, Lenny loomed up in front of him. It scared the crap out of him, that ugly face stuck into his in a dark parking lot. He jumped and let out a shriek.

Lenny laughed out loud. "Come on, man. You're soused. We'll go to my place and sack out. Tomorrow I'll bring you back here for your wheels."

CODE NAME: WHITE MUSTANG

He gently steered Mike toward his Beemer while he talked. To his relief, Mike fell sideways across the front seat without a struggle. Lenny slammed the passenger door shut, walked around the car, waved at Bill and Craig to go on, then tried to get into the driver's seat. Mike was sprawled all the way over, his head under the steering wheel.

"Come on, man, move over there and get your seat belt on. Hey Mike! You hear me, man?" He poked and shoved until Mike sat up and did as he was told, mumbling to himself that "I might as well have my wife here nagging at me…"

Lenny grinned as he turned the key. The engine started with a quiet whisper. It was his love, his pride, his joy, his BMW!

"Mike? We're gonna' finish our talk about buying Harley's. While you were in the 'head', I asked Craig some pertinent questions and I think I have enough information for us to go on, at least for starters. You okay with that?"

As he spoke, they left the parking lot as smoothly as if they were on well-waxed ski's gliding down the slopes on a sunny day. Mike had not responded to his questions so he said to himself, 'Man, I love this car', thinking Mike was asleep. Or passed out.

Not so. Mike finally replied. "I know what you mean, man. This is one smooth mother. Some day I plan on having one just like it. Maybe I can afford one when I get commissioned."

As they rode along, listening to the superior stereo system playing the soft jazz they both liked, Mike was thinking to himself, 'Wouldn't he be surprised if he knew I'm not as drunk as he thinks I am. How I wish I could tell him to go to hell and let me live my life without him. But, I have to play it close until my LDO orders come through. Can't have him getting ugly with me about that. I'll just have to be cool for a little while longer.'

A very long time later, Mike would recall having had those thoughts. By then he would understand that Lenny's role in his promotion to officer rank was minimal, at best. When it was far too late to alter events, he would realize that it was he, Mike, who had earned the commissioning and that Lenny had only been a middle man, called upon to conduct a meeting.

All during Mike's decline and fall, followed by his rise and re-entry into the human condition, he would call upon the lessons learned during the bad times when he was 'hanging' with his nemesis, Lenny the Loser.

20.

It was probably a combination of several factors that contributed to the ease with which Lenny was able to get Mike started on 'crack'. His family had left him, his job had been eliminated, he'd lost the best boss he'd ever had the privilege of serving under, his promotion was hanging fire, he was stressed out big time and it all came together for Lenny's purposes.

Reluctantly, in his mind, Lenny had given Cate the credit. She'd called it. Mike was easy, wishy-washy, the simplest, most effortless conquest he could have hoped for.

Once they'd left the bar and gotten to Lenny's, they talked about purchasing the Harley's. Eventually, Mike figured out that Lenny would be paying cash for his bike. He got pissed! *He* would have to stretch it out for years, probably pay almost as much in interest as he would be paying for the bike itself. What a drag! And he'd have to keep it a secret from Teea too; try to make the payments without her knowledge.

They'd explored the ifs, ands, buts and finally agreed they would get a 'matched set'. That had pissed Mike off too, but he was getting tired and didn't want to hammer the whole thing to death. They settled on FXD Dyna Superglides, fireball cams, Mikuni 41 carbs and porker pipes. Glistening black with chrome trim. Accessories would, of course, be black leather. Jackets, pants, gloves, boots, goggles, helmets, shades…the works. It didn't occur to Mike to ask where and how Lenny had gotten all the literature together so quickly. The answer would have been he'd been lusting after a bike for a long time and it was a part of his scheme to rope Mike in. He knew that Mike would go for it weeks before Mike got around to mentioning it.

Lenny said they would "go zooming around friggin' Italy, man. Bitches will be beggin' for rides, and not just on our bikes." He was leering wickedly. "Know what I mean, man?"

"Is that all you can think about? A piece of ass? There *is* more to life than that." Mike was thoroughly disgusted.

Lenny ignored him. In the end, they had high-fived to seal their agreement. They would send out their orders with their down payments before the end of the week.

"How is it you can afford to pay off yours all at once, man?" Mike asked. "You have a family to support, too. Have you come into a fortune I haven't heard about? I mean, I know you earn more money than me but, give me a break."

The perfect opening, supplied by no other than Mike himself! Without blinking an eye, Lenny got up and walked over to the couch. He picked up a pillow, thrown casually into one corner, and brought it back to the table. It looked like a big, brown, soft, fluffy football.

"See this little item, man? It belongs to Lonzo. Cate forgot to pack it, so I've been using it." With that, he undid a hidden zipper and reached inside. When his hand emerged, it was full to over-flowing with money. Mostly hundreds. Lenny kept reaching in and pulling out. More and more. So much! Mike was stupefied, while Lenny was grinning from ear to ear. "Mike, you heard me earlier when I was talking about dealing?

You think I was blowing smoke up your ass? Hey, man, there's millions out there just waiting for us. It's the truth! You can join my team and make enough to pay cash for your bike in a month. I need you to be my courier, man. Whaddaya say?"

It sounded so easy and Mike was thinking, 'I *need* some of that green stuff. It would solve *all* my financial problems.' Still, he was reluctant to get himself involved, even on the fringe of such an enterprise. He knew it would lead to trouble. Had to. Lenny seemed to be forgetting all about that. He kept saying what a piece of cake it was.

"Man, I've got Nigerians on the payroll, guys on the base, you name it. I want you too, man. Together we can become wealthy beyond imagining before we leave this friggin' filthy place."

Mike was getting sick of listening to all the bragging. If one were to believe everything the guy said, there seemed to be no end to all of the wonderful things he'd done, never mind all the wonderful things he was going to do.

Mike's mind then wandered, and Lenny felt his disinterest. He knew he had to do something in a hurry. While they had been talking, he'd taken his drug paraphernalia from his hiding place behind some loose paneling in the kitchen wall, thinking how clever he was doing it without Mike noticing.

He was wrong. Mike had noticed, all right. He knew what the stuff was. He wasn't totally ignorant! But he *was* curious.

"I've been using for a while now, Mike. No big deal. Trust me. Hell, you don't see me getting myself into trouble, do ya? Do I look sick? Frenzied? Out of

M. L. Verne

control? All that silly shit you hear about? Know what that is, man? A convenient way for the do-gooders to keep us smarter bastards from getting rich, that's what. They're as greedy as we are, but they don't have the balls to take advantage of the opportunities. Now, you and me, it's a different story. We *do* have the balls, man!"

All during the tirade Mike had been thinking 'Hell yes, you're hyped. Most of the time, as far as I can tell. You get started yapping and you haven't the sense to stop. You drink and you get falling down drunk. You miss an average of at *least* a full day of work every week… Your temper is out of control lots…' But, he had verbalized none of it. What good would it do? He watched Lenny snort the coke, drink the beer, get higher.

As he used, Lenny kept urging Mike to "just take one little drag. What can you lose, man?"

Mike fell into the trap. In the end, it was the money. Nothing more, nothing less.

CODE NAME: WHITE MUSTANG

21.

Everything had changed. The compound, all the offices, all the facilities. Gone. Closed down. Locked up. The Admiral was now in Washington. His staff, left behind in Italy, had gathered together one last time to watch on television as he took his new oath of office. For most of them, he'd been the best kind of boss they could ever hope to have. All of them agreed that the Navy would be in fine shape with Admiral Kingston in charge.

Mike's new job was the pits. A nothing. A waste of his and the Navy's time. And after working at something so important!

He spent his days shuffling papers around, feeling like he'd been put out to pasture. It was an insult. Lenny had arranged for his days to be a bore, but he didn't know that. The call he'd told Mike about, speaking with the Admiral, was another of his maneuvers. If Mike were bored to distraction in his office, he would be more open to working the drug business with him.

Mike was also bugged by two officers he was required to work with every day. They were Brits, apparently set on making his life as miserable as possible. They harassed him at every turn, but he was at a loss to know why. Once, he'd asked them up front what their problem was and they had looked at him as if he had a screw loose. Then, they ignored him.

He wondered if they were undercover for the NCIS, looking at the drug thing. He hadn't yet given up hoping that the Navy would get something done about that problem. 'Maybe I've been put here for safe keeping until the investigation needs my input.'

Then his worries turned to the worst scenario. Possibly his use of crack was beginning to show? But Lenny had said, "Don't get paranoid, man. You're acting perfectly normal."

He made a lot of trips to the coffee pot. It was an escape route. The Brits didn't drink coffee. And the coffee area was well away from their sphere of influence. Plus, there were always other sailors hanging out there, people he could shoot the bull with and not feel intimidated.

He decided the best way to handle his problem with the Brits was just to stay out of their way. He did his job, tried to be cool, bided his time, waited for his LDO orders.

* * *

On a routine day in the middle of a week, Lenny called. Just hearing a friendly voice lifted his spirits. He didn't realize how much the foreign guys were affecting his attitude. He told Lenny, "Man, I'm glad to hear from you…"

Lenny wanted to get together for a beer after work. Mike readily agreed. Margo was in Naples again. He needed someone he could talk to without feeling harassed. They were to meet at 'The Place'. Once that was agreed upon, Mike had trouble getting through the rest of the day. He made several trips to the coffee pot just to have something to do He felt nervous and jittery.

'I cannot stand another minute of this', he moaned, and left work early. He rushed to get outside, then felt as if he'd shed an overwhelming case of claustrophobia. He took a gigantic breath, tried to relax. No luck. He was too up-tight.

His drive to the bar could have been labeled helter-skelter. He was in and out of traffic like an idiot, giving the finger to anyone who dared honk their horn at him. Once he almost caused an accident by cutting in front of a semi-truck, barely clearing the guy's left front fender. He got a large, noisy horn blast for that little maneuver.

Arriving at 'The Place', he was pleased to see Lenny's car in the lot. That meant there'd be a cool one waiting for him. Already, he felt like a new man. He'd been too damn high-strung.

Hurrying in, he bellied up and grabbed the beer, downing half of it before he even greeted Lenny who was grinning like the proverbial cheshire cat. Mike's problems in the office were his doing and his scheme was working. Mike would be a hard core user in no time. He recognized the signs.

Mike had wiped the foam off his lips with the sleeve of his uniform. Ordinarily, he'd have changed into civilian clothes. It was not his habit to go to bars in his uniform. That day, he could not spare the time. And could not have cared less that he'd just soiled his last clean khaki shirt. Finally, he sat down next to Lenny, looked into the mirror over the bar and shuddered. He looked even worse that day, he thought, than he had on the day he'd awakened after Teea left him. Teea! His boys! He needed, wanted his family. Turning away, he opened his mouth to speak.

M. L. Verne

Lenny beat him to it. "Mike, I need to get right to the point. That trip out of town I mentioned a while back is gonna' happen this weekend. Are you still willing to take Whitey for me? Will that be a problem for Margo? He's good company. All you'll need to do is feed him once a day and take him out to do his thing when he tells you. I'll only be gone for the two days. Are we cool?"

"No sweat, man. Margo's gonna' be in Naples again, so that dumb dog of yours can keep me company. I've got some hours to work at the mart, but he can house-watch for me during that time."

That taken care of, they had a few beers, talked casually about trivial things, and Mike told Lenny about the on-going troubles in his office. Lenny poo-poohed the whole thing.

Mike was annoyed at his attitude. *He* didn't have to put up with the idiotic accents, the freaky manipulating.

Lenny shouted, "Know what? All they need is a couple of walking sticks and they'd look just like old what's his name? Uh, Alex something or other in that movie, 'Bridge Over the River Kwai?' Know what I mean?"

After that Mike snickered, visualizing the two of them as they sat at their desks with their pipes hanging from their mouths, looking for all the world like nineteenth century nabobs. "I knew you'd think of a solution for me, man. When they bug me, I'll just put that picture into my mind and I'll see humor instead of aggravation."

Lenny didn't have a clue what Mike was talking about. Some weird vision inside his head or what?

CODE NAME: WHITE MUSTANG

He'd been thinking about having Mike stop by for a line or two of 'crack' but, on second thought, decided 'no'. He was fully aware of Mike's jittery need for it and figured if he held off, Mike would be all the more appreciative when he finally did get some. More manipulation. Soon, soon, he'd have the guy right under his thumb, ready to go the last mile, do whatever he needed just to get at the crack.

Two evenings later while Mike was watching Italian television, and thinking about his family, Lenny walked in with Whitey.

'Damn him,' Mike swore inside. 'Why does he think he can do that, just crash into my home without a single knock on the door.' But, as usual, he said nothing.

Whitey started wagging his tail when he saw Mike who was sure the silly dog had a smile on his ugly face. 'Damned if the two of them aren't starting to look alike!' The idea made Mike grin and Lenny figured the smile was for him.

"Mike, sorry I have to rush. Gotta' catch a plane. Here's his food. Just once a day now, and I usually feed him at supper time. Then we go out so he can do his thing. Listen, man, I'll be in touch if I get a chance. I'll be back on Saturday night." And he was out the door.

Whitey made himself at home. He'd visited Mike's place before and knew the nooks and crannies where the best smells were. Once he'd made his rounds, making sure everything was where it was supposed to be, he took over the couch. Burrowed right in.

"Good lord, dog, you not only look like him, you act like him! Get your butt down on the floor, man.

Quit getting hair all over my furniture" He pushed Whitey off the couch, telling the animal "You're arrogant and pushy just like Lenny, man. Who needs it?"

But Lenny was right about one thing. It was better with a warm, fuzzy creature to share the house, to talk to and who did not talk back. 'If I didn't have Margo here, maybe I'd get me a dog.'

When they took a walk, they went to the security gate where the guys were happy to chat with Mike and romp with Whitey. They told Mike he oughta' get a pet of his own. "Be good for you when your woman is away," they teased.

Mike explained to them that he was waiting for his orders and would be going back to the U.S. soon, which brought sad looks to their eyes. "We'll miss you. You've become a good friend."

On Saturday evening his phone rang and it was Lenny calling. "Man, can you pick me up at the Naples airport tomorrow about seven? I can catch a flight out of here in time to get back by then."

"Out of where, man? You never got around to telling me where you were going. Geez, I don't know if I can make that trip on such short notice. Can you call me in the morning?"

The call had given Mike a queezy gut. Lenny said he was calling from Turkey! Must be something to do with his drug business. Mike wanted no part of that shit. He didn't trust Lenny, hadn't for a long, long time. This sort of situation certainly didn't call for a change in the way he felt about the asshole.

As he sat contemplating a way to get out of going to Naples, the phone rang again. An unknown male

CODE NAME: WHITE MUSTANG

voice with a heavy foreign accent asked "Do you know where Lennard is?"

Mike felt a chill go up his spine. This was one of those Nigerian guys that Lenny dealt with. They were the only human beings who called him Lennard. Mike thought, 'Something really weird is happening here. First Lenny. Then, almost at once, this person?'

Out loud he answered, "I have no idea where he is, man. Why are you calling me?"

"Just checkin', man" was the reply. "Hey! Wanna' get a beer? I'm right here at the bar outside your gate. I thought Lennard was at your house."

Mike's curiosity got the best of him so he accepted the invite, telling the guy he'd be there shortly.

He got Whitey settled onto an old, ragged blanket he'd hauled out of a box at the rear of his closet. Whitey snuggled down, his tail thumped once and he was asleep. At least, his eyes were closed. Mike knew that didn't actually mean the animal was sleeping. Whitey often had his ears perked up, one eye open a crack while playing a coy game of peek and grin.

He threw a jacket around his shoulders in case it was chilly out and left his apartment, making doubly sure the doors were securely locked. Sure enough, he caught sight of the tail thumping one time as he exited.

The bar was just a half block from the outside of the security gate so he walked. It was well lit and the Italians were outside of their little hut. He felt safe.

Arriving at the bar after a short chat with the guys at the gate, he walked into the place and immediately had to squint. The air was thick with smoke, there being no exhaust system of any sort. It really was a dump, but the beer was usually ice cold. There was always plenty of company, including the owner, who had befriended him. She was a middle-aged, Greek woman named Diana who had somehow found her way into the heart of Italy.

She'd told Mike she came to Italy many years ago, had stayed single and had the thriving bar to keep her well occupied. Whenever Mike stopped for a glass or two, she sat with him. They exchanged jokes and stories about their native countries and some of the strange individuals who frequented the bar. But not this time. He had spied a couple of men toward the back of the place who definitely looked like the guys he was to meet. Their clothes, their body language and their shining ebony faces gave them away. Besides, somehow they looked familiar. Searching his memory as he made his way to their table, he remembered he'd met them at Lenny's house. They were 'Deitz' and 'Maxo'.

When they saw Mike they gestured, smiling wide, their white teeth glistening as they pulled a chair out for him.

Over the cold beer, they talked some nonsense while Mike struggled to keep up with their guttural speech. It was especially difficult because the place was so noisy. He asked them what they were doing in Italy, knowing the answer but wanting them to tell him that they were drug dealers. Then he'd have a reason to get up and leave when he felt like it. He was already sorry he'd agreed to meet with them.

His question as to their presence in Italy went unanswered but, soon enough, he found out what their purpose in calling him was although it turned out to be an enigma.

CODE NAME: WHITE MUSTANG

"Will you drive up north of here and pick Lennard up?"

'Holy matrimony.' Mike freaked. 'What the hell is this? They ask me this right after I hear from Lenny, asking to be picked up in Naples, *south* of Gaeta? Tomorrow? Too weird!' He was just a little frightened so he stalled, appearing to be trying to make a decision. Certainly he didn't have a clue what these strange people were up to.

Finally, he shook his head, said "Uh, Uh", stood up, looked each of them in the eye and walked out of the place. They shrugged and left right behind Mike, their mission completed. Every patron in the place watched as they went through the door and heaved a collective sigh of relief when they were gone. Strangers like that made everyone more than a bit nervous.

Mike was never to know what their intentions had been that night but there was no doubt the encounter left him feeling extremely uneasy. It should have been a lesson in treachery for him. It only served to rattle his cage, pull his chain as the saying goes.

22.

When the call came from Lenny the next day, they reached an agreement. Mike drove to Naples to pick him up at 'Capo', a shortened version of the airport's name, Capodichino.

'Some agreement,' Mike fumed as he drove the distance. 'The guy calls and I run. He's using me. He's manipulating me. I was maneuvered into this shit.' He castigated himself, called himself stupid, an idiot, a spineless creature.

He worked himself into a small frenzy and by the time he reached the outskirts of Naples, he was full of intensely negative opinions. They were all centered on Lenny and their destructive relationship. His saving grace was Whitey. He'd brought the animal along for company. Each time he spoke out loud, calling himself names, the dog would growl or yip. It was amusing, as if he actually understood what Mike was complaining about.

He had a grin on his face as he pulled up to the curb in front of the terminal because Whitey was sitting up straight, looking out the window as if he expected to see Lenny. Which he did. Before Mike did. The tail was thumping suddenly, a beat a second. There was a contented sound too, almost like a cat purring, coming from Whitey's throat.

It was difficult for Mike to stay mute when Lenny yanked the door open, ordering Whitey into the back seat in a surly tone of voice.

'Doesn't he know, or care, how much the dog loves him?' As he opened his mouth to greet the guy, he noticed there was a second man standing outside of the car. Someone he did not know.

Lenny beckoned for the fellow to get into the back seat with the dog. Then he climbed into the front seat, slammed the door and told Mike, "Take off, man."

As he maneuvered through traffic he thought, 'More weird stuff. No introductions, no 'hello how the hell are ya', no thanks for driving down...nothing!' Now, he was pissed all over again.

By the time they were back on the highway traveling north, Mike had shrugged it off. He'd figured the guy was another of Lenny's Nigerian 'business partners', someone he didn't need to meet in any case.

The return drive was made in silence. Lenny dozed, Whitey whimpered and the Nigerian stared out the side window. The miles clipped by unnoticed except for Mike. He was going to be very relieved when this day was over.

Abruptly, Lenny sat straight up, told Mike to pull over and stop, opened his door, stepped out, let the Nigerian out, climbed back into the car and told Mike to keep driving. Then he dozed again.

Mike supposed he was beyond being surprised. He simply drove, didn't ask any questions and at last pulled into Lenny's driveway.

Before the car came to a stop, Lenny was out and running up on his porch, fumbling for his keys, hurrying into the house while Mike sat still, his mouth hanging open. 'This is not normal.' Quite frequently, Lenny was rude and crude but this behavior was beyond Mike's experiences with the guy.

M. L. Verne

It was twilight, the lights went on in the kitchen, Mike let poor, ignored Whitey out of the car and then took off.

'Enough already!' Driving slowly, he tried to put some sort of spin on the events of the weekend. Nothing surfaced that made much sense. Lenny went to Turkey after leaving his dog behind. Lenny returned from Turkey towing some Nigerian stranger with him who got dumped out in the middle of 'Nowhere, Italy' and Lenny was delivered to his house. End of saga.

Actually, the story was, Lenny had run out of crack and was desperate to get home for a fix. He'd never been asleep on the trip back to Gaeta. He'd been clenching his teeth to keep from screaming, scratching and heaving his guts out. He wasn't ready for Mike to see what deprivation did to a guy. Might scare him off before *he* was totally hooked himself. It had been the ride from hell. And yet, in his agony, Lenny was into denial. *He* was no addict. No way! Just ask him.

Pulling up to his parking area, Mike saw all the slots were full. This had been happening a lot lately and he was getting sick of it. To make matters worse, it would do no good to report it to the landlord so he drove around the building twice. Finally, someone pulled out. He pulled in behind them and though he had to hike back around the place, at least he was finally parked. What a pain in the ass! Would his orders *ever* come?

He had forgotten to turn on his porch light and almost fell over a bunch of roots sticking out of the ground where he'd been digging, thinking he'd plant some sort of greenery, try and make his front yard a little more pleasing to the eye, give himself a little

CODE NAME: WHITE MUSTANG

exercise outdoors, whatever. Grabbing hold of the little fence enclosing his patio, he put his key into the lock and heard his phone ringing. Even before he answered he knew it would be Lenny. He heaved a disgusted sigh, picked up the phone, said hello and sure enough he heard, "Hey, man, thanks for the ride home." He was himself again.

'What now?' Mike wanted to slam the phone down. He remained silent, too angry to speak.

"Hey, man, you there? What's goin' on? Can I come over? I wanna' pick Whitey up."

"Your dog is out in your yard somewhere, man. Don't bug me any more, okay? Just leave me the hell alone!" And he *did* slam the phone down, proud of himself for finally taking some kind of a stand on his own behalf.

'I've had it with the son of a bitch. Who does he think he is, using me like he does? To hell with him.'

He lit his water pipes, smoked a cigarette while he waited for the water to heat up, then stripped and climbed into the shower. As usual it was frustrating, not one bit satisfying.

'How I would love to get into a shower and just stand there for half an hour letting the water run all over me instead of the way it is now—warm, cold, warm. I *hate* it here! I want my *family*!'

He scrubbed his body quickly, shampooed in a hurry, rinsed off and got through just as the water turned icy cold.

As he was toweling off, he heard his front door slam. The walls of the place shook and that raucous voice boomed through the house.

M. L. Verne

"Hey, Mike, you here? It's me, Lenny. I came over to thank you in person for the ride. I need to explain a couple of things too. Where the hell are ya', man?"

Mike was now in a murderous rage. He hurriedly put on some jeans, then stepped into the living room, ready to kill the bastard who was making things worse by occupying the one comfortable chair available.

"Lenny," he began and was rudely interrupted before he could utter the rest of his opinion.

Lenny had reached into his pants pocket and was saying, "Mike, hold that thought a minute." He pulled an enormous wad of money out, waving it under Mike's nose. "I owe you an apology, man. That dude that rode part way back with us? I couldn't introduce you because I didn't know who he was. I met him in line at security. He was right behind me and if he hadn't been there I would presently be in jail I think. The guy at the checkpoint told me to step to one side and wait for someone to come for me. Why? I do not know. That Nigerian spoke quietly to the guy and he waved both of us through. After that, he asked me for a ride. How could I say no?"

While he talked he continued peeling bills off his roll.

"That guy saved my ass. I'm convinced of it. I couldn't deny him the simple courtesy of a ride. Here, man, this is for you."

He handed Mike a handful of money, saying "Thanks a lot. It's for taking good care of Whitey…for picking me up."

Mike was shaking his head 'No', knowing it was drug money and not wanting any part of it. Besides, he

CODE NAME: WHITE MUSTANG

also did not believe one word of the story Lenny had just told him.

"Don't be a fool, Mike. This stuff is easy come, easy go. I already told you that. No sweat. Just *take* it."

It looked as if they were all hundreds so in spite of himself, Mike was tempted. He needed money. Who didn't? All he'd done was watch a dog for two days and drive a guy from Naples to Gaeta. Nothing. No big deal. But hell, if he felt that way, why not? He took the money. It was five hundred dollars.

He said, "Man, I enjoyed Whitey's company. You were right about that. If I was gonna' be staying here I'd get me a pet too. Thanks for the payola. I can use it as you know."

"Mike," Lenny began, "I need to tell you about this trip I made. I was in Istanbul. The business deal I was taking care of? I was buying heroin. I brought it back with me. I suppose that security guy at the airport suspicioned as much. Anyhow, now I have to get it out on the street, distribute it to my guys out there. There's so damn much money floating free I can hardly stand to think of it. You can't even *begin* to imagine. Just today, I brought in a very small bag of stuff and it'll sell for thousands, in the blink of an eye. And there's more than plenty to go around. I need your help. Then we can both leave this friggin' country wealthier than Croesus. The thing is, I have a problem getting through security. For you, it'll be a breeze. Those airport guys *never* stop white military people. Whaddaya' say, man? You game?"

Unexpectedly, Mike's thoughts turned to Admiral Williams, his total disregard of his, Mike's, attempts to reach and speak to him. 'Could he be covering for

M. L. Verne

Lenny? Is it possible he knows about Lenny's drug dealing and is keeping it under wraps to save the Navy from more embarrassing notoriety while the 'Tailhook' incident is still fresh in the minds of the world population? Or the cheating at the Naval Academy that has just become public knowledge? No, that's absurd. I refuse to believe it.' Somewhat disoriented with his thoughts, only half listening to Lenny as he spewed words a mile a minute, Mike felt exhausted. 'Why don't I accept what this man tells me? He is a senior officer, after all. I ought to hold him in high regard, trust his integrity, yet I don't have any faith in him. So what is my problem?'

Out loud he said "Man, I do *not* want to hear any more of this shit. You are putting me in a hell of a spot. Gimme a break! Go home. Take your information and your money with you. I'll act like I never heard any of this. I do *not* want any part of your operation."

He was livid. "Just get out of my house, man. *LEAVE!*"

But Lenny was on a roll, high on crack and the beer he had consumed since getting to Mike's. He ignored Mike, over-rode his tirade. He was getting louder by the second with only one goal in mind; to woo Mike, have him totally involved in his 'business', entice him with money, get him hooked on crack. He kept saying, "You and Teea could live in the lap of luxury. Pay all your bills, save a bundle for the boys' educations, pay cash for a new house, man. There's no end to the possibilities."

The temptation was too much along with his inability to stand his ground and forcefully over-ride Lenny's powerful personality. Not to mention, he was already addicted to crack, which he would have denied if confronted about it. As he tried to shut out Lenny's words, his voice, Mike came to realize it was an exercise in futility. He put his hands to his head, wagging his body to and fro.

Lenny grinned internally. 'Leered' would be a better word. He knew he'd scored! He got out of his comfortable chair and grabbed a small bag he'd had beside him on the floor. Walking into Mike's kitchen, he sat down at the table and began taking items out of the bag. "Mike, come here" he coaxed. "It's time for a teaching session."

He motioned for Mike to sit across from him while he placed a small length of a car radio antenna on top of the table. In spite of himself, Mike was curious. He'd read about this sort of thing but had never seen the actual technique.

Lenny stuffed some cocaine from his bag into one end of the 'pipe', lit the other end and began smoking it. Soon, he re-stuffed the make-shift pipe, giggling like an idiot. He was high, wide and addle-brained. "Here, man. Now it's your turn." He'd gotten the pipe lit again and handed it over as he spoke. Mike took a drag and Lenny doubled over with ear-splitting laughter.

"Man," he choked out, "you don't smoke this shit like a cigarette. I can see right now you're gonna' need some serious instruction."

He stood up and staggered out the door without another word.

For his part, Mike floated into his bathroom, relieved himself and fell onto his bed. Before he drifted into a whirling, unstable sleep, it occurred to him he'd gotten no explanation for all the weird things that had happened over the weekend. Lenny had skated right on by the few questions he'd managed to ask.

'The man is a piece of work. I suppose I'll never understand how a senior officer could get involved in illegal, immoral activities.'

23.

There were three vehicles in the parking lot out side the mart. Except for that, Mike didn't notice anything unusual as he carried out the trash. Ordinarily, his was the last and only car at that late hour. He heaved the bags into the receptacle. As he turned to re-enter the mart, he caught a movement out of the corner of one eye. An icy chill snaked down his spine and the hair on his arms stood up as his body alerted him to possible danger. Grabbing for courage he turned slowly, looking in the direction of the movement. He saw a black man, very tall, very intimidating, very Nigerian. He knew the differences.

The native Africans carried a peculiar aura about them, a subdued arrogance, a different strength of character not often found in black Americans. At least, that's how Mike saw it. And generally respected it. But, right at that moment, he was alarmed.

He had a difficult time seeing the man clearly and was not able to determine if it was someone he'd met previously. Carefully, he stepped sideways in order to allow what was left of the waning light in the west to reflect onto the face of the individual.

Briefly, he caught sight of the setting sun's rays glinting off the trash on the beach. Junkies, homeless persons and drifters had littered the place to such an extent it was life-threatening to walk there.

In fact, while he tried to focus clearly on the man's face again, he was recalling that the daughter of one of his friends had written a paper after collecting a large plastic trash bag full of hazardous items. It had been

M. L. Verne

her choice for a school project, the subject being pollution. She'd gotten an 'A' on her paper and had then deposited both her paper and the trash-filled bag in the office of the area Commander. She had written a note asking, "Why must children be exposed to these dangerous things?"

As far as he knew, nothing had ever come of it. Kind of like his attempts to reach Admiral Williams once upon a time.

While he'd been thinking those thoughts he'd been watching the man, trying to place his face. He realized he'd seen him some where at some point in time. Then he smiled and Mike's memory clicked in. Lenny's house of course. Where else? His name was Martin.

'Funny about these Nigerians. None of them seem to possess last names,' Mike thought.

Martin approached him, still smiling, revealing a mouth full of strong, white, gleaming teeth. Mike envied that smile while he ran his tongue over his braces. He didn't think his smile would ever be so strikingly attractive.

"Hey, man, remembah me? Lennahd's place? You interest in make big money? Fast? Easy?"

"Don't think so, man." Mike hurried back into the mart and quickly locked the door behind him. The guy may very well be on a mission for Lenny, but he had scared Mike who peered through the window in the door and watched as Martin walked toward the parking lot. Quickly he went to the front door and looked out the small window. He was just in time to see Martin climb into a neon blue Geo Prism. Very flashy. As he left the lot, Martin double-clutched, his tires squealing like an angry monkey caged up at the zoo. Mike made

CODE NAME: WHITE MUSTANG

a mental note of the license tag. AFI! 'Hmmm, isn't that interesting. What's a foreigner doing in a car with American tags?'

But, in his relief that Martin had gone, he promptly forgot it. He supposed Lenny had sent the guy but had no idea why.

While he finished stacking shelves, Mike thought about the other strange people he'd met through Lenny. For instance, there was Deitz and Deitz's wife whose name he'd never heard. Now that he was concentrating, he remembered having seen those two a couple of times, loitering outside the mart. Again, he wondered why.

Moving along the aisles, checking everything to be sure the place was ready for the next day's business, it finally came to him, clear as daylight. He slapped himself on the forehead and knew the people within Lenny's circle were, in one way or another, all tied up with his drug deals. '*Hello!*' he mused. And Lenny was sending them around to keep an eye on *him.*

'He thinks he's gonna' back me into a corner. I get it now. He wants me so intimidated I'll fall for his sales pitch, start working for him in his 'business'. He has tenacity, I'll say that for him. When the time comes for a confrontation, it's gonna' be quite a show.'

But he was reckoning without taking into consideration his increasing use of, his need for, crack. It was a creeping, ugly, sinister kind of addiction that had taken over him without any warning. Mike was already hooked, he just didn't know it. Yet.

* * *

M. L. Verne

As Mike was leaving his office one afternoon, walking to his car, looking forward to a quiet evening at home with Margo, maybe broil a couple of steaks and have some wine, he bumped smack into Lenny. He was startled, not having expected anyone to be there. He'd had another bad day dealing with the two Brits who were on another roll, hassling him.

'Badgered to a frazzle' is how he'd been thinking of it lately.

One look at Mike's face told Lenny he'd be scoring again. He immediately invited Mike over to his house and without a second thought Mike accepted.

If Mike had asked himself why Lenny happened to be in that place at that time, if he had questioned Lenny's motives for what appeared to be an off-the-cuff invitation, if he had wondered about those things for even one second, would he have refused the invite, gone home as he'd originally planned? If. If. If...

He followed the beemer and as they pulled into Lenny's driveway, Mike noticed another car parked around the side of the house. He immediately became apprehensive.

'Why is it,' he asked himself yet again, 'why is it I wise up only *after* I'm already suckered in?'

Nothing was stopping him from backing his car out of that driveway and going home. Why didn't he? More if's, ands, buts

He followed Lenny into the house, and there sat Deitz and his 'no name' wife. They were high on crack. No one could talk that fast and not be. Even he recognized that. Also, he could make no sense of their conversation, if it could be called that. Meanwhile,

Lenny had already taken his crack paraphernalia out of its hiding place and was readying a fix.

"Want some, man?" His query was directed at Mike.

At that point, he could still have walked out. Was it curiosity? He wasn't tied down. He still had a chance to make the right choices. No one was holding him hostage.

The longer Mike listened to Deitz talk, the clearer his agenda became. It was all about money. Fortunes. Six and seven figures in one night wasn't unheard of.

He was dragged into the reality of the wealth that was available. The temptation was staggering! He saw what his role could be in the enterprise. True, the people were disgusting. They appeared slovenly, their conversations were disruptive, their interactions repulsive. 'But hey, I can do the job and not become like them. I can stay sober, deal and get rich. So why not?'

He was smoking crack again and before he knew it. They had cajoled, tempted, manipulated, recommended, urged. Now he was getting high. They'd fixed him up with the purest stuff available.

His body had jolted as he fell into submission. His heart had pounded, his pulse had raced, he had gotten so 'into it' he'd stopped thinking in terms of being human. He was soaring. Stars and comets. Colors and music. Suns and moons. Laughter. Shrieks. More laughter. Babbling. Incomprehensible words. More screams. Flying on invisible wings. Swooping in loops and circles. He was *TRIPPING*, was unaware of his behavior. His companions rejoiced. He was in their pocket!

M. L. Verne

They waited for him to come back down. It took some time but they were in no hurry; they were high too.

After an infinity, or so it seemed, they were able to talk to Mike, educate him about the methods they used for getting in and out of Turkey undetected.

They told him how contacts were made, how to reach the dealers in Istanbul, the procedures to follow in the purchase of the heroin, how to pay the runners.

It was an enormous amount of information to be absorbed all at once. Lenny knew he'd need to go over it again after they both sobered up. Maybe tomorrow.

They smoked a little more. Then the Nigerians left. Lenny offered to take Mike home. "Gotta' take good care of my number one courier. My main man!"

"Forget it. I can do my own thing." Mike floated to his car. He never remembered how he got there.

The streets, recognizable to him only because of the lights along the way, enthralled his visual perceptions. How had he managed to get home without becoming a statistic? A major miracle.

Margo was waiting for him. As he came through the door she gasped, appalled but not surprised. She'd been involved with another crackhead once and knew the signs, had recently seen hints of them in Mike's demeanor. It was a disappointment to her. She'd have thought Mike was above such things, taking into consideration his love of his family if for no other reason. If she tried to interfere it would be futile. She had learned that the hard way.

He'd have to 'come down' alone but she was able to get him into bed. Then she made love to him. He was putty in her hands. Their activities that night bordered on the animalistic. Together they rode the waves. Up and down, in and out, sideways and upside down. They peaked at the crest of an enormous surge of ecstasy and were transported into sleep with smiles on their faces, sighs on their lips.

It was destined to be a night they would never forget.

24.

The time had arrived. He was going to Turkey. Lenny got himself and his gear together and drove over to Mike's house. He had long since ceased knocking at Mike's door, had never once given his rude conduct a second thought.

He parked, walked in and found Mike lying on his couch with a wet cloth over his eyes.

"Hey, man, what's up? We got stuff we gotta' do here, stuff we need to talk about. If you're going to Turkey, this is the time."

Mike groaned as quietly as he could so his migraine wouldn't worsen. He didn't need any of Lenny's aggravation.

He whimpered as he lifted the cloth off his face, squinting, looking at Lenny through a haze. He'd swallowed a double dose of his pain pills. The Navy docs were more than generous with them, handing them out like Hershey kisses. But that day, they weren't touching his pain. It meant he'd be out of commission for a couple of days at least. He was all too familiar with the signs.

Lenny was talking non-stop about the trip to Turkey. He was on a mission. He needed to refine Mike's ideas, make sure he had all the pertinent information down pat. He insisted Mike sit up and pay attention. His voice sent throbbing twinges of pain through Mike's brain, making him wish he had the strength to stand up and punch the jerk. If only he could. 'Just go away. Leave me alone.' It even hurt to think.

Lenny was not deterred. "Sit up, man. Come on. Lying around feeling sorry for yourself isn't gonna' make you feel better *or* put tons of money in your pockets. I'll fix us a smoke. That'll do the trick. We've got work to do, man. It's already Thursday. Plus, you have to go to work tomorrow."

The last thing he *needed* was crack, didn't want to *think* about it. He already had enough narcotics on board to knock a healthy horse over. Prescribed shit.

It didn't matter. Lenny fixed the crack and they smoked. Mike couldn't have resisted under the circumstances. He was too sick. He had no physical strength. The migraines always did him in, left him on death's door. Or at least he wished he could die. Good god. What agony.

Several moments later Mike sat up, flabbergasted. His headache was gone! Could that be? Was smoking crack the answer to being freed of migraines? He'd heard people were smoking marijuana for pain. Maybe *he'd* just discovered a new medical breakthrough.

He looked at Lenny, his eyes suddenly clear, head free of pain. "Man, I can't believe this. It's the sensation of the century!"

Lenny snorted. "What do you think I've been trying to tell you, Mike? Maybe now you'll have more faith in me."

While Mike was still euphoric, pain free and vulnerable, Lenny briefed him again. Step by step he took him through the course of action he would undertake in Istanbul. Along with the directions were remarks meant to bolster Mike's eagerness to go.

"We're gonna' be wealthy, man. But none of it will happen without you."

M. L. Verne

To a degree, Mike was convinced. He said, "Man, I'm really not into this shit of yours long term, but I'll go along for a while. If I can make enough to pay off a couple of outstanding bills that's all I'm interested in."

Ignoring those comments Lenny said, "Here's the rest of the drill, Mike. You'll need to bring along an empty video camera bag. If you haven't got one, I do. Either Craig or Bill will drive you to Naples where you'll catch your flight to Istanbul. When you get to Turkey, hire a cab. Go to the Hilton Hotel. Check in, go right to the room, memorize this phone number I'm giving you, then throw this paper away. Call the number, ask for Amadi. This dude is known as a 'small boy'. It means he's a local runner."

They went over and over the routine until Mike had it down to perfection. Lenny's mouth was watering. He was thinking about all the money that would soon be his. Finally, he felt there was no more to tell Mike for the time being. So he left.

It was just in time. Mike had been wrong about the crack. The migraine was back with a vengeance. He swallowed some more narcotics, hoping he'd be well enough in the morning to go to work. The last thing he needed was to have to call in sick. That would only give the Brits more ammunition.

He slept fitfully, awakening several times throughout the night. In the morning he was good to go, so he thanked his guardian angel for the welcome relief from his pain.

Somehow he got through the day, trying not to give any thought to what he'd be doing over the weekend. He was antsy about it but determined to get it over with.

CODE NAME: WHITE MUSTANG

When the work day ended he went directly home, packed a few things and made certain he had a full dress uniform right on top. Lenny had explained that this was one of the most important things he needed to remember. It would save his ass if he got stopped and questioned at the airport. He'd only need to explain he was on 'official business'.

As he was zipping up his carry-on, Lenny walked in. 'Good lord, if that guy only had a few manners' he fumed. He supposed walking in on *anyone* would be no big deal for the ass hole.

"Here, man. We're gonna' have a smoke before you take off."

'What the hell', Mike sighed. 'I'll be on a plane long enough for it to wear off.' He simply did not want any controversy.

"This'll relax you and get you into Turkey without worrying. It'll be no sweat for you, you'll see. Craig should be here in a minute. He said he's happy for something to do right now."

If the truth were told, Mike was relieved. He'd been worried there'd be some last minute glitch and he'd have to ride to Naples with Lenny. He knew he'd never manage to listen to all the bullshit and then get on the plane in a relaxed condition if that's how things had turned out.

They sat at the kitchen table smoking their crack, looking at each other, Lenny asking Mike if he had any last minute questions. Mike shook his head 'no', feeling better by the second.

Lenny hummed a tune, but it was so off-key it hurt Mike's ears. They both laughed. Loudly. It was a rare and humorous interlude.

M. L. Verne

"Mike, before Craig gets here I'll tell you this. You'll need the cash to purchase the stuff. Here's thirty thousand. It's enough. Tuck it into the black bag and wrap it in black plastic. Have you got any? A garbage bag? X-ray will not penetrate black plastic."

While Mike pulled a plastic bag from a kitchen drawer, Lenny continued his instructions, repeating himself ad infinitum.

"Do not let this out of your sight. You see? That's the whole idea about the plastic. Very clever. Wish I'd thought of it. Now, this is all one hundreds. That makes the wad less bulky. It'll fit perfectly into the little bag. I suggest you place it in your jacket pocket or under your belt. You taking that blue vinyl bag over there? How'd you get your full uniform into it? Good job!"

Mike felt a little shaky. He supposed from the crack. He grabbed the back of a chair as he stood up so Lenny wouldn't notice. He didn't want another lecture. He tucked the black bag holding the money into his belt, fully intending to stash it in his carry-on once he got free of Lenny. He'd packed snugly and there was more than enough room.

Then Craig showed up and they chatted for one or two minutes, then agreed it was time to get going. Lenny said "Mike, one last thing. This venture is being financed by Deitz, me and Maxo. You need to know that. And don't be showing any nervousness. It would be a dead giveaway. Call me if you need to. I'll be at home."

Mike was scowling as he climbed into the car with Craig. He said, "The guy treats me like a kid, like I

CODE NAME: WHITE MUSTANG

don't have any common sense. Man, I am so sick of him. Can't wait to get this over with."

Craig glanced at him, eyebrows raised, and shrugged.

They rode in silence most of the way. For starters, they really didn't know each other. Secondly, they were military personnel involved in an illegal activity and did not want to talk about it.

The other thing was, Mike was discovering that 'a little crack' did *not* go a long way. He was jittery and wanted *more*! He scratched himself, felt conspicuous and scratched some more.

Craig glanced at him again. Mike shrugged, grinned sheepishly and tried to fall asleep. He gritted his teeth. It was a tortuous ride.

When they pulled up to the curb at the 'Capo', Mike jumped out quickly, thanked Craig and hurried into the terminal. He was very nervous but trying not to show it. He lit a cigarette hoping it would calm him down. There was no time to hang out. He had checked the reader board and saw his flight was loading. He took a few more drags, put the butt out in a convenient ashtray and walked up to the security checkpoint.

Grudgingly, he admitted Lenny knew his business. Piece of cake! He was waved through security with only a glance at his blue bag. The guy even smiled at him.

He walked down the ramp, entered the plane, found his seat and sank into it with a huge inward sigh of relief. At once, the flight attendant appeared, asked what he'd like to drink. He was in first class. Lenny had arranged his ticket.

"May I put your bag overhead for you, Sir?"

M. L. Verne

"Oh gosh no. But thanks. I'll just put it here under the seat. It'll fit nicely and be out of the way." Phew! Dodged a bullet!

Once the plane was airborne he tried to relax. He'd had one beer before take-off. Now, he asked for another. Teea had taught him how he could take deep, slow breaths and feel better when he was up tight. That old familiar lump formed in his throat again at the thought of her. Whatever would she say if she knew what he was up to? He didn't want to think about it!

Instead, he went through all the steps he needed to take to get the caper over and done with. 'Caper. Good word.' He grinned at his cleverness, finished the beer, relaxed and fell into a light sleep, erasing his need for crack. Temporarily.

CODE NAME: WHITE MUSTANG

26.

The flight must have been uneventful. He slept the entire way. When he felt the wheels touch down, he awoke with a start and looked at his watch. It had taken longer than he'd been led to believe. Not that it made any difference.

The landing was smooth, his exit from the plane routine. Customs was a breeze with another smile, this time from an attractive woman.

There was a very long line of taxi's out front, every driver eager for a fare. They gesticulated, bowing in their eagerness to accommodate the travelers.

Mike waited in line hoping for the sounds of the English language. No luck. When it became his turn, he climbed into the front seat and asked, "Istanbul Hilton?"

The driver grinned a toothless grin nodding 'yes' and they took off with a jerking motion. Mike was thrown against the back of the seat. He felt gratitude that he hadn't been ejected from the vehicle. 'Crazy. As bad as, if not worse than, the Italians. If that's possible. Must be a European thing.'

They careened around corners, barely missing cars going in both directions. There didn't seem to be much order to the tangled traffic pattern.

There was a great deal of horn tooting and fist shaking. By the time they pulled up in front of the hotel, Mike was sweating profusely. He was never happier to pay someone off and see the last of him. He threw several thousand lira down on the seat, got out and almost ran into the hotel lobby without once looking back.

Lenny had said he'd make the reservations and by god, he had! For once, the guy hadn't been bullshitting. Mike signed the register using a phony name. Sam Crandell. Sounded okay…

He picked up his bag and decided to walk up to his room. He needed the exercise. It was only on the third floor. Even so, by the time he got there he was out of breath.

'And out of shape,' he scolded himself. 'Gotta do something about that.'

He opened the door, walked in and fell onto the bed. This whole thing was getting to him. He closed his eyes, tried to relax, had no success. His heart was still beating like a tom-tom after minutes of taking deep breaths.

He picked up the phone, dialed the number he had memorized. It rang twice and then it was answered by a rough male voice speaking in a language Mike supposed was Turkish. He hadn't been told that might happen and it threw him. He sputtered and then said "I need to speak to Amadi."

The person on the other end didn't understand. He was asking questions judging from the inflections in his voice.

Mike hung up. 'What the hell?' bubbled up through his frustration.

The phone rang. "This is Amadi. You just called? You are Mike?"

"Yes." Mike didn't care if the fool noticed he was pissed.

CODE NAME: WHITE MUSTANG

"Sorry, man, I could not get to the phone on time. My friend answered for me. As you noticed, he does not speak in your language. My English is excellent. We will do our business now, yes?"

It was agreed they would meet in twenty minutes in front of the Hilton on the sidewalk. "You will know it is me. I will be having on a Denvers Bronco jacket. That is the best American team. Lennard gave the jacket to me. It is a gift."

Mike had just reached the front doors of the hotel, over- sized and glass paneled, when Amadi walked up with a swagger, wearing the jacket. As they met, they smiled at each other and shook hands cordially. Mike took an instant liking to the fellow. There was something intriguing but uncomplicated about him.

"Hand me your little black bag, man. You have it? Yes? We can not loiter. You will come with me to my home for a beer?"

There was a taxi at the curb waiting for them. Mike was sure Amadi had arrived in it and had asked the driver to wait. As they rode along the crowded, noisy streets Mike hung onto the strap, trying to keep himself upright. The driver's erratic maneuvers didn't seem to phase Amadi. He was talking a blue streak.

"The place where we are going I share with my friend King. He is my boss, too. We do our business all under one roof. That is the way American's say it. Yes?"

They pulled up to a building that looked decrepit. It's paint was peeling off, there were a couple of cracked window panes on the ground floor which looked uninhabited and the whole place appeared to be hundreds of years old. So the reality of the apartment on the third floor, which they reached via an elevator, was more than a bit of amazement for Mike. In fact, he thought, one could say the place was luxurious.

Amadi grinned when he saw the astonished expression on Mike's face. "You are surprised Mike. Yes? King was thinking a robbery would not happen in a building that looks so shabby on its outside. You must look at the treasures here. I will get us some beer."

Mike was not an expert on art, an understatement, but even *he* could tell that the things sitting about the room were priceless. Jade and ivory oriental figurines primarily. But there were also paintings on the walls that were surely originals and a couple of sculpted nudes on pedestals that held the eye for long moments.

'Obviously, buying and selling drugs in Turkey is a profitable enterprise.' Mike was bedazzled.

Amadi returned with a couple of icy cold bottles of beer, some vague brand Mike had never heard of but, when he sipped it, he was pleasantly surprised. It might be foreign but it was damn good.

The two men visited for a few minutes, talking of trivial things, having another beer together. Amadi asked Mike if he'd brought any American videos with him. "Lennard promised he would send some with you."

"No, he didn't mention it to me," he answered, thinking, 'Quite typical of the jerk.'

Shortly, Amadi asked Mike if he was ready to leave and they said their 'ciao's', Amadi grinning at the use of an Italian word. He had called a taxi for Mike and walked as far as the elevator with him, telling him he would be in touch.

CODE NAME: WHITE MUSTANG

"No later than tomorrow morning, man.'

The day was warm and sunny, vibrant with color. So Mike asked the driver to drop him at a bazaar near the Hilton Hotel. For a reason Mike had no clue about, his request seemed to make the guy deliriously happy. He looked back at Mike, grinning ear to ear. What Mike saw made his belly spin and lurch. The guy had a few crooked, tobacco stained teeth in a mouth that was wide open, brown slime running from one corner. Just gross. Chewing tobacco. Had to be. Mike was disgusted.

When they arrived at the bazaar Mike tipped the guy even so, simply because he had driven sedately, sensibly. It had been an unexpected relief. The amount he gave the driver must have been appropriate as he was rewarded with another foul smile.

The bazaar was exciting. It was the only description Mike could think of. He walked around leisurely, checking out the booths, savoring the delicious, spicy smells wafting up from the food stalls. His saliva glands started working over time, reminding him he hadn't eaten since the day before. He followed the aromas, found a place where the tables were full of freshly cooked meats and warm breads that had flaky looking crusts. He bought a huge plate full, then looked around for a place to sit down while he relished the feast.

Mike had been around the world a couple of times during his navy career and had always found foreign countries, their customs, their unique foods, the people, richly fascinating.

He had learned many interesting things over the years, and that day was no exception. He watched the mothers scolding their children while they bought fresh vegetables, the men standing around in groups talking, gesticulating and smoking, the children running wild while they played their games, laughing, giving their parents a bad time.

Mike grinned. 'Children are the same the world over, and so are the men. Look at those dudes over there, hanging out while their wives do all the disciplining and marketing. Probably when they get home the wives will have to carry all the groceries inside too.'

He finished his meal entirely sated, even going so far as to pat his stomach. He was ready to look at some gold pieces when a couple of boys about the age of his twins popped up in front of his face. They smiled, showing very straight white teeth. Mike was moved to give them some money while he thought about Jason and Joel. They hadn't been begging but they just reminded him of how much he missed his sons. They jumped up and down with happiness when he handed them some American dollars. Quickly they ran to their mother to show her their treasure. She waved at Mike, smiled, nodded. Mike walked away feeling jubilant.

The choices in gold jewelry were astounding and quite reasonable He had been told that would be the case. He would definitely buy some. There was so much of it he was dazzled. He shopped and finally purchased a lovely gold ankle chain for Margo, a gorgeous gold necklace for Teea. As he made his rounds, he spied a watch that he coveted for himself. But by then he was exhausted. He needed to return to the hotel. He made himself a promise to come back the next day for the watch.

Once back in his room he washed up, put his purchases at the bottom of his carry-on and fell onto the bed, planning a short nap.

Damn! No sooner had he closed his eyes when the phone rang right in his ear, causing him to jump up, startled. He looked at the time and was surprised to see it was nine o'clock.

'Must have dozed off after all' he mumbled while reaching for the shrilling phone.

It was Amadi of course. "When will you leave, man?"

Leave? The question threw him off balance. He wondered, 'Why would he ask me that at this hour?'

"Huh? It's nine o'clock, man. I just got in bed a little while ago. I'm not leaving until some time tomorrow."

"Mike, it is tomorrow. You are not up yet. Yes? It is beyond time for breakfast."

He climbed out of bed and looked out the window into blinding sunshine. Incredibly, he had slept the soundest sleep he could remember. When he stopped to think about it, he felt better than he'd felt in a long, long time. Rested, refreshed, calm. No shaking.

"Amadi, I'll be getting something to eat downstairs and then I need to go back to the bazaar for one more item. After that, I'll be ready for you. What're your plans?"

They arranged to meet in front of the hotel again at twelve noon. It was a good hour Amadi told Mike who thought, 'Whatever.'

After a satisfying, lengthy shower, he went down to the café and ordered American but requested Turkish spices for flavoring.

M. L. Verne

"No problem," the waiter told him.

Everything was wonderful. It seemed like he couldn't fill his belly. He ate eggs, ham, potatoes, toast, peppers, he used hot sauce. And the coffee! Turkish, heavy, black, aromatic, biting. It was *good* to feel *good.*

The waiter told him about a back way to the bazaar, a short cut. The walk was refreshing and did him a lot of good. Crack was the farthest thing from his mind. The air was crisp, not yet heated up like it would be later in the day.

He found the watch kiosk easily, made his purchase and left. He was pretty much without funds by then so any more shopping was out of the question. He needed to hustle back to the hotel if he was going to be on time to meet Amadi. He was suddenly anxious to be done with the trip, to get back to his own apartment and get on with his life.

Promptly at noon as agreed, Mike walked out of the hotel lobby and Amadi was there waiting for him. Wordlessly, they walked toward yet another taxi, Amadi having taken Mike by the arm, steering him. Not a word was spoken as they rode along. After their friendly visit the day before, Mike thought it was more than peculiar. But he said nothing.

Shortly, they arrived at King's home. Amadi paid the cab driver and they rode the elevator back up to third floor luxury. Just as before, no one was there. Amadi wasted no time giving Mike the black video bag they had exchanged the previous day.

The strange thing was, Mike felt sure it weighed exactly the same as it had when the money was stashed in it. Did heroin and money, one for one, weigh the

CODE NAME: WHITE MUSTANG

same? Well, he wasn't about to ask. He did glance around the room, looking for any travel bags, but saw nothing.

"Well, okay Amadi, I'm out of here," he said. "Call me a taxi will you? I have to get to the airport."

Amadi complied, reached out, shook Mike's hand, opened the door to the hallway and waited while Mike walked out. Then, he closed the door, leaving Mike standing alone in front of the elevator. Throughout all of it, Amadi had not spoken one word. It was very, very weird.

Mike stood at the curb waiting for the taxi, shaking his head in wonderment, again thinking 'Whatever.'

When the taxi arrived, he told the driver to take him to the Hilton. Once there, he packed swiftly, went to the lobby, took care of last minute business, hailed another cab and was on his way to the airport. It had taken about fifteen minutes max.

'Piece of the friggin' cake,' he told himself as they approached the airport. He felt no trepidation as he went through security.

He'd had to make some changes in his original flight plan but that had been no problem. It had taken only a few minutes but required an overnight stop.

Now, it was the next day and once the plane was back on the ground he exited, went through customs without blinking an eye, walked out of the airport, took a deep breath, started to cough from the filthy air and knew he was back 'home'.

As he looked around trying to spot his ride, whoever, he thought, 'Now I can collect my fee, tell Lenny to go to hell, forget this whole business and get on with my life.'

27.

Before Mike began his trip to Turkey, Lenny had purchased the round trip tickets for him on Alitalia Airlines. While he gave Mike his last minute instructions he'd cautioned, "It's always a good idea to create a bit of confusion, just in case. When the deal is done over there, change your return ticket. There's a travel agency office in the lobby of the Hilton. Get a one way return on some other airline via a different route."

Following those instructions, Mike had stopped briefly and purchased his return ticket to Naples with a stop in Zurich for a plane change. It was a local commuter plane and bumpy. But the scenery out his window was spectacular. They flew over the Alps which were snow covered and wondrous to look upon.

The change in Switzerland meant another trip through customs. There were no hitches but he was getting tired. His nerves were twitchy. He tried to sleep but it was no use. He fidgeted and drank too many beers. It wasn't long before he developed a pounding headache. At least it wasn't a migraine.

To add insult to all of his imagined injuries, the plane made an unscheduled stop in Turin. It was the last straw so Mike got off, too worn out to go any further. He flagged a taxi and asked to be taken to the nearest decent hotel. Obviously, the cab driver didn't know what decent meant. It was a sleazy, rundown place but the towels and sheets were clean and crisp, there was plenty of hot water and it was quiet.

He asked the switchboard to put in a call to Lenny while he was toweling off, then almost fell asleep while he waited. After what seemed like a hundred clicks and strange, hollow noises, the phone rang and Lenny picked up right away.

"I am back in Italy, man. Turin to be exact. I did it all, just as you ordered. Now, you can have your frigging enterprise."

"Hey, man, cool it. You're tired out. I can hear it in your voice. Kick back and sleep well. You'll feel better in the morning. But first, before you hang up, I gotta' tell you to be sure you get on the very first flight out of there in the A.M. You may have to change your ticket again. No big deal. Just do it. The thing is, Italian security uses drug detection dogs at 'Capo' but they don't get their show on the road until after ten o'clock. The first flight in lands much earlier than that, I'm sure. I'll check on the arrival time and someone will pick you up. Count on it, man. Now, get some sack time." And he hung up.

'The ass hole didn't even give me a chance to say anything.' Mike was fuming again. 'The hell with his black ass. Who needs it?' He fell back on the pillows, took a couple of deep breaths and the next thing he knew his phone rang.

It was the desk with his wake-up call. He was up and out quickly because he had no idea how long the ticket change would take or, for that matter, what time the first flight out would be.

On the way to the airport, he marveled at the deep, peaceful sleep he had enjoyed. Who would think it, all things considered? His anger at Jones, in and of itself, foreboded a restless night.

Not so. He hadn't even dreamed. 'Perhaps,' he thought, 'because I've been away from Jones and his crack pipes.'

He'd begun to think of Lenny by his last name only, telling himself, 'He doesn't deserve any respect.'

He threw some lira on the front seat of the cab as it pulled to a stop at the terminal, grabbed his bag, walked swiftly up to the counter and saw he was in luck.

There were only two individuals in line, one of them already being helped. When his turn came, he got his boarding pass and still had time for espresso and a croissant. It made his day.

Soon enough the flight was called. He boarded after passing neatly through security, settled into his assigned seat, smiled at the flight attendant who vaguely resembled Margo and buckled up. Now he was almost frantic to get back to his lover.

Before the plane left the runway he was asleep, a small grin on one side of his mouth as he dreamed of the night to come.

In seconds, they were landing. Amazing! He'd barely closed his eyes he was sure. He was feeling *excellent.*

Until he walked into the terminal. Then, he broke into a sweat.

The place was literally crawling with dogs. They were in every corner sniffing, yipping, pulling at their leashes, dragging their handlers along behind them. A nightmare.

'The son of a bitch lied to me again.' Mike railed, in a rage. 'He has put me at risk for the last time.' He

CODE NAME: WHITE MUSTANG

was shaking so hard with anger he almost dropped the items he was carrying.

To make matters worse, he saw they were having an unscheduled security check. As he stood in yet another line, expecting a dog to bust him at any moment, he perspired copiously. By the time it was his turn to be checked, he was a basket case. His shirt was soaking wet, his face red, his breathing rapid.

The security agent stared at him with black, emotionless eyes, his eyebrows almost touching his hairline.

"Man, I got airsick. I am gonna' heave some more in a minute. Can you hurry? I need to get to the head."

Quick thinking! Later, he would congratulate himself. Meantime, the agent shrugged and waved him through.

He ran as fast as he could. He *was* sick. He barely made it. He vomited while the perspiration ran down his body. He hung onto the walls, shook, trembled, gasped, wiped saliva from his chin.

Even in his wretched condition, he briefly wondered why there were never any seats on the toilets in Italy.

Hating to, but having no other choice, he sat on the filthy edge of the toilet until he could catch his breath, be sure he was done heaving. Then he got up slowly, made his way to the sinks, filled his cupped hands with water, splashed his face the best he could and it helped somewhat. At least he felt he could walk out of the head and not feel as if he were a spectacle.

The door hadn't even closed behind him when he spied Lenny, pacing like a caged animal. He had a vicious looking scowl on his face, his skin glistening with sweat and when he saw Mike he started across the floor yelling. "Man, where the fuck you been? I was about to throw up my hands and leave. What the hell…?"

By then he was nose to nose with Mike and got a whiff of Mike's stench. Several strings of his vomit were stuck to his clothing and his breath reeked. Lenny took a couple of steps backward as Mike said, "Don't *even* say throw up to me, man. That's where I've been. Throwing up. Have you seen the dogs in this place? Hell, man, I am sick of your friggin' lies. Don't involve me in your shit any more. I have had it. I mean it, man! Fuck your money."

It was the first time Lenny didn't have a comeback. He shrugged and walked away with Mike trailing behind him.

'Well, I must have gotten all shook up for nothing as it seems the dogs are gone.' Mike shuddered in relief. Obviously, they'd been on a mission that had nothing at all to do with him.

'How was I to know?' A guilty conscience does strange things to people. He had been led to believe he was carrying heroin in his luggage. Even though he had never seen it, that's what he'd gone to Turkey for. It was a fifty-fifty chance those dogs had been there to sniff him out.

Lenny's beemer was at the curb. 'No wonder he was so up tight. His beloved car was parked in a no parking zone. Guess I can't fault him for that.'

They climbed in and peeled off. Usually, they didn't give seat belts a thought which was strictly against Navy regulations. If they were to get killed,

CODE NAME: WHITE MUSTANG

unbuckled, no benefits would be paid to their families. Navy rules.

Still, when he rode with Lenny, he gave it serious consideration. That day was no exception because Mike could now tell when Lenny was high on crack. He could finally discern the differences.

They were flying along the highway and Mike would have liked to say something about the speed but knew it would only cause a row. 'Not worth it,' he decided.

Instead, he thought of the biker meeting the two of them had attended a week or so back. Their Harley's had come and they were both delighted with their purchases. They'd talked with the guys at the meeting, shown off their bikes and let it be known they hoped to be included in the club's traveling plans. Their reception had been cool, to put it mildly. At the time, Mike thought there might be racism behind it. After mulling it over in his mind though, he decided it was probably Lenny's personality. And perhaps his military rank. It wasn't easy, or proper, for the lower grades to hang out with a senior officer. He was not aware that all of the guys knew about the drug dealing and using.

Matter of fact it was common, wide spread knowledge. Some personnel were beginning to suspect that Mike was involved too because he hung out with Lenny so much; the old adage, 'You're known by the company you keep.'

As a result, respect for Mike was on the skids. If Mike knew about their attitudes, he didn't acknowledge it. Not even to himself. Especially not to himself!

Mike drifted into a surface-like sleep while Lenny raced in and out of traffic, barely stopping to drop coins into the toll collection boxes as they went. The undue stress at the airport had wiped him out. He'd told Lenny when they left 'Capo' that he wanted to go straight to his place. So when Mike sensed the car was stopping, he expected to be home. Instead, he saw they were at Lenny's. "Man" he began, "I need to get home. I told you that."

"Be cool, man. Today is payday. You did a job and you need to be compensated. Besides, I have to hear how it all went down over there while the details are still fresh in your memory. Come on in, man. We'll have a beer, chill out, talk."

At the mention of money, Mike ceased resisting. 'Damn straight I did a job,' he agreed silently. 'I've earned some cash. A share of the profits.'

As they approached the house Whitey came running to greet them, tail going a mile a minute with, Mike was positive, a grin on his ugly face. He couldn't help it. He laughed out loud. He was moved to reach down and scratch the animal behind his ears. Whitey, in turn, drooled all over his pant legs.

"Come on in and leave the mutt alone, man. You'll spoil him worse than he already is. I haven't got the time or inclination to fool with him. Got more important things happening. Know what I'm sayin'?"

Lenny's house, as usual, was an eyesore. It reeked of old cigarette butts. No wonder. There were ashtrays all over, full to overflowing with half-smoked tobacco. The sink was stacked high with dirty dishes. The table was crammed with crumpled up, empty bags of potato chips and pretzels as well as crusty, used paper plates that he no doubt had to resort to after running out of regular china, all of which was in the sink. There was a Mr. Coffee that hadn't been turned off in time. The bottom of the container was black with burned-on dregs. 'He's lucky the place didn't burn to the ground.' Mike was fed up.

"Sit, man. Here, have a beer. Unwind. Did you meet the man? Have you got the black bag? Listen, I apologize for the mix-up in my advice about the airport dogs. My wires got crossed. Next time, I'll double check my source, have everything running on smoothly oiled wheels."

"Lenny, I told you, man, I am finished with this. No more!"

He continued his diatribe, on a roll, not willing to stop. "There ain't gonna' be a next time. Forget it, man. Just get Whitey out of my way and I'll go get your friggin' black bag. He's already ruined these pants with his slobbering."

He got up and walked out while Lenny sat where he was, taking no heed of Mike's request to corral Whitey. Instead, he pulled out a wad of bills, hundreds, from his hiding place in the wall, then put his crack tools and rocks on the table next to the money. Quickly he fixed a couple of hits, began smoking his, counted out money for Mike who was coming back into the house with the black bag in hand.

"Sit, Mike. Here's some cash for you. There'll be more as soon as this deal is over and done with. This is a grand, for starters." He peeled ten bills away from the wad and handed them over.

Mike thumbed through the money while Lenny offered him a smoke of crack. "Man, I truly appreciate your help with this undertaking. We'll both turn up wealthy, never fear. Now you see how easy it is, right? Oh yeah, I know we ran into a glitch at 'Capo' today but, you know what? This is like any other job. New ins and outs, a screw up here and there, then it's cool."

As usual, the more crack he smoked, the faster and louder he talked. Mike took a few hits if only to ease the monotonous drone of his dialogue. He was paying half-way attention while deciding how best to leave without a problem. He sat up when he heard "and you know, man, when we began this partnership, I toldja you were gonna' be my courier? That's what ya are, man. Know what I'm sayin'? But that's not the jive talk on the street. You gotta' hear this from me 'cuz I know you're gonna' get pissy about it and I don't wantcha out there punchin' some dude out over trivia. You hear someone calling you a mule and you shrug, walk off. Hear me? It's just a word. Won't mean nuthin' personal."

Mike recalled he'd left his bike in Lenny's garage a few days before he went to Turkey. 'Thank god I don't have to rely on him to take me home.' He stood and left quickly before his temper got him into an uncontrollable rage. He might kill the bastard!

'A mule? An ass, more likely. Same damn thing.' He rolled his bike out, crammed his payola into the saddlebag, climbed on, revved up and roared off. The small amount of crack he'd smoked didn't impair him, or so he thought. But he *was* extra careful. 'Last thing I need is for some cop to stop me, find the money.'

As he rode, he thought some more about the guy who was beginning to feel like an enemy. 'It's like, when I tell him I'm done '*MULING*' for him, he doesn't hear me. The extra money is great but I've had it. I can't figure him out. Can *not* understand where he is coming from!'

The gates to his compound were open. The fellas had heard his bike coming. He waved, they waved, everybody grinned at each other, Mike slowed as he drove through and around to his parking place. He turned off the engine, wheeled his bike up onto his patio, unlocked his door, pushed the bike ahead of him into his apartment He had been doing that ever since taking possession of his new toy. It was the only way he could figure to keep the bike out of harm's way, undamaged. The complex might be gated, but who knew who lived *inside*? It was an enormous place, several buildings that accommodated hundreds of people. His pals, the guards, had told him there were thieves among the tenants. And they would know.

Margo wasn't pleased with the situation but Mike kept reminding her he had a large investment involved. She'd just have to put up with the inconvenience, overlook the oily odors.

However, she was in Naples again and Mike was glad. He needed to get beyond the trip to Turkey before seeing her. He was still in a quandary over what he was going to tell her about his absence for two days and nights.

He took a fast, incomplete shower, fell into bed and drifted off thinking how desperate he was to get away from Lenny and the illegal activities he'd gotten caught up in.

* * *

M. L. Verne

Several days passed. Along with the time, his initial panic and guilt waned. He was finally able to think about Turkey with calm logic. He'd gotten away with a crime and had gotten paid for it. And, he was never going to do it again.

He had stashed enough money to make a couple of bike payments, then sent the rest to Teea to pay on bills. If she should happen to ask him where the extra money had come from, he'd tell her he'd gotten lucky playing poker. That would appease her. She knew he wasn't much of a gambler so it wouldn't worry her.

He'd begun to feel like himself again. He'd had no crack since the last time over at Lenny's and, to be honest, he didn't seem to need any. Wonderful! That was the good news.

The bad news was, he had forgotten one very important detail. In the aftermath of that scary trip, he neglected to destroy the left-over return airline ticket. He'd crammed it in the back of his closet along with his luggage and several other items that he intended going through and sorting out one day soon.

In the important business of his everyday life it was a minor detail and he never gave it another thought. With the passage of time, that seemingly harmless oversight would come back to haunt him and would be the ultimate ticket to his oblivion.

28.

In America, at the Pentagon, the newly appointed CNO, Admiral Bradley J. Kingston, was faced with some dilemma's which his star-studded career had never before been subjected to.

For instance, there was the lingering debacle of the 'Tailhook Incident'. The ever present, prying media would not let it alone. So he was compelled to face the cameras, the questions, on a daily basis. It was not the sort of 'learning experience' anyone would be inclined to look at with enthusiasm.

Now, there was more crushing news, personally devastating. The Command he had so recently left in Italy was under investigation for drug problems. The NCIS had contacted him, briefed him, informed him that he would be expected to help them, to analyze their findings.

"Get a group of trusted people together Admiral, and let's start cleaning up this mess. It's something that cannot be put on the back burner. Top priority is the word of the day."

First, Tailhook. Then, the cheating at the Naval Academy. Now, this! Plus, that morning he'd been told there were probably drug problems at the Academy, too.

He was going to need all the help he could get for the business of cleaning up the image of his beloved Navy. For America. For the Planet.

He'd been going through personnel files searching for profiles of persons he knew personally and trusted. It was not an easy task. He'd begun returning to his office after dinner the past couple of evenings where the phone would be silent, where there would be no interruptions. His wife had agreed to make plausible excuses for his absences at social functions. It was the only way.

He'd gone through a dozen or more service jackets rather quickly, piling the non-contender's on a chair for re-filing. It was interesting, amazing, how much information came to light within the confines of just a few pages of type. He'd run across persons who he'd served with years before and had, basically, forgotten about. If the reason for this activity were not so serious, anything but what it was, he'd have enjoyed renewing old memories.

After a few days, he had managed to weed out everyone he would not be recommending. It hadn't taken quite as long as he'd thought it might. He'd decided he would need a total of four people for the assignment. One of them would, necessarily, be his personal Aide, sharing information between the NCIS, his newly appointed group and himself.

For starters, he chose Commander Irene Kelly. He'd worked with her occasionally in Italy, knew her as an outstanding officer of the highest caliber. She was already in Washington on another mission, one not as crucial as his. She was, he knew, an excellent choice.

Secondly, he chose Lieutenant Commander Christine French. She was an attorney who had been involved in a few significant Navy investigations in the recent past. She was not personally known to him, but her file told him she was a first rate candidate. He felt the group would need her sharp legal mind.

CODE NAME: WHITE MUSTANG

The two women were going to want a junior officer as a kind of sounding board, someone who was in touch with 'the outside world' by virtue of youth and having come into the Navy recently. He selected an up and coming Ensign, an Academy graduate, one Preston Matthews, for the third spot. His record implied he was a shining star with a very promising future. Admiral Kingston was always on the lookout for rising stars.

He'd needed to spend as much time deciding about an Aide as he had choosing the other three collectively. That individual would have to meet with the press when he, as CNO, was occupied elsewhere. He/she would need to keep everything coordinated, chair the meetings, report to and from the NCIS. Good public relations skills, the ability to respect the opinions and suggestions of the rest of the group; a very tall order. He had three remaining persons to choose from. He agonized over the choice for a day and a relatively sleepless night. This person would make the difference. In the end, he allowed personal feelings to influence his final choice. It was the only tool left to him because all three were equally qualified.

Ultimately, he opted for Commander Gus Keef, the man who had been his Aide in Italy. They too shared history, having worked together on a few other assignments in the past. He held a respect, a personal liking for Gus Keef and he trusted him.

By Monday of the following week, the newly selected group had assembled in Admiral Kingston's office. He welcomed them and immediately launched into a detailed briefing, stressing the importance of the mission.

M. L. Verne

"With hard work and some good luck, we should have this matter taken care of in a minimum amount of time. It's an undercover investigation. You will be working hand in hand with the NCIS. Two of their agents will be here in a few minutes to brief all of us. I've selected each of you for your individual merits as well as your documented abilities to work well with others. This will not be an easy task because heads will roll".

"The subject of the investigation is drugs," he continued. "Dealing, using, transporting across international borders, you name it. That's about all I know for sure. Until the NCIS agents arrive, why don't you have some coffee and rolls. Putting something into your stomachs will be beneficial when the going gets rough."

During the Admiral's talk, Gus Keef had become convinced he'd suddenly developed an acute case of worms of the spinal cord. He itched, he perspired, he coughed, he squirmed, he crossed, then uncrossed, his legs every few seconds and finally became aware of his distracting behavior. "Irish" Kelly, sitting next to him, scowled and shook her head at him. It was a wake up call so he tried desperately to control himself.

When the unexpected orders had reached him in Italy, telling him to report to D.C., he'd been stunned. His guilt clicked in at once. 'I've been found out.' He'd lifted his phone immediately to call Admiral Williams whose Aide stated, "The Admiral is out of his office for the remainder of the week escorting and entertaining visiting Senators while they gather information for their peers. He cannot be disturbed."

That left Gus hanging out all alone on a very shaky limb.

After a while, he'd settled down and thought rationally. 'It has nothing to do with my minimal involvement in the drug thing. I've known Admiral Kingston my entire career, served with him more than once, know he is not a devious person. If there was a problem with me personally, he would handle this summons differently.'

Later, as he got settled on the flight to Washington, Gus was feeling much better about it. Whatever *it* turned out to be, it was bound to help his career. He expected to be promoted to Captain shortly. Then, he was going to retire. He was ready. And he needed this break from his dull routine in the meantime. His wife would keep a tight reign on the family during his absence. She was as good if not a better sailor than he was. He fell asleep almost before the plane left the runway and slept the entire way across the Atlantic. It was always a boring trip.

The briefing, then, came as an absolute shock to him. He'd had to use all of his reserves to remain outwardly calm once he got his jitters out of the way. He'd given himself a mental heads up. 'The Admiral does not play games. Remember that!'

Just about then, the two NCIS agents entered the room and the briefing got very serious very fast. They had everyone's full attention. The group heard, "It's a helluva mess. Drug rings involving many Navy personnel and other branches of the military as well. We're going to be extremely busy for the next several weeks getting all the information compiled so we can begin making arrests. We must get this hideous situation under control as quickly as possible."

They explained the entire scenario as they knew it, up to that point in time, and their listeners were horrified. Even Gus had not known how widespread the problem was. All along, he'd believed it involved only a handful of people and was contained locally, there in Gaeta. *Maybe* Naples. How naïve' of him!

As the meeting wound down, Gus resolved to tread extremely carefully. He'd cover his backside, work extra diligently, get through this assignment with no fallout soiling his reputation. He closed the door on his guilt and put his worries in limbo.

After the agents left, the Admiral asked the group to put their heads together and come up with a name for the job at hand. Following much discussion and a great deal of laughter, they decided. It was to be "Operation: White Mustang".

29.

Some of the many alarming things about the use of crack cocaine are the ways the various systems of the body speed up. Heart rate, pulse, breathing, thought processes, metabolism; everything leading to an inability to sleep or eat.

Lenny had been awake and on the go for days. His mind raced right along with his pounding pulse. He'd decided he would need to know about every single one of Mike's activities. He was obsessed. He wanted Mike hog-tied, unresisting, available as his mule, in and out of Turkey every weekend.

In the interim, he was trying to unearth some kind of glitch, a major screw-up, in Mike's past. Believing everybody has a skeleton in the closet, he wanted to find Mike's and blackmail him into total, complete submission. He was a little concerned because Mike had shaken off his insistence that he was the one man in charge of Mike's commissioning. That was to have been his, Lenny's, major leverage.

Subsequently, he'd gone through Mike's service jacket, found nothing negative that he could use for his purposes. All things being equal, he should not have had access to Mike's personal data but he had his ways and they usually worked to his benefit. He noted that Mike had, at one time, applied to the CIA for a position. The ensuing security check had been routine and it was obvious Mike had never completed the application. 'Humm, that's interesting,' he murmured. The thoughts led nowhere.

Finally, his last resort was to check out the complex where Mike and Margo lived. He knew they were both in Naples on that particular day, Mike on Navy business and Margo to visit her family. So it was as good a time as any. He hopped onto his Harley and rode out there thinking to make a huge impression by roaring up, skidding in on a cloud of dust, slamming to a stop.

The Italians were totally unimpressed. They thought Lenny was a horse's ass and they didn't attempt to hide their opinions. They couldn't understand why a great guy like Mike would hang out with such a '*pazzo asino*'. Still, Lenny had a way about him. He had their full attention with the first words out of his mouth.

"I'm here to talk to you about Mike. He's my pal, you know? We are into dealing drugs together. Margo doesn't know. It's just me and him and a few foreign dudes. We've got a good thing going and I need his help to keep it that way. What I need from you is a little information once in a while. When he comes home, when he leaves, who is with him...know what I'm sayin'? Not any big deal and I'll pay you for your time and effort."

Initially, they were shocked. *Their* Mike into drugs? Not to be believed! 'The Family' had never gotten into that kind of thing. 'Way too much trouble,' the Don had decreed.

As Lenny prattled on, they listened against their wills. By the time he finished his sales pitch, they *knew* he was *pazzo*. Not only did he want them to spy on Mike, which was bad enough, he wanted to know all about Margo, too.

Didn't he have any idea she was untouchable, her son a member of 'The Family'? *Dio Mia*!

Lenny pulled out an enormous wad of American money and they were snagged. He'd known exactly at what moment he needed to do that in order to score. Their grins quite literally lit up their faces, stretching from ear to ear. They shook hands all around indicating a deal had been done.

But Lenny was ignorant about 'Family' rules, had no idea there would be no revelations with regard to Margo. And, they would be asking their Don what to do about Mike too.

Until *he* spoke, there would be nothing done at all. They felt no qualms about taking Lenny's money. A deal was a deal, even if it wasn't yet a deal.

When his betrayal was exposed, Lenny would chastise himself for not having done his homework. He had allowed his cocaine- ridden ego to rule his good judgment, had jumped in with both feet, having no clue about the ways of the Mafia; had acted irresponsibly and recklessly and ultimately paying a huge price for rushing in where any individual, not part of 'The Family', would fear to tread.

* * *

As soon as their shift was over, they went to the Don.

While they told him of Lenny's offer, carefully spelling out the details, his fury mounted. There would be a price on Lenny's head. Mike would be feeling the repercussions because he had involved himself in an activity which had the potential of bringing trouble to

M. L. Verne

Margo. It was not allowed. She was the mother of his nephew's son. It was simply a matter of the all-important blood ties

30.

It was one of the last lovely evenings of the fall season. Very soon winter, with its cold rains and winds, would be upon them. Margo told Mike she was happy about the season's turn because her mother had a villa in the Italian Alps and she was looking forward to taking him up there for a little get-away weekend. Mike hadn't skied in years and so was as eager as Margo, looking forward to the invigorating air and exercise. He'd been excellent at the sport once. Could he still cut a fine swath through the snow?

Margo had a day off in the middle of the week, a rare event. She was visiting Mike as he busied himself getting the mart closed up for the night. They had been chatting about their ski trip which was coming up soon. There was already more than plenty of snow at the ski levels according to the reports.

A few customers roamed the aisles, as if they had nothing else in the world to do. The cashier, a newly hired girl, was hoping they'd soon leave so she could get home. She'd had to leave her children with a neighbor because her husband, a Marine assigned to the Navy mission, was on duty.

Mike had stepped outside to have a cigarette, get a feel for the cooler air while Margo, a non-smoker, remained inside the mart talking with Margaret. They had a few things in common and enjoyed each other's company. They were laughing over a silly joke when the phone began to shrill. Margaret had a hand full of bills she'd been counting so she motioned for Margo to answer the call.

M. L. Verne

"*Pronto*" she said, then quickly followed it with "hello" having forgotten for a second...

"Hello...may I please speak to Mike Steele?" It was Teea.

Margo recognized her voice from Mike's answering machine. Later, she would ask herself what had come over her, why she'd done what she did. At the time, it felt good.

"He's just stepped outside on a break. This is his girlfriend. Can I take a message for him?"

Teea began to shriek. "Who the hell is *THIS*? You get Mike on the phone. Now! I need to speak to him about our sons! This is his *wife*, you *bitch*!"

"Sorry," Margo piped sweetly, "he's unavailable right now." And she hung up.

Margaret looked at her with saucer eyes, eyebrows raised to the ceiling. Shaking her head she said to Margo, "You don't know what you've done, girl. You might be living with the guy but there's stuff you aren't privy to in that marriage. If I were you, I'd be telling Mike right now what you just did."

Margaret shook her head again and doubled her efforts to get her last minute chores finished up so she could get out of the place as soon as the last customer exited. There was going to be fireworks!

Margo was still pumped up and ignoring Margaret's advice when Mike came back inside and she smiled coyly at him. She felt no apprehension as she told him about the call she'd just fielded.

"I knew you'd want to finish your break, Mike."

His reaction stunned her. He was livid. Heedless of the people still shopping, he shouted, "How *dare* you! That was my *wife*! If she called *here*, it means she has

CODE NAME: WHITE MUSTANG

a problem with the boys. You *idiot*! You *know* the agreement was you are *never* to talk to her! What the hell....?"

The customers were enthralled, thinking they were witnessing a real life soap opera. Margaret was torn with divided loyalties. She was fond of both Mike and Margo. She'd noticed the customers peering around the shelves, curiosity all over their faces.

"If you all are finished with your shopping, could you bring your items up here so we can get you checked out? It's time to close for the night. Thank you."

Sheepishly they came forward and did as Margaret had asked. She quickly rang up their purchases, gave out change and bagged the groceries. She wanted to grab them by the arms and pull them outside. Restraining herself, she simply locked the door after them.

Mike and Margo had stopped speaking. The atmosphere was vibrating with bad electricity. She closed her till and went out the back way, avoiding eye contact with her friends. She was a romantic at heart and felt sure they would get their problem solved, certainly faster if she was out of the way.

Mike was actually stomping up and down the aisles in his fury. Margo had trailed out the back door behind Margaret and was sitting in Mike's car, crying silently, wishing she could rewind the clock, re-do her foolish, impulsive mistake.

Soon enough, Mike secured the building, walked out to the car, climbed into the driver's seat, started the engine and tore out of the lot as if the devil were chasing him. He was lucky the guys at the gate of his complex knew the sound of his car and had opened the gate for him. Otherwise, he might have driven straight through all the wrought iron, running into and killing everyone.

The guards couldn't believe what they were seeing. Mike was always so friendly, waving and smiling, slowing down as he passed through. The scowl on his face was ferocious and Margo was obviously very upset. What was happening?

By the time they pulled into the allotted parking space, Margo was ready to cry out loud. If the truth were told, she'd never been involved with a married man before, had never been married herself. So she truly did not understand the horrific implications of her thoughtless actions. She had no skills when it came to dealing with a wife. Her game-playing with single guys was a totally different scenario.

Mike stormed into the apartment ahead of her and grabbed the phone without even turning on the lights. He dialed long distance and, predictably, there was no answer. He slammed the receiver down and paced, mumbling to himself.

"Friggin' bitch," Margo heard, not knowing if he was referring to her or Teea. She was subdued, silent, shaking inwardly. She'd fallen in love with Mike contrary to all of his early warnings. She wanted him both for herself and as a dad to her child. She'd long since put their initial agreement regarding his family priorities out of her mind. She was determined to separate him from his stateside family so she could have him to herself.

Mike had gone into the bedroom and slammed the door shut. Gone to bed, she had to assume. She congratulated herself.

"I've made the first dent in their marriage. With perseverance and good luck, it will end up in divorce. Then I can have him!"

The idea cheered her up considerably. She smiled as she curled up on the couch not the least bit bothered by the fact Mike would never know, or care, where she'd slept that night.

31.

He finally caught Teea at home and she berated him, both in English and Spanish. When she did that, he knew he was in for it. He couldn't help wondering if she'd actually been right there in the house when he'd tried to get her on the phone the past several days, just determined not to speak to him. To be honest, he could not blame her.

He was still perplexed and angry with Margo and had begun to ask himself if he could ever forgive her. Why had she done that? They'd had an agreement! Or, he'd thought it was an agreement. Maybe she didn't know what an agreement was? 'Whatever,' and he shrugged.

Meanwhile, as his thoughts wandered, Teea was reaching the peak of her tirade. "Who do you think you are? You have a *family* here. The three of us are supposed to be your top priority. I am sick to death of the games you play. I have a problem, I call you and your *girlfriend* answers the phone? Give me a break! You are screwing your boys, you are screwing me and all at the same time you are screwing that bitch? All you ever think about is sex. You need to get your act together. Until then, just don't call us and we won't call you either." And she slammed the phone down.

Mike was frightened. Did she mean that? Was he cut off from his boys? 'She's killing me.'

He was going to have to deal with Margo whether she liked it or not. He'd tried, the past couple of days, to talk with her about what she'd done but, so far, she

CODE NAME: WHITE MUSTANG

had emphatically denied having any knowledge of an agreement.

"Mike," she maintained, "when I moved in here, I thought the understanding was that we were going to be lovers forever. And I would have thought you'd told your wife by now so she could get the divorce started. Now, all of a sudden, it's my fault that you are in trouble with her. It is *not* my fault, Mike!"

By that time, she was sobbing and hiccuping like an adolescent. "You should have told me she doesn't know about us."

In the end, he was at a loss. He'd had training in how to handle people problems. 'Get to the point. Talk it out. Settle it.' Fine! It worked quite well on the job. It was not working with Margo. She was lying, of course. How to get around it? He didn't have enough experience in this kind of situation to solve the dilemma.

They had another go-round after Teea hung up on him and he felt like he was strangling. He needed to get some air before he lost his mind.

He stepped into the bedroom, shut the door, took his jeans and t-shirt off, got into his leather. All of it. He walked out of the apartment without one word to Margo who sat looking at him with a smirk that she covered up with her palm. 'Can't have him seeing my satisfaction.' She was feeling quite smug and in control.

Mike climbed onto his Harley and took off angry, bewildered, shaken up. The gate wasn't open so he had to stop; some new kid he'd never seen before. The pause gave him a chance to simmer down a little bit. It

M. L. Verne

had been raining and the air smelled fresh for a change. It cheered him up. Finally, the gate swung open.

He took off thinking he'd just tool around and try to enjoy the sweet smelling air along with his relative freedom.

It was not working. The further he rode the more distraught he became. He was in a terrible quandary. Women! Was there a man on the planet who could figure them out?

Of course! Who else? He headed his bike in the direction of Lenny's place, feeling enlightened before he'd gone a mile.

Whitey, as usual, came flying off the porch with his tail going a mile a second. Mike stooped and scratched him behind the ears. That brought out Whitey's doggie grin full bloom across his furry face. When Lenny stepped outside, his grin was as wide as his dog.

"Man, great to see ya'. Come on in here and sit. We'll have a beer and get caught up on the news. Do some jive talkin'."

All of Lenny's entertaining took place at his kitchen table. Mike often wondered if it was a habit he'd grown up with or if he'd adopted the custom since being in Italy. Certainly, it was an Italian custom. Not that it mattered one way or the other but, it was a three story house and he'd never been invited to see the other rooms. Just the kitchen. Where Lenny kept his stash of so-called designer drugs.

They sat across the table from each other. "Beer okay, man?" Without waiting for Mike's answer, Lenny took two bottles out of his fridge, uncapped them, sat down and handed one over while chug-alugging his own, finishing half the bottle in one fell swoop. They chatted about Navy stuff, nothing of any importance, gossip that added zip to their day or to their intellects. It was a way to pass the time. Then Lenny said, "Your LDO package is at the Pentagon, man. I got a fax today from my source. It's under final review. I checked on the latest info while I had the guy on the line. He assured me you're on top of the pile of applicants and he is gonna' see that it gets reviewed first. The word isn't out yet about assignment dates but I got the definite feeling it will be any day now. So how you feeling? Good news, eh? Let's do some rocks and celebrate. Here, let me get our stuff out."

"Hey, man, hold it. I came by for a specific purpose. I need some advice. About a serious problem. I don't need an addled brain messing up my thought processes."

Too late. The stuff was out and on the table. But Lenny did respect Mike's request. He sat back, waiting for the words to come bubbling out. Once Mike got started, there was no stopping him.

The whole sordid tale of woe was revealed. Lenny, incredibly, listened without saying a word. He maintained a calm, interested look while internally he was rejoicing. Ecstatic. 'The man will *need* the rocks now! No other way for him to get calmed down. He's totally miserable and I've got just what any good pal would order to make him feel a whole lot better.'

Mike eventually wound it up with a last question for Lenny. "What the hell am I to do with these two women, man? They're making me crazy."

"Man" Lenny began, "just be cool. Not to worry. What you need to understand here is that women always come back. I told you that before, man. You give 'em their space, let 'em simmer a while, treat 'em like pets, man. Pat them, scratch them where it does the most good; it's gonna' get them every time. Buy a piece of jewelry, a bunch of flowers, whatever. Soon they come begging on the doorstep. Trust me, man. It works."

Mike was disgusted. Again. 'No wonder Cate left' he thought for the hundreth time. 'I came here looking to hear some kind of profound suggestion or a solution. He'll always be just a friggin' asshole.'

All during his dissertation, Lenny was very busy getting his cocaine ready. The paraphernalia was spread out all over the table.

"Man" he grinned at Mike, "we're gonna' cook us some mashed potatoes here. Before this night is over, you are going to know every single thing there is to know about crack. It is heads up time. Literally." And he cackled like an old crone stirring a hot cauldron full of magic potions

"Mashed potatoes? What the hell is that s'posed to mean?"

"That's what you and me are gonna' be callin' this stuff from now on. A secret code. Clever huh? I thought of it just today."

Mike had never seen the full compliment of gear until that point in time. His curiosity was running rampant. All thoughts of leaving had vanished. Up to then, he'd been handed just the finished product to smoke, except for the antenna episode which really didn't count.

He watched intently while Lenny put a small amount of cocaine, in white powder form, on a dollar bill he'd smoothed out on the table top. Next to that he put a proportionate amount of baking soda. Then he poured both piles into a glass vial which contained a little water. He held the mixture over a small, burning candle until it bubbled gently. He then removed the bottle from the flame, allowed it to cool off slightly, then reapplied it to the flame. Once it was bubbling again he pulled it back, swirled it around in circles and in a few moments a small white rock formed. He turned the bottle upside down and shook the rock onto the table, carefully drying it off with a paper towel. He said "There you go, man. Easy as falling off a rock," giggling again. Like a school girl enjoying a silly joke.

"It's ready, man. Let's smoke and toast your commissioning."

Much, much later, Mike would recall that night and admit to himself that it had been his final chance to flee the ever widening hole he would eventually fall into, a hole so deep there was no way for him to escape from the ensuing horrors.

32.

How he got home safely would forever be unknown. By rights, he should have lost control of his bike, ending his life in a ditch or up a pole. He'd ridden full throttle, never slowing down, never stopping. Not even at intersections or traffic lights.

The gate was open but if it hadn't been, he would not have cared. He'd have driven right into the wrought iron, full speed ahead. He was too high, too far out of the world, too much a master of his own private universe to care about mundane things like survival.

The guards shook their heads in disbelief. They were convinced, after that episode, that Lenny had told them the truth. Each of them in their own way, and also collectively, had formed a high regard for 'the *Americano*'. They were all disappointed.

Margo waited for him until her eyes wouldn't stay open any longer. Then she had lain on the sofa, sleeping lightly, still waiting.

The roar of the bike woke her. He was in the parking lot revving the engine like some demented teenager. It was the middle of the night for gods' sake! The neighbors would be raising holy hell with them. The racket faded a bit and she wondered if he was leaving for more places unknown. But no, he was riding around to the other side of the building. That meant he would be bringing that smelly, oily machine into the apartment again. She'd begged him a thousand times to stop doing that. God! She was *SO* pissed.

CODE NAME: WHITE MUSTANG

He walked in dragging the bike alongside, placed it by the closet door, grinned at her and began taking his leather off. She had her mouth open, ready to start in on him, but he beat her to it. He'd thrown his gloves, helmet, jacket and boots into a corner and grabbed her. On the way home he'd been planning his strategy, knowing he'd be in trouble. He hadn't left her a note. Big number one sin. They had agreed early on they would always remember to do that. He'd forgotten. In his rush to find solace, he'd forgotten a lot of things. Well, no matter. Now it was her turn to forget.

He walked toward her, scooped her up, carried her into the bedroom and laid her down on the bed ever so gently. He smiled into her lovely green eyes and slowly removed her robe. This unusual behavior startled her, rendering her speechless. Mike began to fondle her breasts and she sighed contentedly, resigning herself to pleasure. She could tell that Mike was high. She knew the signs. But she also knew that, for some reason, crack made some men better lovers. They put their inhibitions on hold while they were in the grip of drugs.

Mike was tender, gentle; it was a switch. She'd had no previous indications that he could be like that. Their sexual life together had always been on the wild side, their emotional co-dependency demanding it.

This time, as they came together for mutual satisfaction, it was soft, velvety, quiet, delicate. They were, each in their own way, overpowered by the forces engulfing them.

They gasped with pleasure, gazed at each other, smiled, embraced. They felt each other's bodies delicately, little butterfly touches here, there and everywhere. It was totally sensual, eventually leading them into pillow talk.

Her head was on his shoulder and he held her close. She could feel his heart beat. Very fast at first, then slowly abating down to a strong, steady beat. With each passing second, she fell deeper and deeper in love...

'I can never live without him. He's everything in a man I've ever dreamed of. In some way I will find the answer to make him mine forever.'

They murmured to each other, not saying anything that made much sense but it was satisfying for them. All of their recent troubles and misunderstandings seemed to fade into nowhere. Neither one of them said 'sorry' but, for the time being, it wasn't important. They were getting very sleepy. As they drifted off, Mike suddenly said, "I was at Lenny's tonight. Guess what.?" Then, he told her all about the crack, how they had smoked it, how he'd ridden home on cloud nine, didn't know for sure how he'd arrived safely. The talking took him into reality. Sleep became the furthest thing from his mind. He was on a roll! He told her all about his trip to Turkey, the journey back, the scare in the airport and, "I think I brought heroin back but I never saw any. The whole thing was really weird."

Margo was not shocked or surprised. His association with Lenny presupposed such activities. She had a pure, unadulterated hatred for 'that black man' as she'd begun referring to him. 'He's a corrupter.' She'd long been expecting Mike to tell her about his involvement. Her only reaction was, again, disappointment.

CODE NAME: WHITE MUSTANG

Now, in a complete reversal of her earlier lovely thoughts, she got really angry. She made up her mind, in that very instant, she would use his confession, his corrosive activities, to her own advantage. 'A girl has to do what a girl has to do to survuve in this world,' she assured herself. 'This will be my weapon to hold over him, blackmail him if I have to, to get what I want and need from him. It'll work!'

She knew she was not above telling Teea, if it came to that. Now there would be a paved street into the divorce courts. She felt content; she had a plan.

Not knowing her thoughts, Mike still felt charged, euphoric. Then, suddenly, he crashed. Hard. 'Thank the lord Lenny warned me about this' he gasped. 'I need to get up, find my pills. He said I'd have to take at least a tranquilizer, if not a narcotic, or I'd be depressed and unable to function.'

He got up quickly, dumping Margo unceremoniously onto the mattress to fend for herself, offering no explanation. None was needed. She already knew what his problem was.

He rushed into the head, turned on the light, fumbled in the drawer for his migraine pills. He never thought he'd end up thankful for the headaches. Now he was. Where would he be without these narcotics? And he had plenty thanks to the Navy corpsmen. They were generous to a fault with both Valium and Percodan.

He swallowed several Percodans without even bothering to count them or fill a glass with water. He was actually panicky. Lenny had done a number on his psyche having warned him about the bottomless pit of depression.

When he finally went back to bed, Margo was sound asleep, curled up in a ball, looking like a soft kitten. He even thought she was purring. He drifted off, proud of his sexual prowess.

Later, his saliva glands woke him up. They were volcanic in their effort to get him moving. It was espresso! One of Margo's many accomplishments. Hers was the best in Italy as far as he was concerned. He'd developed a strong addiction to caffeine long ago. Most sailors did in fact. On any given morning, espresso was a great source as a wake-up call. On that day, it got him moving, sure as hell.

After a short stop in the head, he walked into the kitchen and was greeted with an ear to ear smile.

"Sit, Mike. Here's a mug full of your favorite. First thing I want you to know is, you mean everything in the world to me. I count on you for my happiness and I hope I make you happy, too. I know I get out of hand now and then so I thank you for being tolerant. I do promise to try and behave myself from here on."

"Of course you make me happy, Margo. You should know that by now. You've brought sunshine into my life. I honestly don't believe I could have made it through the dark days after my family left without you. And, when you go off to Naples, I get quite lonely for you. You're good company, *very* good company!"

Inside his head, Lenny was saying 'Treat them like pets...' Although he was ashamed of his thoughts, he had to admit it was looking like the jerk knew what he was talking about.

Mike and Margo had been developing devious thoughts about each other subconsciously for several weeks by that time. It was a dangerous game, full of hostility, negativity and pure meanness.

While he'd been thinking of her as a pet, she'd thought of him as a yo-yo. 'He can never seem to make up his feeble mind. First he says, 'my friend' when I tell him how much I dislike that black man. Then he says 'you're right, I need to get away from him.' This has been going on almost since day one of our relationship.'

After a while she had ceased talking to him about Lenny. But she had not stopped thinking of Mike as a man who could not make a firm decision about his companionship with a loser.

She had settled for sharing Mike with 'that black man' but only for as long as Lenny kept his distance and did not bother her personally. It was a kind of truce. The latest, this crack business, had gotten her riled up but she was mature enough to admit it was Mike's choice to do what he was doing and she knew if she was going to keep him she'd have to put up with it.

For Mike's part, he'd formed a resolution. Margo was on trial.

If there was any more trouble where his family was concerned, he would have to tell her to move out. He'd have no other choice.

'In spite of her denials, she knows where I'm coming from. She's known from the get-go. My family comes first. Period.'

Thus, the seeds of animosity had been planted. The ground was fertile, the growth would be rapid. Eventually it would blossom into bitter, vicious rancor.

33.

Mike no sooner finished breakfast, dressed and left for his office when Margo, having straightened up the kitchen, got ready and went to visit the Don. She was neatly and carefully attired. No short skirt in the Don's presence. She'd learned *that* the hard way! Her makeup was minimal, just a touch of pale pink lipstick and a dab of mascara. She needed a favor.

The Don was very old fashioned about women and their 'place' in the world.

Just as she had anticipated, he was in his office holding court. The room was enormous. It had to be to contain the desk he sat behind, 'probably all day long,' she suspected.

He was rarely seen in public. Only very special occasions got him outside of his mansion. A funeral usually, depending on who the departed was and the circumstances surrounding the death. In his younger days he had attended baptisms and weddings. No more. Now, he was old. Frail. However, he had lost none of his mental acuity.

Margo was ushered into his presence after only a short wait. She had come to expect courtesies from the old gent being well aware of his feelings for her son. They exchanged some banal pleasantries, mostly Margo reporting on the health of her baby. She assured the Don he was well cared for by her mother, that he was loved to excess. Very smart. Very handsome.

"*Bene, Bene.* I remember your Mother. *Bello Donna*! So why are you here today? What can I do for the mother of the son of my nephew?"

CODE NAME: WHITE MUSTANG

He was needling her in what he thought was a subtle way, giving her a bad time because she refused to marry the nephew. She ignored his comment. Instead, she got right to the reason for her visit. Briefly, she explained about Mike, the drugs, his dealing, his using, his American Navy position and "I love him."

The Don peered at her, asking what business any of that was of his. He gave the impression none of what she'd told him was important. She knew then that she had to get to the point in a hurry. If she wasted his time she would not be treated congenially next time. Secretly, she sensed he didn't have anything else to do at the moment. Nevertheless, she didn't waste any moments. "Because of the illegal activities Mike is involved in, he is going to be in big trouble. Very soon. When that happens I will need your help to keep myself out of it. I must think first of myself and of your grand nephew."

"Clever girl. There is already an easy answer for you, Margo. You can leave this American now. That will be the end of it. What is keeping you with him other than *sesso*? It is a sin outside of the marriage bed. You should marry my nephew, the *padre* of your son. Be a proper family. Family is the most important thing in the eyes of the Church."

He smiled at her, raised his eyebrows, shrugged his shoulders, spread his hands in a pleading gesture.

She returned his smile, gave it her all, wanting to dazzle him. 'He might be old but he is still a man,' she thought. She said nothing out loud, having the good sense not to bad-mouth his nephew who was, as far as she was concerned, a loser. She was not going to marry him. Not then, not ever. Since the day she had told him she was pregnant, he'd never been in touch with her. Not once. She would enjoy telling the Don that but never had.

He was waiting, watching her, knowing she would not conform to his wishes. He didn't push it any further because he knew all about his nephew shirking family responsibilities. It saddened him. 'Young people in these times...the old ways are nothing to them.' Finally, he spoke. "We have family members on the west coast of Cypress. If you need to go away, we will take you there. At the same time, we will take your son and Mother out of Naples. Tell her so she will be prepared. That is all I can do."

She thanked him and left immediately. It didn't set well with him if anyone prolonged their interview. She had learned that the hard way too. But she was well satisfied. He had come through for her and she knew she'd be taken care of.

Driving to work, she re-explored her feelings. No guilt. No remorse. Only relief. She had asked nothing for Mike. There was no other way. He was an American military man. His welfare was in someone else's hands. It was, for her, a matter of looking out for number one. She had done that.

Nearing the Exchange, she tried to get her thoughts off her problems so she could do her job efficiently. As she pulled into the parking lot she had a sudden vision of Mike with a huge black cloud hovering over him dripping with white drops which she instinctively knew must be crack fallout. It jolted her. It was, in her mind, an omen of terrible things to come.

There wasn't anything she could do for him. He could only help himself. As surely as she loved him, she knew that he would do nothing, would drown in the dark depths of the self-made calamity he was headed toward. She would have to stand by helplessly.

34.

His escalating use of crack was beginning to tell. For one thing, he was paranoid. The problems with the two Brits in the office were worse than ever. He'd decided they were out to ruin his career. He still had no idea why. His imagination, paired with his paranoia, was giving him nightmares. He'd been feeling sick lately too but couldn't put a finger on the reason. It wouldn't occur to him it was the crack.

His weight had always been within the normal range for his size. Now, he looked like a cadaver. He had no appetite. His eyes were circled in black, making his face into a parody of a raccoon. He seldom slept. His clothes began to hang on a body that was getting scrawnier by the day.

He was a nervous wreck. Irritable, difficult to be around. His true friends, once amounting to a couple of dozen, were at a loss; bewildered, beginning to avoid him.

One morning his boss called him in. "Chief, you look like shit. What the hell's the matter with you? Your performance is falling off and I'm hearing unsatisfactory things about your personal life. We need to discover the problem and fix it. Right?"

Mike explained, for what seemed like the millionth time, "Sir, since my family left, I'm unable to find a way around my need for them. The Brits are still hassling me and I don't seem able to brush them off. I know they're a temporary glitch but still, I really think the bottom line is that I so despise this stupid job. It's a nothing, Sir. And it's driving me bonkers. I feel as if I've been put out to pasture."

"Chief, you need some time off. Get away for a few days. Go on over to Istanbul. They tell me it's a great place to relax, rest up, do some people watching, spend some money. Splurge."

He couldn't believe what he was hearing and that wasn't quite the last of it.

"Chief, I am putting this in the form of a verbal order. We will label it a mental health day or two. Or three, if that's what you need. Take off. Now! I don't want to see you again before next week"

He had a huge pile of dirty clothes in his car and needed to go to the laundromat. This would be a good time to do that. He had the rest of the day so why not? He gathered his briefcase and a couple of soiled uniforms together preparing to leave.

First though, he called Lenny. "You'll never guess, man. My boss just ordered me to take some time off and go to Turkey. Can you believe it? Is that bizarre or what?"

The Navy Lieutenant Commander actually jumped out of his chair with joy. His eyes bugged out and he had difficulty keeping his voice under control. "Let me get a thing or two taken care of here, man, and I'll meetcha' at my place. We'll have some mashed potatoes. Celebrate your hiatus. Give me an hour."

No time now for laundry. Maybe Margo could be sweet-talked. Not once did he question himself as to why he had called Lenny, why he was in a hurry to get to Lenny's place, why he felt he had to hurry, hurry and not keep Lenny waiting.

M. L. Verne

If someone had told him 'Hey, Mike, you are *addicted* to crack, that's why you do what you do,' he would be astonished and would go into instant denial.

Sure enough, when he got to Lenny's, the man was already there. Whitey was no place to be found. 'Probably out hunting a bear,' Mike snickered.

He was still smiling when he walked into the house. He didn't bother to knock. He'd picked up one of Lenny's rude habits.

Lenny saw the grin and snarled "What's so funny, man?"

"Be cool, huh?" Mike answered. "I was just thinking funny things about Whitey. Where the hell is he? I missed his happy greeting. And don't be yelling at me. I had some errands to take care of, okay? You aren't the only person in the world with priorities you know."

Lenny backed off and said, "Sorry, man. I get nervous some times. Let's have a smoke and a beer. We'll both feel better. All the stuff is ready. Come on. Sit down, man, I got bad news. I had to deal with a message regarding random urine testing. Know anything about that?"

He was holding a vial of cocaine mixture over a flame as he talked. His hands were shaking. Mike took no notice. He had his own addiction to contend with. He just didn't know or admit it. Not yet.

"Well," he answered, "I got what probably amounts to the same message across my desk first thing this morning. That got me a little shook up at first. Then the boss called me in to tell me 'you look like shit' and that didn't help my frame of mind. Until he told me to take some time off and go to Turkey. But hey, man, not to worry. I've been assigned to be the coordinator for urine testing for the command. In charge, man. How's that grab ya'?"

Hearing that brightened Lenny up considerably. He'd been fretting, knowing he'd never pass a urine test. He'd had a vision of himself carrying an uncontaminated bottle of urine around in his pants pocket and didn't have a clue where he'd find any....

As they smoked, Mike felt another foolish smile on his face. The stuff always made him feel so damn good.

"I think I should keep a stash of this at my place, man. I can't be running over here every five minutes for a puff."

A red light flashed in Lenny's brain. He'd been hoping he wouldn't have to face this quite yet. "Man, you have to be careful with this shit. You aren't experienced enough to be left alone with your own supply yet. People have been known to o.d. on it, you know? I have to take care of you. You're my responsibility. You have to trust me on this, man."

The last thing he needed was to allow Mike free access to cocaine. No way! Not until he had Mike securely in his pocket and ready to do anything for a fix.

Mike grinned and smoked, fantasizing while he soared to his own personal mountain top. Eventually, he wasn't even aware of Lenny's presence in the room. In turn, Lenny was already on top but he was getting angry as opposed to Mike's pleasure.

"You listen to me, man. There's a package in Istanbul ready to be picked up. This order from your boss to go over there came like a gift from the gods. As

M. L. Verne

long as you *have* to be there, you *will* pick the shit up. Right?"

He was pissed because, in his view, Mike was acting stupidly. Grinning like a fool. Not listening. Or so he was convinced.

"Roger that." Mike giggled. "No problem, man. What ever you say, man. I'm your main man, man." He sounded ridiculous.

Lenny was pissed. "Go home, Mike. And for shit's sake, be careful. If you get picked up in this condition it's curtains. You're higher than a kite, man. Maybe, on second thought, you better stay here."

But Mike was already up, almost skipping as he went out the door. He came close to falling on top of Whitey who was stretched out full length on the porch. "Oops" Mike sputtered, "Out of my way, dog. Gotta' go home, man."

He got into his car but apparently thought he was on his bike. He screamed out of the driveway, threw the car into second gear and roared away; high on crack, low in the saddle. He felt like he was riding a bronco in a rodeo, a possible accident as remote from his mind as alpha was from omega.

Just as before, his safe arrival home was nothing less than miraculous.

35.

Gus Keef loved the Pentagon. Whenever he got the chance, he wandered the halls breathing in the hustle and bustle of the place, getting pumped up with all the activity. He realized, at some point, that he'd been so bored in Italy he'd begun to lose sight of what he'd long considered his destiny. He'd believed for years he would become an Admiral, an important Admiral who might end up running the Navy. When he left Gaeta for this assignment, he had long ago resigned himself to making Captain, then retiring. Now that he was back in the thick of it, he renewed his dreams of Navy immortality.

He was spellbound with everything going on, liking the job Admiral Kingston had given him. He was doing something vitally important for the Navy, for the country.

It hadn't taken any time at all for him to settle into the work. In many ways it was like most of the jobs he'd been assigned to over the years. Tons of paperwork always but he had a bright young Yeoman to help with the 'white blizzard' as he called it.

She was a stunning, elegant black girl, tall and statuesque with mocha skin that was blemish free and teeth that lit up the room when she smiled. Which was often. She was a Senior Chief Petty Officer, a career girl with a very bright future indeed, someone he would go to bat for any day of the week. Her name, Deanna, charmed him too. In the short time they'd been working together, he'd come to depend upon her skills without reservation.

M. L. Verne

He'd been given the title Aide to the CNO, a prestigious position that made him very proud. Among many other things, it was going to be a tremendous boost for his career. That was probably an indication of why he'd renewed his goals. In the past few days he had managed to block out all thoughts of the shameful activities he'd gotten involved in when he was in Italy.

One of the NCIS agents had come to give a briefing to the Mustang group. He seemed somewhat frustrated because things weren't progressing as rapidly as everyone had hoped. They'd run into several snags, primarily due to the problems being more widespread than originally assumed.

It had meant finding more agents there being a shortage in the general vicinity of the ongoing investigation.

"So far we are aware of one very large group operating clandestinely, mostly between Naples and Istanbul. Back and forth. This involves military personnel from all branches but primarily Navy. Plus Nigerians. We simply don't know much more than that at this time. However, we need as much input as you can give us from your end. We'll supply you with names and you will research each individual's records. Before we wind up this operation, we'll be dealing with the Italian and Turkish governments too. As I mentioned, this is much more widespread than we ever could have imagined."

After the briefing, as everyone rose to leave, Admiral Kingston called out to Gus. "Commander Keef, if you would. Please remain for a few moments?"

CODE NAME: WHITE MUSTANG

In spite of his newfound, workable, clear conscience, Gus almost panicked. He may have thought he'd buried his guilt. In truth, it was hovering just below the surface, lurking like a man-eating shark. He began sweating. His hands shook. He placed them behind his back hoping the Admiral wouldn't notice.

"Gus, thanks for waiting" the Admiral said, smiling. "I need to have a little private chat with you before we go any further into this search for the culprits. I should have taken this up with you sooner but I've had so much going on. What I want to share is simply that this endeavor must take top priority. I know you realize it but I want to reinforce it in your mind. This involves more than just Navy people and I'm afraid, by the time we finish, it's going to be a national catastrophe. Yesterday, I attended a meeting involving the DEA and several other government agencies. The subject was drugs and what can be done. I got to thinking; if we can find a way to solve the problem we're faced with right here, perhaps it can become a solution for the entire country in due time. I suppose that sounds like a wild daydream but stranger things have happened. In any case, I wanted to encourage you. Also, I want to tell you I'm depending on you while I'm occupied elsewhere. In particular, you're exceptionally good with the media so I want you to handle that chore yourself at all times. The word will be out before much longer and there will be a barrage of reporters camped on our doorstep after that. Well, thanks again, Gus." And, typically, he was gone.

Gus stood as the Admiral left, so relieved he almost toppled over. The instant the door closed he fell back into the chair. He wiped his forehead with his

M. L. Verne

sleeve, took a handkerchief from his pocket and dabbed behind his neck. Once the trembling eased up he went directly to his office and locked his door. He sank into his swivel chair, sighed enormously, buried his face in his hands and leaned over his desk trying not to sob. He wasn't sure if his reaction was from fear or from relief.

"God, I hope I can survive this." It came to him that he was caught between two admirals. He was going to have to protect both of them the best he could, juggle the odds of being discovered, keep his recent activities undisclosed. Play it close and continue to pray for guidance.

He had been selected for this job because of his outstanding abilities to get the job done. He may have been distressed because of guilt but he still had his pride and his solid reputation. It would be enough to carry him through the worst of whatever was coming.

'Clearly, I must take it one day at a time. Keep busy. Stay calm.'

He felt better. It would not last.

36.

He was going back to Turkey. One last time. Well yeah, he'd said that before. But what the hell? His terror and near panic from the previous trip had vanished. He had no memory of it. Perhaps it was an unconscious blocking out of a most unpleasant experience. Or, it may have been because of his escalating use of crack. He was half high half the time, using at random or whenever the notion grabbed him. He hardly slept, he seldom ate and when he did, the amount was so minute as to be just about zilch nourishment. Margo was concerned but unable to help him. He lived in another orbit, on some other plane.

Although he had yet to receive any of the big time money Lenny kept talking about, he'd already spent thousands in his dreams. He'd paid off every bill including the balance on his Harley. He'd made some sound investments for the boys' educations. He'd seen that Teea had a grand new wardrobe, a ton of valuable jewelry, better than any he'd seen on Cate. Teea had come back to Italy with the twins for a visit and they'd gone on a wonderful vacation together.

It was the crack. As he flew around with his dreams on his mind and his body on his bike, he never thought that maybe his behavior was getting weirder with each passing day. Even if he had known he wouldn't have cared.

He had to get over to Lenny's for another last minute briefing. His last and final trip. He'd be going over there in a couple of days. He zoomed in and out of traffic at high speeds causing more than one driver to pull over a few feet to give him some extra space. He felt invisible behind his black helmet and his mirrored goggles. Alive. Indestructible.

There was another car in the driveway when he got to Lenny's. It was a blue Geo Prism and it looked familiar.

He pulled up behind it and parked, wondering briefly who it might belong to. Well, no matter. He shrugged as he stooped and patted Whitey's head, then walked into the house as if he lived there.

There sat Lenny and two people who were strangers to him. It crossed his mind that there always seemed to be strangers at Lenny's house. 'Whatever.' He shrugged again. There wasn't much more that was going to surprise him, for sure.

Lenny introduced them as 'Prine and his wife.' Apparently, the woman was nameless. Mike looked long at her, waiting to hear. There were no further names spoken. He was embarrassed for her but she appeared to be oblivious to the slight. Perhaps she didn't understand the language. Mike was sure they were both Nigerians and some of those folks did not speak English.

As Mike sat down, Lenny handed him a smoke and Prine said, rather tersely, "I suppose you've been waiting for this." Lenny lifted a magazine off the table revealing a stack of money. Again, it looked like all hundreds. American. He pushed the entire pile over toward Mike saying, "It's yours, man. Payday."

'About time,' Mike thought but didn't say it. He began counting, estimating about nine thousand total. He was ecstatic but he feigned nonchalance. 'I earned it,' he assured himself.

"Lotsa' cash, man. Guess it slipped my mind I had this coming."

"Yeah! Right! Who's gonna' believe *that* shit, man? Forgot, my black ass. Gimme' a break. You better do a fine job this weekend if you expect any more of the green stuff." He'd been drinking beers along with the crack so he was in his usual vulgar mood. Surly, petulant, mean, aggressive.

Mike didn't even finish the crack. He gathered up the money and left. He was in no frame of mind to listen to Lenny's crap. He climbed back onto his bike and, as always, stroked it lovingly before starting it. The large amount of cash he was carrying had sobered him up enough to be very careful going home. He sure as hell didn't need to get stopped and have to explain where the money came from. Or, worse yet, get in an accident, be unconscious, have some Italian cop steal his reward from him.

'Seems like I've had these ideas before. Somewhere. Sometime. Oh well. No big deal. Way to go, man! Makin' big bucks after a short trip over the border and a small scare at the airport.'

As he drove he talked to himself, enjoying his own voice, his own company. *And* the thought of his newfound wealth.

Once back in his apartment he spread the cash across the table. Then he just sat and stared at it. He'd never seen so much all at once. And it was his. Right then and there, he made up his mind he was going home for a visit with his family. *Now* he could afford to do that. So why not? There would be more money after this next trip too. 'Matter of fact, tomorrow morning I'll get a chit in for more time off. By the beginning of the week it ought to be all approved. Then I can make reservations and be on my way home.'

* * *

His phone rang and woke him up. It was Lenny. "I'll be there in a few, man. You ready to go? I'm taking you to Capo."

Once in a while it occurred to Mike to wonder how Lenny was able to take so much time off from his work. Even a Lieutenant Commander had to answer to *someone*! 'Guess he knows how to cover his ass' was all he could come up with.

Less than ten minutes and Lenny came through the door.

'Must have broken every traffic law on the books.' Mike shuddered at the thought of having to ride to Naples with the maniac.

There was no choice, of course. Not if he was going to do the gig. Get it over with once and for all time. He could only hope his guardian angel would ride along with him.

He'd called Teea to let her know he'd be coming home shortly. They weren't there. He left a message on the answering machine. He made reservations for one week hence. He had dropped into his boss's office to tell him his plan. Up front, the Commander had said "Chief, it's an excellent idea. You need to do that. I should have thought of it myself for you." He'd signed Mike's chit without giving it another thought.

After securing the drug money in black plastic, like the other time, they got on the highway going south.

CODE NAME: WHITE MUSTANG

Speeding. Weaving in and out. Back and forth. It looked to Mike as though even the Italians were trying to stay out of their way.

The speed of the car took second place to the speed of Lenny's conversation. He spewed words non-stop. "Man, yesterday I was briefing this Italian Admiral? You shoulda' been there, man. It was *fantastic*! The guy was stunned at my delivery. Naturally, he didn't know I had a short smoke just before he got to my office. But I was on a roll. That Admiral told me it was the finest intelligence briefing he'd ever attended. And I was high as a kite, man. It was so cool!"

It wasn't a question of whether or not to believe him. Mike knew he was telling the truth. It was just, being cold sober, he was saddened to think a senior officer would get off on walking such a tight rope.

As they approached Naples, the devil's own stench assaulted their nostrils. Satan's halitosis! Sulfur. Belching out from the bowels of the earth. In clouds that polluted everything. Ugly!

Speeding along, Lenny continued his soliloquy, Mike only half listening.

"I've been over to Turkey a few times myself, but just since Cate left. Usually she traveled to set up the buys. The guys we deal with took an instant liking to her and because she's an Italian native there was virtually no risk involved."

That got Mike's full attention. He felt sorry, had no idea Cate had been involved in the drug deals. He hoped Teea would never find out. She thought so much of Cate.

"I bought a stereo for the Nigerians, man. At the Exchange naturally. They really appreciated it. Said they could make a bundle peddling it on the black market."

Was there no end to the man's treachery? Mike felt at his wits end. 'You'd think a man of his status would be extra cautious not to break military regulations.'

"And you need to get yourself an official passport, man. As soon as possible. Just in case you ever get held up at some airport. Official paperwork will get you through where a personal passport might raise some eyebrows. And you need to stay at a different hotel every time you go over there. You don't need to run the risk of being recognized. Know what I'm sayin'? The guys we traffic with take care of the packaging of the stuff. That's not for you to worry yourself over. They use vacuum-sealed bags that are coated with some kind of heavy oil. It thwarts the dogs. The first bag is placed into a second one for extra insurance. They'll sew the bags inside of your luggage. In the lining. They have it down to a science. No way anyone would ever detect the drugs they conceal for us."

The information did nothing to make Mike feel more secure. Once again he was sorry he'd agreed to do this. The butterflies were back. Full force.

"Just make damn sure someone picks me up, man. The last thing I'll be needing is having to sweat a ride home. This is *not* the way I plan on spending the rest of my life. So forget your jive talk about *next time*'cuz there ain't gonna' be no next time, man."

Lenny was quick to assure him he would be waiting for him. "I'm still sorry for the last time when you got so nervous. It won't happen again, man. Not to worry; just get the job done. That's all I ask."

Then they pulled up to the curb, Mike jumped out, grabbed his bags, slammed the door, Lenny pulled away and Mike was on his own.

The security check was no problem. He was on the plane in minutes, strapping himself in after stowing his bags, one under the seat, the other overhead. Maybe he could sleep.

No use! By the time the plane was airborne, his mind was turning as rapidly as the jets that were propelling the flight. The events of the night before kept buzzing around in his head demanding his attention.

He had ridden his bike over to Lenny's who was waiting for him outside, pacing back and forth on the porch. As soon as Mike pulled in, Lenny ran to his beemer, beckoned for Mike to join him and they'd taken off immediately for Prine's house. When they arrived, Mike was taken aback because Lenny actually knocked on the door. They were asked to come in and there sat yet another woman, another stranger. Prine introduced her as 'my sister'.

'Right!' went through Mike's mind. 'Whatever.' He rolled his eyes in Lenny's direction only to see those eyes rolling too. They both had to look away to keep from laughing hysterically.

Then Mike started coughing. 'Damn,' he mumbled, 'I was afraid I was coming down with a cold. Bad news. I *always* get *so sick*.' The worst of it was he was going home to see his boys in a week. He didn't want to carry any bugs to them or be miserable himself. If he was smart he'd go home, crawl in bed, let Margo nurse him.

Instead, here he was on a flight to Turkey coughing again. The flight attendant asked if he'd like some tea with lemon. No, he ordered a beer, thinking the coolness would soothe his throat which was feeling like raw meat, like ground hamburger.

Sipping the beer, he thought some more about the previous evening. Whoever the woman was she had remained silent for the entire visit. The men had talked up a storm, mostly about this trip he was now taking. Obviously, Lenny and Prine were expecting an enormous take following the culmination of this deal.

Eventually the woman had stood up, walked to a door half concealed in the wall on the far side of the room, opened it and reached inside. She brought out an old fashioned cosmetic case the likes of which Mike hadn't seen since he was a kid and his grandmother had paid the family a visit. Hard plastic, light green, the size and approximate shape of a large loaf of bread. She lifted the lid and Mike had to smile. It even had a mirror on the under- side of the cover. Could have been the same one as Grandma's. The 'sister' reached inside and withdrew dozens and dozens of bills. 'There must be a million bucks in there!' Mike's eyes bugged. When it was all counted, it added up to just over forty thousand.

The woman had handed the cash to Prine, who had counted it, then handed it to Lenny, who had counted it. It was then passed to Mike, who was told to count it.

"This is the biggest deal so far for us, man. We need to be absolutely correct. Know what I'm sayin'?"

Shortly thereafter, the two of them began to argue. Lenny and Prine. Who was going to provide the proper bag in which to carry the money to Turkey?

CODE NAME: WHITE MUSTANG

Mike thought, 'How can they get so uptight over something so trivial? We're talking forty g's and they're in a row over a tote bag. Or whatever. It's an exercise in futility!'

After awhile they seemed to come to an agreement of some kind. Mike had stopped listening. Prine reluctantly handed him a sports bag, zippered, brand new.

The woman and Prine wrapped all the money in black plastic and put it into the bag. Lenny grabbed the bag quickly and said to Mike, "We are out of here." By then they both needed to fix up a couple of smokes to get rid of the jitters.

Once inside Lenny's house, he got the stuff going while Mike paced. His nervous movements made Lenny angry.

"Be *cool*, man. One thing you never want to do is use this shit when it's still hot. Know what I'm sayin'?"

No, he did *not* know. And, it did not matter. He just wanted to smoke some crack!

Thinking about it on the plane, he got jittery again. He'd brought a little stuff along, thanks to Lenny. But he'd die before he'd use in flight. The woman sitting in the seat next to him was frowning at him. He had to do *something* to stop his tremors.

He strove to get his thinking away from his physical needs. Lenny, last night, had said "You have to exchange some of your cash into lira. It will be much easier to pay your way 'cuz lately the American dollar is under suspicion. You know? The other day, at the hardware store, some chick at the cash machine had the balls to look at my twenty to see if it was counterfeit. Can you dig it? I was so pissed. Gave her a piece of my mind on the spot. Like *I'd* spend phoney money."

Mike had to wag his head, remembering. The guy sold drugs all over southern Europe and was incensed when checked out for counterfeit bills. Talk about a double standard! Go figure. He had no problem believing Lenny had given her a piece of his mind. He was notorious for it. Mike's only question was how long it would take before Lenny had no mind left, after giving all those pieces away!

So they had stopped on the way to the airport to exchange his dollars into lira.

"Five hundred bucks worth should see you through the weekend." Famous last words.

The exchange left him with an enormous pile of bills. The rate was somewhere in the neighborhood of 1680 lira to one dollar. If Lenny hadn't had a couple of rubber bands in his glove box it would have been a ludicrous situation. As it was, Mike had trouble finding room for all of it.

His pockets, the area around his belt, his bag, all crammed full. He sighed and wished himself anywhere but where he was going, praying he'd live to go see his boys next week.

The flight, smooth and uneventful, ended while he was still trying to get his scrambled thoughts together, get his shaking under control.

He got antsy and sweaty again. Customs was no problem. It was the 'snoopers' who did a number on his nervous system. But the gods, whoever they might be, were still with him. He walked out of the terminal in three blinks of an eye, flagged a cab, and told the driver, "The Marriott, please."

Once checked in, he decided on a cold beer in the lounge. His throat was on fire. Plus, he felt he had to collect his thoughts. It was late evening, he had nothing else to do and was hoping he might get a decent night's sleep. As he sat, sipping the beer, swallowing painfully, his thoughts zeroed in on what he was doing, what Lenny was doing, asking himself why either one of them would jeopardize so much, *everything*, to do it. Hundred dollar bills floated through his mind like autumn leaves in a fall breeze.

He finished the beer, returned to his room and showered hot and long. 'Yes!' He was jubilant. For once it was very satisfying, even steamy enough to at least give him the *illusion* of feeling better, his throat less scratchy, his cough a little looser.

Climbing into bed, piling everything he could find on top of his body, hoping to sweat the bugs out, attempting to chase the demons out of his brain so he could sleep, at last he felt himself drifting off. The dreams were anything but comforting. Even in his sleep, he knew his time was short, his freedom in jeopardy.

37.

His throat felt a mite better. His chest was buried under several tons of wet sand, his head pounding with a thousand jackhammers. He had to get finished with his business and get back to Gaeta for medication.

He made the call. It went down the same way, the young stud faking ignorance of the language. Mike was sick and in no condition for games. He slammed the phone down, shaking at the clatter.

Predictably, it rang immediately. It was Amadi.

He croaked "Hello", wincing with pain. His throat wasn't better after all, rough as an emery board, hurting like hell as he began coughing.

"This is you Mike. Yes? You sound different, man. Like I told you last time, we must be careful with telephone calls. Yes? I will come there soon. In ten minutes. You will meet me in front just as before."

He got up, did a few necessary things in the head, got dressed, went to the lobby to try and find some cold remedies in the gift shop; aspirin, cough syrup, lozenges. All available. He swallowed four aspirin with a slug of the syrup. Gross! Better than nothing.

Walking out front, waiting as he'd been instructed, the fresh air perked him up, got him past feelings of imminent death. He inhaled deeply and coughed until his eyes bugged out. Pedestrians. It seemed like hundreds were staring at him, frowning. 'To hell with them. I can't help it.'

The time crept by. He didn't have a hint how long he'd been standing there, becoming more conspicuous by the moment. He went back to his room disgusted, fell on the bed, struggled to catch his breath, coughed some more.

The phone rang. He answered, gasping for air, sneezing twice. The hair on his arms was vibrating, the back of his neck felt infested with creepy crawlers.

"Where were you, man?" came Amadi's voice. You should have gone outside as I told you to do. Yes?"

"What the hell's goin' on, man? Don't give me any shit. I *was* there like you told me. So? Where were *you*?" God, it hurt to speak!

Something didn't feel right. Mike was *sure* someone had been watching him the entire time he'd waited outside. If he was getting paranoid he felt justified. Again his skin felt creepy.

He moaned as he rode the elevator to the ground floor, too sick to walk the stairs. Not even down.

Reaching the lobby he saw Amadi to his right, standing directly across the way from the lounge. He nodded and turned to walk out the doors, indicating Mike should follow.

Talk about being noticeable. He was still wearing his flashy Bronco jacket. Denver had lost its bid for the Super Bowl but Mike supposed Amadi didn't know. 'Whatever.' Mike shrugged.

Going through the doors Amadi and another man, looking to be no more than twenty years old, stepped to either side of him, steering him around the side of the building.

All the while Amadi kept checking over his shoulder as if expecting someone else, looking like a spy in a grade 'B' who-done-it. His behavior did nothing more than draw attention to the three of them.

Suddenly Amadi said "Give me the money, man." And the two of them took off. They got into a taxi idling at the curb, probably the one they had arrived in. And they were gone, leaving Mike standing there with his sore throat and his cough and nothing else. Not a thing to show for the large amount of cash they had just relieved him of. And no instructions.

'What now? I wonder how this will sit with Lenny?' He scratched his head, shrugged and slowly walked back into the hotel, took the elevator up, re-entered his room. He barely managed to call the front desk to request he not be bothered until the next morning and he left a wake up call.

He tried a hot, steamy shower again, hoping it would help break up some of his congestion. It didn't work. He climbed into bed and swallowed another half dozen aspirin with a huge slug of cough syrup. Then he laid back down.

The phone rang.

It was morning and he jerked awake. In spite of his stuffiness, difficulty breathing, coughing, he'd slept soundly. Remarkable.

He stretched his aching muscles as he lifted the phone to stop the ring of his wake-up call. Right on cue, he began to hack. He had to struggle to sit up, struggle some more to stand up. He stumbled into the head coughing, peed, tried the shower to see if there might be extra pressure so he could get the steam to fill the room. Everyone in the hotel must have showered at the same time. No hot water at all. 'Just my friggin' luck!'

Then the phone rang again. "We have a problem, man. Can you stay over for another day or two?"

Amadi sounded like he was in a cavern filled with echoing scrapes and bumps.

Again, the hair on Mike's arms stood up, quivering. "No way, man. I'm out of here. I'm sick as hell and need to get back to Italy on the next flight." He hung up.

As fast as possible, he threw his belongings into his bag, checked the room for any forgotten items and walked into the hall toward the stairs. He could manage them this morning in order to get the hell out and away. Something very weird was going down. He had to hurry.

Stepping into the lobby from the stairwell, the first person he saw was Amadi. 'The guy must have called me from the courtesy phone.' He was sweating with exertion and sickness.

'Let me get the hell out of here in one piece,' he begged silently as Amadi beckoned to him. Mike approached carefully as Amadi extended his arm to shake Mike's hand. As he did so, he slipped Mike a shopping bag, then turned and left without one word having passed between them.

'Too weird!' Mike was freaked. He paid his bill, walked out, hailed a cab and said "airport" before he'd even slammed the door shut. He got as comfortable as he could in the back seat, then took a peek in the bag he'd been given. It was crammed full of money. He couldn't believe what he was seeing.

"Holy shit" he breathed, 'it must be the same cash I brought over here. How the friggin' hell am I supposed to get through security and customs with *this*!'

Gazing out the window as he rode along, not seeing any of the scenery or thinking of anything else, he began to ponder his serious dilemma. Then, an idea began to form. It started as a supposition but by the time he was deposited at the airport, he was well into a solid plan. He checked in for the flight, noted he was a little early, sat in the midst of all the travelers milling about and tried to stay unobtrusive. Getting enthusiastic.

'Yes! I think it'll work!' He crossed the floor, went into the head, entered a booth that had a lock on its door. He placed the shopping bag on the toilet tank, undid his belt, lined his waist with as many bills as he thought would stay in place, secured them by tucking his shirt tightly under his belt, pulled the belt as snugly as he could and still breathe. He dug his sweater out of his bag which was now sitting on the filthy floor. Thinking, 'I'll have to throw it away once I get home because now it's probably crawling with vermin.'

The sweater was bulky, just the thing to hide his bumpy waist. He took his boots off and stuffed them with bills.He knew he was going to have very sore feet by the time he got home. He'd have to try and walk without limping but if that proved impossible, he could say he'd twisted his ankle.

There was a small stack of bills left over. He put some in his front pockets, the rest in back pockets and felt comfortable enough with that as a final act. It was unlikely he'd be asked to empty his pockets. If he were, it wasn't enough money to get into a quibble about. He was as ready as he'd ever be.

Stepping out of the booth, he splashed cool water on his hot face, washed his hands, began coughing again. It was repugnant.

He'd hacked up a huge clot of phlegm which he spit into the receptacle for used paper towels. Carefully he took in a deep breath to see if that little exercise had cleared out his chest. Sure enough, he managed it without another coughing spell.

'Maybe I'll live to see another day,' he joked, feeling better.

There were no problems getting through to the plane and, once on board, he was able to relax completely. The rest of his plan was foremost in his mind as he leaned back with his eyes closed. He'd decided not to drink on the return flight. He'd be needing his wits about him if his plan was to work.

Initially, he had carried forty-five grand into Turkey. He'd spent about two thousand for room, food, taxi's and so forth. That was what Lenny had told him he could expect to spend. It seemed like a lot, but what did he know?

Okay! This time, he was going to pay *himself.* That was the bottom line. No more waiting on the whims of a couple of crack heads.

As he'd stashed the bills around on his body in the head, he had counted it and, by god, he *was* going to steal some of it! He had to change planes in Rome. There, he'd decide how much.

His mind made up, his chest less congested, his sore throat feeling lots better, he asked the flight attendant for a glass of ice water. "Very large, if you can." It would do him good.

Then he fell into a contented sleep that lasted until he felt, then heard, the plane's engines reverse on the runway.

38.

Landing in Rome, Mike felt upbeat as he deplaned. He had dreamed the impossible dream during the flight. Riches beyond the imagination. He thanked all of the flight attendants as he left. They smiled broadly at him 'the perfect passenger.' He'd slept the entire way.

Passing through customs, carrying his bag, feeling jubilant, he was not prepared for the look the agent gave him. 'Uh-oh' he worried. The man's eyes shifted down to Mike's waist, then back to his face. His look said, 'I know you're carrying contraband of some sort, man. What?'

Mike gave him stare for stare. Somehow, it worked. Instead of blowing the whistle, the guy surreptitiously rubbed his thumb and forefinger together, the universal sign meaning money. Mike quickly reached into his back pocket, extracted the bills he'd stashed there, carefully handed all of them over while he prayed no one could see what was going on. The agent took the bills in one hand while waving him through nonchalantly with the other. Obviously the guy was a pro, had done this sort of thing before.

As soon as he was free, Mike hurried toward the head. He'd gotten nervous again and was hoping he wasn't gonna' get sick like he did the last time. He ran cold water over his face and felt better right away. He took the opportunity to re- count the money and redistribute it. He'd seen on the reader board that his flight to Naples had been delayed.

CODE NAME: WHITE MUSTANG

He realized the agent had gotten three thousand bucks for his discretion. 'Not a bad day's work for the bastard,' Mike grumbled. But he couldn't complain because he had gotten away with something himself. If that agent were honest, he'd be on his way to an Italian jail about now and that was the worst fate imaginable, Italian jails being notoriously inhumane.

He replaced the money; about twenty five grand, around his waist, a little over ten thousand in his boots. As he walked out of the head he heard the first call for his flight. He took a minute to call Lenny to let him know his arrival time.

"Will you be picking me up, man?" He would.

Mike ran for his plane.

The short hop to Naples gave him just enough time to finalize the story he was going to tell Lenny. He had his fingers crossed, hoping Lenny would be high. He, Mike, was sober. So if that's how it turned out, he'd have no trouble convincing the fool he was telling the truth about where the rest of the money had gone.

By the time he got off the plane in Naples, he was wiped out. His cold had him feeling lousy again plus, he admitted, he'd been under more than plenty of stress. His limp was noticeable now because of having walked too much with his boots full of money. His feet were killing him. Lenny was nowhere to be seen. Another little stroke of good luck. The limp might have given him away.

He wasn't about to hang around waiting for the ass hole. He caught a bus to Gaeta. He was all clogged up and needed to get into bed. He caught a cab once he arrived in Gaeta. He stuck his head out of the cab window as it approached his security gate. The guys opened up with a wave and their usual friendly smiles. Going around the corner toward his front door, Mike spied Margo's car.

'Son of a bitch!' he swore under his breath. 'She's supposed to be in Naples until tomorrow night.' He paid the driver, grabbed his bag and walked up the sidewalk.

No sooner had he opened the door and she was on him. "Where the hell have you been and who with?" He'd expected to be back a whole day before her so had never said a word to her about the trip he'd just made. He tried to placate her. No success. She was on a tear. They shouted back and forth until finally Mike began coughing so hard he thought he would throw up his lungs.

"Margo," he gasped, "you know what? If you're that unhappy here, why don't you just move out? Here, let me help you pack. There's no use of us making each other so miserable. Take your clothes now and I'll see the rest of your stuff is delivered to you in a few days. I'll be leaving for the states next week anyhow for a visit with my family. This is as good a time as any to finish off this deteriorating relationship. It'll work for me."

"Fine!" Amazingly, she was in full agreement. It had been so easy. She went into the bedroom and packed. As she did, she looked into herself, was pleased to note that she'd handled all of it very well indeed. Bottom line, she knew it would be best for the both of them. He could do what he had to do to get right with his wife and she, Margo, would be free and clear of the trouble he was headed for. He was on the skids and she had a pretty good idea how he was going to end up. She thanked the gods she'd had the foresight to cover her ass by letting the Don know about her situation. It was comforting to know the Mafia would take care of her, her son and her mother.

If Mike should try and pull any funny stuff later, he'd be right in their sights.

She reminded herself that no guy had ever dumped on her and gotten away with it. After all, she did have her pride!

Shortly, she was ready to leave. She asked Mike to take her bags to her car for her. They stood together by the driver's door looking at each other. There'd been some wonderful times and the memories were reflected on their faces. She leaned forward and kissed Mike softly on his cheek. He felt a lump forming in his throat. Then he started to cough.

The moment was gone. She climbed into the car and drove away without a second glance. He wondered fleetingly where she'd spend the nights until she could find another apartment, shrugged, reminded himself she was a very resourceful young woman and went inside.

He lay down on the couch after taking more aspirin and cough syrup and smiled quietly while he thought about going home in a few days to see his boys. The next thing he knew, his phone was ringing and it was morning.

"Where the hell were you, man? I waited for hours at the airport." Lenny was as rude as ever.

Mike thought 'Yeah. Right.' and said "Man, I didn't hang around. You weren't at the gate so I came right home. I am very sick and besides, things went totally weird over there. No deal went down, man.

Nada. I spent a couple of grand for the essentials and it ended up with Amadi returning the money to me in a paper bag. Strange? Ever have that happen before? They wanted me to stay a couple more days, man. I freaked and got the hell out as fast as I could get onto my flight. I had to put the money some place besides in a paper bag. You know? So I stashed it wherever I could find room and got busted in Rome. The customs agent took a look at me as I checked in. Some way or other he *knew* I had cash on me. Don't ask, man! I don't have a clue. Anyhow, I paid him off and he let me go. I finally got home and Margo was here. I thought she was gonna' be in Naples. She started in on me, man, and I kicked her out. I fell asleep and now you've gotten me up. That's it, man."

He didn't tell Lenny that he'd stashed ten grand away for himself. 'If he notices and asks about it, I'll shrug and insinuate Amadi must have kept it. It'll be my word against some Nigerian that Lenny probably doesn't trust in the first place.'

His conscience didn't bother him in the least over the theft. For starters, it was dirty money. Who was Lenny gonna' tell? Plus, he had earned it! All the stress, the anxiety, the terror he'd suffered and struggled with during two dangerous trips to Turkey justified it. And he would never again be doing it.

That decision was written in stone as it would eventually turn out. He would, most definitely, never again go to Turkey. Not in *this* lifetime!

39.

After showering, shaving and having a bite to eat, Mike rode his bike over to Lenny's. He'd told Mike they needed to get to Prine's place and settle matters. Mike had the rest of the money in his saddlebag so he drove carefully. Once again it was not a time to chance getting pulled over.

As always, Whitey was ecstatically happy to see him while Lenny, already high, was rude, crude and socially unacceptable. Without so much as a 'hi' he growled, "Let's go, man." Mike handed him the bag of cash as he was climbing into the BMW. The car began rolling before Mike had even gotten inside.

"Hey, man, *hold* it! You tryin' to kill me? What the hell's the matter with you?" Under his breath, Mike grunted, 'ass hole.'

They shot out of the driveway, left some rubber on the street and screeched off. Mike, who seldom bothered with a seat belt, buckled it as fast as he could. After traveling at top speed for several blocks, Lenny pulled the car to the side of the road. He put it in park, reached into the bag Mike had given him and pulled out a wad of money. He handed all of it to Mike and told him "Don't say one word, man. You've earned this for your troubles. But we can *not* tell Prine."

Mike did as he was told. He didn't say a word. But he thought plenty. It was clear to him Lenny was going to dip into the honey pot himself and was buying his silence. It felt like he'd just become the recipient of another ten grand. Certainly *he* wasn't gonna' rock the boat.

Prine was not home. The 'sister' was there, whoever she was. They left the bag of cash with her, repeating several times she was to have Prine get in touch as soon as possible because there had been a problem in Turkey during Mike's trip.

She nodded that she understood. Time would tell.

Driving back, Mike told Lenny he had to get home ASAP. "Man, I have had it. I've got this friggin' cold and it's getting worse by the minute. I have to get some serious sack time or I'm gonna' end up dead. I am serious, man. Besides, if I'm going home to visit my family next week, I'd just as soon not take any Italian germs across the ocean with me."

He rode to his place carefully again, this time because he had *his own* bank roll in his pocket. He wasted no time, once he got into the apartment, but went straight to bed with more aspirin and cough syrup under his belt. And slept.

He dreamed that his brothers had found out about his drug involvement and they were crushed. They'd never verbalized their pride in his military career, or in him, but he'd known. It was the way they were. In his dream, they confronted him with their disappointment. When he woke up, he was filled with shame. He considered the dream an omen, a tool. It would bolster him in his resolve to disconnect from Lenny and his enterprises.

There *was* help for Mike. He could have turned himself in to the medics as an addict but he feared if he did, his career would be destroyed. He was a prisoner within his own body.

40.

An NCIS agent was placed in the midst of the NATO forces. He was given the rank of Warrant Officer. Members of the NCIS were civilians but, when working undercover, often had to assume false identities. As a Warrant Officer, agent Cy Woodall would have access to both officer and enlisted groups. No questions would be asked.

Commander Keef had learned of the assignment. At the first opportunity, he telephoned his pal Greg Williams. He felt Greg needed to know about the 'spy'. Just in case. He was still depending on Greg to be there for him in the event of unexpected disruptions.

"Gus, I won't forget you, or your tenuous position. Trust me. Try not to be too worried about things. Until this blows over, until everything is resolved, I think it best that we not be in touch. There's no use tempting the fates. I'm sure you agree."

Any debts, real or imagined, were history then as far as Gus was concerned. He could get on with the tasks at hand and with his life.

The investigation was finally picking up steam. Mind boggling drug activities were coming to light. The entire milieu was like an octopus, tentacles reaching into every corner of vulnerability, sucking the honor and decency from each individual it came in contact with. It was going to take longer than the original plans had presumed to clean up the mess. And it would be tricky because of the international aspects. With each passing day, it began to look as if some members of Congress would have to be informed.

Meanwhile, Gus's respect and admiration for Admiral Kingston had been growing by leaps and bounds. No matter what the job, large or small, who or what was involved, what the eventual outcome would probably be, the man was in control. He made incontrovertible decisions based on simple common sense.

It came as a wake-up call then when the admiral began to show signs of weariness beyond the norm. He had also become disturbingly remote, quiet, withdrawn, pressured. He fidgeted in meetings. His attention wavered.

'Something is wrong,' Gus told himself. 'Maybe I'm not as safe as I had thought. Maybe he's found out about me and what I've done…' That nasty, old, ugly guilt trip again!

Reports crossed Gus's desk with increasing frequency. He scanned them closely, word for word, especially when lists of names appeared. He expected to see persons he had known being targeted. If and when it came to that, he had no idea what he would do. Nothing? Remark on it casually? Mention he had known this man or that woman? He shrugged, unable to answer his own questions. But the longer the lists became, the more he saw no name or anything familiar on them, the easier he breathed.

In truth, he would have done well to resist relaxing. Instead, he should have remained alert to signs of trouble brewing in his own back yard. Very soon, he would regret not heeding his sixth sense, not acting when the best interests of the admiral were at stake

After the fact, he knew he should have pried, should have attempted to discover *why the admiral had made several under- cover, unannounced, unscheduled trips back to Italy!*

He, Gus Keef, might then have been able to step in and avert the historically tragic event that would soon take place.

41.

Mike went home to Colorado where Teea was waiting for him. She looked ravishing. He couldn't take his eyes off her. He longed to embrace her and never let go. The look in her eyes held him off. Also, she hadn't brought the boys along. And, she had an attitude. None of it felt good. He hoped he wasn't going to regret having made the effort. But no, there was no effort too great when it came to spending time with his sons.

"What is *wrong* with you?" she began. "Have you got AIDS? You look like a scarecrow!"

People were staring. She was shouting at him. He was mortified. He actually did not know he looked wasted away. Anyone who loved and cared for him would have reacted the same way. He was pale and skinny, beyond emaciation. His cheeks were sunken, his clothes hung on his sparse body. It was the crack and his bout with pneumonia, finally diagnosed, for which he was still taking antibiotics.

He took her arm and led her out of the terminal. Enough already! His teeth were clenched. On the long flight over he had lectured himself. 'She's gonna' be hostile, and it's your own fault. Be tolerant. Give her a chance to hear you've finished with Margo. That's what her biggest problem will be."

She had not kept the boys out of school because she had learned not to trust Mike and his plans, had lost faith in his promises. She could never have found a way to explain to her boys what the deal was if Mike didn't come off that plane. They knew he was coming home but she had not told them when. She simply wanted to avoid hurting them again.

She drove directly to the boys' school. Mike had insisted he needed to see them at once. The secretary informed them their children were in the gym and directed them where to go.

They were wrestling. Mike was thrilled. That had been his sport in high school.

"It was their choice," Teea told him.

They spotted him in the same instant. Just like everything else, together they had sensed his presence. They finished the holds, got up and walked to their parents with grins on their faces.

"Hi Dad. What are you doing here?" Like, he just happened to drop in on a whim! He grinned back at them, understanding where they were coming from. They didn't want to get emotional in front of the guys. He wanted to grab and hug them but held off so they wouldn't get embarrassed. He remembered how it was.

He spoke briefly to the coach, making it short because it was an unannounced visit and the man had the whole class to handle. Including a couple of girls!

In the boy's wrestling class? 'Things sure have changed since my day' Mike thought, shaking his head in wonder.

The coach had only good things to say about the Steele boys. "Jason seems to have more interest in athletics than Joel. In time, I think Joel will be more suited to the arts but for now, this is good discipline training for them. Their Mother comes to all the matches and is very supportive. It's great you've been able to visit because they miss you and talk about you all the time."

M. L. Verne

Mike had to swallow to keep the lump from his throat, the tears from his eyes. He told the boys he'd see them at home soon, then he and Teea left. She felt he was on the verge of breaking down. Excluding everything else, she knew well how important their boys were to him.

Driving to the house was difficult. Each of them had tons of issues that had to be explored, talked over and resolved. They wanted to 'fix' their marriage but neither of them knew where to start. Teea was sorry she hadn't asked Ev, her therapist, for some advice. Their conversation was carried on in fits and starts involving only trivial subjects.

When the boys came into the house yelling, their parents were relieved. Now they could lean on their sons as a diversion.

They all went to the super market together. Mike loaded up two shopping carts with everything imaginable, determined to fill the fridge, the freezer and the cupboards. He planned on cooking up a storm while he was home. Teea had said, "Go for it! You've always liked to cook more than me."

A couple of times she'd wondered out loud where all the extra money had come from. He was flashing wads of it around, had given her two thousand to 'pay down on the bills', told her he'd gotten lucky in a crap game. She didn't know anything about gambling so he knew he could get away with the fib.

While Mike cooked a wonderful dinner, Teea did some laundry. It was a comfortable domestic scene. Mike felt totally relaxed, wishing he could stay right where he was for the rest of his life. Still, he was also

CODE NAME: WHITE MUSTANG

on guard, waiting for Teea to bring up the subject of Margo.

She stalled until the boys got settled in for the night. Then she got down to brass tacks. He assured her over and over again that Margo was out of his life, that he'd sent her packing, had not heard from her since. She kept at him until he was running out of patience, not knowing how else he could convince her he was telling her the truth. Her distrust was painful for him but he suffered it because he knew he had it coming. Only he, himself, was to blame. He silently promised he would spend the rest of his life making it up to her.

They spent the night together in the same bed. There was no desire involved, a typical impasse with long married couples. In particular, long married couples with huge problems.

Mike was up early in the morning fixing his boys a big, nutritious breakfast, glad to let his wife sleep in while he fed the kids and drove them to school. He wanted to have some 'man to man' talks with them, try to re-establish their previous camaraderie. When he dropped them off in front of the school, he told them he'd pick them up too. That got him a couple of big white smiles. But he knew they were wary, not sure how much they could depend on him. 'Poor guys, they've lost faith in their dad.'

The ensuing days improved everyone's acceptance of each other. Teea stopped being nasty and sarcastic and began smiling occasionally. The boys poked at their dad and the three of them rolled around on the floor, knocking things over, laughing up a storm. They played catch in the yard and the four of them ran

M. L. Verne

together in the early evening hours. Once, they agreed to a race. Teea won hands down. Mike was proud she was still in such excellent condition. He complimented her vigorously.

One evening, his parents called. He couldn't begin to guess how they'd discovered he was in the states. He loved them dearly but had wanted to limit his visit exclusively to his own family.

It seemed his mother was scheduled for potentially dangerous lung surgery. They thought he'd want to know.

Teea insisted he had to go to be with his dad during the ordeal. 'Just for a day or two until your mom is okay.' She purchased a gift for her mother-in-law, sent her love along with Mike and a 'get well fast' order.

Her surgery was to be at the Mayo Clinic. He flew to Minnesota. Both his parents were at the gate when he walked off the plane. He'd ridden first class and why not? He had all the money in the world in his pocket.

His mom, Norma, didn't recognize him. He walked past her toward his dad, Jack, who was standing closer to the gate than she was. She called out "Mike?" and almost cried when he turned to look straight at her. 'He's just a sack of bones.' She was horrified. Gazing into his eyes, she saw that something was very amiss. He grinned at her, braces and all, trying to look like himself. But she was his mother. She *knew* he was in trouble.

They'd secured a two-room suite in a small hotel next door to the Clinic which was specifically for patients and their families. They went there from the airport, visited for a while and caught up on 'the news'. Then they drove to a restaurant. They feasted on Lake Superior trout, the catch of the day, with all the trimmings. Mike ordered an expensive bottle of champagne to toast the success and good news they were expecting the next day from the surgeons. His mom said the docs were worried about cancer. He poo-poohed the idea. His dad, usually very verbal, was silent. Mike knew he was worried and mentally thanked Teea for insisting he come to be supportive.

It had been a lovely evening and a joyful reunion with their son in spite of how he looked. They were sorry it had to come to an end. When the check came, Mike grabbed it.

"Put your checkbook away, Dad. This is my treat."

Norma and Jack were nearly knocked out of their chairs when Mike pulled out an enormous handful of money. A red flag went up immediately in their minds.

Mike was always complaining about how broke he and Teea were. What was this? They looked at each other with eyebrows raised, worried expressions on their faces. But, Norma was going in for surgery in the morning and needed to be free of major family concerns. The outcome of the operation itself was enough to be uneasy about. So they shelved any discussions between them about Mike until later.

The surgery did go well, the news was good; it was not cancer. Just as Mike had predicted. He'd hung out with his dad during the wait and they celebrated together afterward. Norma was released on the third day during which time Mike had hunted up some old school chums he'd lost track of over the years that he'd been gone. They'd gotten together for beers and had reminisced, evoking many laughs and a very good time. He'd shared some of the fun with his parents but they weren't fooled. Their son was in some kind of trouble and they knew, by the time he went back to Colorado, that he was not going to tell them about it. It was very painful emotionally and very worrisome.

They told Mike, the night before he left, that they were going to visit him in Italy. He took that news with a large grain of salt. They'd said before they would be visiting him at other places where he'd been assigned but had never made it. He'd been disappointed previously. Now, he was terrorized.

The way his luck had been going, this time they *would* show up! Then what would he do? His mom had been chiding him about his 'anorexic look'. God forbid she should find out *why* he was looking that way.

So he did not encourage them. In the end they would do whatever they wanted anyhow. And that's how it was left. Undiscussed and unresolved.

* * *

It seemed to him he'd barely returned to Italy and gotten back into the swing of things when his parents called to tell him they would be coming for sure. They would let him know the exact time he could expect them but 'be assured, we *are* coming.' From their tone of voice, he knew the decision was made, they would definitely come and they would pry. *That* was why they were coming. He had no doubt about it.

He'd have to get his act together. Beginning at once. Clean up the apartment, get some food stocked, get off the cocaine. Mom would figure it out if he didn't. Knowing her, she'd find out everything she was coming to Italy to find out in any case.

It was his own stupid fault. The dumbest thing he'd ever done in his life was flash that money around under their noses. He should have realized they were onto the fact that something strange was going on just because of the way he looked. He'd finally admitted he appeared shrunken up, after Teea made another big scene about it when he'd gotten back to Colorado.

He *had* to get off the crack. It was *killing* him.

He called Lenny.

"Come on over, man. We'll cook up some mashed potatoes. We can make some solid plans for their visit. Decide how we want to entertain them. Right? See ya'."

Mike rode over with trepidation. What he *really* wanted to do was call the folks back and tell them not to come. Talk about foolhardy! *That* would cook his goose forever.

Lenny had the beers open and the crack ready. Mike had gotten so worked up over the 'visitation' he almost forgot to pet Whitey who, as usual, was thumping the porch with his tail, sounding like a bass drum that was out of sync.

"Man, I need to get off the crack before they get here. You don't know my mom. She'll spot it right away, man."

"Right. We all need to do that." Lenny was very agreeable. "All in good time, my man. For now let's just visit and make some plans."

They accomplished exactly nothing. Lenny kept steering the conversation around to Mike's next visit to Istanbul while Mike steadfastly refused to discuss it.

M. L. Verne

He'd grown weary of telling the guy he wouldn't be doing that ever again. It was a battle of wits. No one was winning. They were just wasting time and getting high.

"Hey, man," Lenny grinned, "I been tryin' to figure out what went wrong during your last trip over there. Amadi assured me 'Man, it'll never happen again.' Well, how am I supposed to know what 'it' means? No one can tell me. Anyhow, I raised holy hell with them, gave them a big chunk of my mind. And I gotta' tell ya', they are *humbled,* man. They know there's plenty more people where they came from and it'd only take a minute to switch my loyalties."

Mike believed that. In fact, he was sure Lenny *had* no loyalties. Except to himself! He might be loaded with crack, but he could still think straight. He suddenly *knew* that he'd be able to resist Lenny from that point on. Why the change? The feeling that he could do it? Because his parents were coming! It was that simple. He loved them enough to do it. For them if not for himself. Such positive thinking had bolstered him to the point of getting sober. He got up to leave. 'Might as well start right now,' he decided.

As he was walking out the door, Lenny suddenly grabbed his arm and said "Hey, man, just a sec; I had this brainstorm. Know what you can tell your folks when they get here? About why you're so up tight, lookin' so scrawny? Use the situation at your office. You know. With the Brits. They'll buy that, right? How's that idea grab ya'?"

Mike thought about the suggestion as he rode home. It was possible. God knew the whole friggin' mess was enough to drive an admiral bananas.

While he showered, he prayed to God that He would stay by his side during the coming weeks, guide him down the right path. As he fell asleep he felt good, wondering if it was due to the fact he'd just spoken to God for the first time in months.

42.

The plane was due to land in a few minutes. He couldn't believe how nervous he was. They were his *parents*; he had no reason to be afraid. His story was all ready. He hoped it would sell.

He'd been tracking their journey, had telephoned them at the terminal in Spain where they'd had a plane change. They had been pleasantly surprised and curious how he'd known where they were. He could follow their progress with the communication devices available to him at work. They were flying on a military plane, his dad being a retired serviceman. It was one of the benefits allowed, after twenty-plus years of dedication.

He watched them through the fence as they crossed the tarmac. He whistled, they waved. He could tell they were wiped out. His eyes filled with tears as he watched their progress. He loved them so much, was so sorry for the evil things he'd been doing. If they ever found out, it would very likely destroy them.

In their happiness to see each other, they almost knocked themselves down. "Mom, Dad, you don't look any the worse for such a long trip. How was the flight?"

"Long. Boring. Tiring. Ho-Hum." Jack was worn. He'd slept only in short spurts all the way. Norma fared better. She had swallowed a mild sleeping pill as they left the eastern shores of America anad had slept the entire way across the Atlantic. Jack's choice had been to tough it out. Now he was feeling the effects of jet lag.

CODE NAME: WHITE MUSTANG

"Let's get a bite to eat on the way to my place," Mike suggested as they waited for the luggage to be unloaded. He launched into his story about how the Brits were making his life hell on earth. They listened to their son, noted his pallor, his lined face, the black circles under his eyes and did not trust what he was telling them. Something wasn't ringing true.

'Maybe I can at least put some weight on him while we're here.' Norma was beside herself with concern.

Mike could sense their skepticism. 'Shoulda' known they'd see through me. They always have.' But he kept at it until he got to the end of his tale of woe. By then, the luggage was unloaded. Mike led them to his car in the parking lot and when Norma saw it, she burst out laughing.

"What?" he asked. She told him she was delighted with his 'wreck' The humor of it lasted until she climbed into the back seat. Both the rear windows were cracked and the springs were popping out of the seat. She couldn't find a spot to sit that felt safe. "This seat is deadly, Mike. Am I going to get stabbed to death back here or what?"

"Mom, there's a pillow back there. Find it? Sit on that and you should be just fine."

Jack was finding the situation amusing too but when he climbed into the passenger seat it fell sideways, him with it. Mike had never taken the time to fix it, put it back on the tracks. The men had to climb back out and Norma had to move to the other side of the seat. Then they worked on fixing the problem. It took a while. Finally it was solid and felt much safer.

Mike was very pleased that his Dad could still fix things as well as he always had. "I owe you one, Dad. I'll buy dinner."

His parents were appalled at the 'scenery' along the route they were driving. Garbage everywhere. They watched in horror as people threw plastic sacks out of their car windows into the ditches alongside the highway. "What's the story here, Mike? It's disgusting."

"The southern Italian people have no pride in their country. Their attitude is that the world is going to come crashing down around them in the form of hot lava from the volcanoes, so why bother? In northern Italy, it's quite the opposite. I hope we can get up that way while you're here."

Jack was stunned by the traffic. "I can't believe the way these people drive! I have some bad habits but this is suicide. It looks to me like they'd as soon hit you broadside as pass you legally. Have you had any accidents, Mike? I can't see how it could be avoided for very long in this madness."

"Yup. It's pretty bad. But you get used to it. You learn to go with the flow. A guy ran into me recently, a local. Believe it when I tell you car insurance means nothing here. Especially if you are American military. The cops showed up the day I got hit, shrugged their shoulders and walked off. I have gotten exactly nowhere trying to collect. Now you know why I'm driving a wreck, Mom. It doesn't much matter if someone runs into this car 'cuz it's already all banged up, right?"

They pulled into a restaurant parking lot which was almost empty. Norma wondered what sort of place it could be with no customers. Inside, it was cold. And silent. They walked between linen draped tables that were devoid of centerpieces, china, silverware, glasses. To Norma's practiced eye, some of the tablecloths looked soiled. There wasn't a wait person in sight. Mike led them to a side room containing a huge oven-like fireplace that was black with soot and empty of any visible energy- producing equipment.

"Not to worry, folks. They serve wonderful pizza here," Mike assured his parents. Norma didn't know about Jack but she had her doubts.

"I've been here before and it has always been very busy. Must be the time of day. It is mid-afternoon after all."

He got up and went to look for someone to wait on them. Jack and Norma took the opportunity to compare a couple of notes.

"Why, he looks as if he's been in a concentration camp." Jack complained. "He looked bad enough when he came for your operation. If you ask me, compared to now he was downright robust back then."

Norma was shaking her head. "There's something very wrong here, Jack. I hope to God my suspicions are wrong but I think he's mixed up with drugs somehow. The way he looks and acts is indicative, not to mention all that money he had when he came to see us. I'm afraid I'm going to have to trust my instincts."

"By God, it better *not* be drugs. I'm gonna' ask him straight out. I can't believe he'd do that to himself and to Teea and the boys, not to mention his career." He was irate.

"Shh, here he comes with a waiter in tow. We'll talk more about this later." She didn't relish a

M. L. Verne

conversation dealing with drugs but knew it would have to be taken care of in due time. Just not on the very first day of their visit.

Mike ordered a carafe of the local wine he'd grown so fond of. He told the waiter they'd be having pizza and would the chef please come and prepare it in the oven so they could watch the process?

"*Si*. I will tell him." The waiter smiled and spoke a few words in Italian to Mike who answered briefly. "I've picked up some phrases, as you can see," he told his parents. "A bit from Teea, some from listening to the civilians in my office building. Not from the Brits, of course. They're too stupid to even speak decent English."

"Oh now, Mike, you're just angry about them. I bet they speak excellent English. Better than we do. After all, it was their language first."

She wanted him to lighten up. He was too intense. She grinned when she chided him so he'd know it hadn't been a lecture.

The chef showed up and began preparations. He lit the fire in the oven, now apparent that it was fueled by hidden gas jets. He molded the pizza crust, poured some tomato sauce over it and baked it. That was it.

Now it was Mike's turn to grin. "That is pizza, Italian style. I wanted you to experience it. Only in America can a person get the sort of pizza we're used to. There's Italian and there's ours. Actually, we lucked out. We got a hot meal. Ordinarily they serve their pizza cold here. It's not an Italian dish, originally."

They didn't finish their meal. It truly was tasteless and gummy. Mike paid the bill and they went directly to his apartment. The folks were now so tired out they could hardly stay awake. The guards waved cheerily, knowing Mike had his parents in the car with him. He'd told them about the coming visit. There was an empty space to park, right in front for a change. After he unlocked the door he told them to go on in while he carried their bags for them.

They checked out the apartment, Mike telling them the sleeping arrangements and they remarking about his Harley sitting in the living room. Then, they collapsed.

The next thing Norma knew, it was morning. She had slept soundly right on the couch, hadn't moved an inch, couldn't believe it. Jack, it seemed, had found his way into the bedroom. Mike had closed the door. Jack was notorious for his snoring. People avoided him at night if at all possible. She looked around and saw that Mike was sleeping on the extra cot he'd set up in the kitchen area.

He'd fallen asleep thanking God his parents had arrived safely. He had also asked, again, for guidance in the days to come because he was going to need all the help he could muster.

'Cold Turkey'…no laughing matter…withdrawal was going to be a bitch!

He had drifted into an uneasy sleep filled with weird images and ideas. None of it made sense and even in his sleep, Mike tried to avoid figuring out what it all meant.

At last, his sleeping mind cleared and when he woke up he felt rested, eagerly looking forward to spending some quality time with his visitors.

43.

Mike took them to visit Lenny. Later, in private, Jack and Norma would discuss the event and agree it was the first page in a book of debacles. At the time though, they were polite, Jack more so than his wife. She sensed trouble when she entered the house.

It was a 'villa' they were told. Three stories tall. The furnishings seemed shabby. The entire place, up and down, reeked of cigarette smoke and unwashed bodies. In the master bedroom there were piles of clothes everywhere. Norma *had* to mention it. "What would your mom say if she saw this mess?"

He was embarrassed and showed it. Mike thought, 'Way to go, Mom,' grinning to himself.

Lenny said "She'd have my ass. You're right. I will be cleaning this place up. Been meaning to do that for a while now. Just been too busy."

'Right,' Mike thought. It was his first time in the upstairs areas of the place and he wasn't much impressed. There were a few expensive pieces of art sitting here and there but, for the most part, it was a barren, chilly place.

Lenny invited them to have a beer with him but he'd hardly gotten the words out when Norma said, "Well, thank you Lenny. Mike has promised to take us shopping, a couple of errands we need to take care of. So we'd best be going. Perhaps another time?"

She, for one, needed to get out of the place. The vibes were all negative. She glanced at Mike and saw he was edgy. Jack would have taken Lenny up on the invite but he was out-voted. They headed for the Navy

Exchange. As they drove along, Mike told his parents about Margo. He made no excuses for his behavior. There was no excuse. For starters, they were fond of Teea. Then, there were the grandsons. Close upon that, they were Catholic. He told them how sorry he was to have done such a thing, that he had learned a valuable lesson. It was over and they could rest easy.

Jack made no comment. Norma sighed. Audibly. Mike got their message.

They shopped for food and wine. They checked out a few items they might like to take home as souvenirs and were pleased with the prices. Mike pointed out a girl behind a counter, told them she was Margo. They were not interested. On the way home Mike pulled into an outdoor stand where foods like cooked chicken were being sold.

"These chickens are so good. As tasty as any you'd buy back home. 'Road kill.' Ask me no questions, I'll tell you no lies. I have no idea where the term originated. But you'll see. They are delicious."

The ensuing couple of days were slow, relaxed, a time for enjoying each other's company. They spoke of a hoped for trip to Germany They presumed Mike would be going with them.

On the third day, Mike had to go to work. He came home full of apologies. "I can't go to Germany with you; I'm so sorry. My boss says he can't let me go, can't spare me. I have an idea those Brits have something to do with it but I have no way to prove the truth. I really am sorry and I'm just as disappointed as you are. I was looking forward to the time away with the two of you."

They didn't believe him. They were sure it had something to do with the trouble he so obviously was involved in. Norma made up her mind. If he didn't share with them soon, she was going to start quizzing him. She was determined to get to the bottom of his dilemma so they could help him. How? She didn't know. Yet. But she was sure something would turn up.

She'd been watching him closely and was thankful to note he ate good meals along with them. Once or twice she asked herself if she could be wrong about the drug thing. But no, she knew there was *something* amiss. That's what it *had* to be.

Eventually, it was too heavy for Mike to conceal any longer. He made up his mind to tell them some. Not all.

Lenny was the first part of his story. Mike figured his mom, at least, already had a whole lot worked out. Jack, on the other hand, was bowled over. Being retired military himself, he had no way to relate. A senior officer? Dealing drugs? Impossible!

"When Teea took the boys and went home, I was devastated. I know it's not an excuse but once they were gone, it was so painful I didn't think I would survive. Lenny was there for me. A part of his support was introducing me to crack cocaine. *Of course* I knew it was wrong. But at the time it helped me. I was able to pull myself out of hell, finally able to cope with the loneliness, get my act together. I'm indebted to Lenny for that."

He talked on for a while but it wasn't washing. His parents were well acquainted with military life, knew that the Navy was the one branch of the service that separated families consistently. It was the way of life.

Navy people were expected to cope with it. Mike and Teea had been apart more than they'd been together during their marriage. Mike should be well used to that by now. He shouldn't need any 'crutch' to get over yet another separation, no matter what the reason was.

Nevertheless, they loved their son unconditionally. They would do whatever they could to support him and help him.

Since he couldn't go to Germany with them, they changed their plans and left a couple of days earlier than they'd intended. Their tickets were pre-paid, purchased before they left home. No reservations required. Mike drove them to the train station.

They stopped on the way to pick up his friend Bernadetta. "She speaks both Italian and English and will be very helpful at the train station for interpreting purposes. Besides, she is an interesting individual. She's only twenty three and is already studying for her doctorate. I think you'll like her."

She certainly was different! Long, black, curly hair and in more places than just on her head. Huge dark brown eyes, a big sunny smile. And she used the 'f' word indiscriminately. That clearly startled his folks. Mike was chagrined. He'd been used to it.

But she was invaluable at the train depot. Without her they would never have found the correct train. The ticket agent they approached for information did not speak English. Bernadetta interpreted for all of them.

They got settled in their compartment, bid Mike and his friend goodbye, told Mike they would call from Germany when they got ready to return and sat back in anticipation of a new adventure.

M. L. Verne

Bernadetta invited him in for a drink. He told her he'd take a rain check. In the months and years ahead, he would recall the invite, his decision to turn it down, the events that ensued. It was his last chance. After that night, nothing would ever be the same.

44.

It pissed him off but he couldn't help himself. He had to see Lenny. The need was overpowering. When he got there, he was welcomed as if he was expected.

"Man, I have an excellent idea. When your folks get back from Germany we'll take them down to the 'boot' to visit my in-laws and spend the weekend. That way, they can see what *the real* Italy is all about."

"I don't know about that, man. My Mom may not do it unless she has an invitation. The social niceties are a stickler for her."

"Not to worry, man. You know me. 'Mister Persuasion.' I can handle that."

Oh yeah! Mike knew all about Lenny's persuasive traits. It would be interesting to watch the interaction between Lenny and his mother when the subject came up.

"Come on, man, let's go for a bike ride. We need to stop over at Prines' anyhow so I can finish up some business with him."

Mike had taken his bike over to Lenny's a couple of days earlier just to clear it out of his living room for the rest of the folks' visit. "Why not? I have nuthin' else to do. It's gonna' be a long few days now that I'm used to company."

"After we leave Prine's place, we'll go over to Fronz's. He's got a fresh supply of cocaine for me to pick up." It was now obvious that Lenny had planned the entire evening ahead of time.

Along the way they stopped at one of their favorite beer joints for a sandwich. Mike pigged out. Since getting off the crack, he was always ravenous. Lenny was impressed. "Go for it, man!" They drank a couple of beers and got back on their bikes. Mike was determined to get the hell home ASAP.

Soon enough they reached Prine's where Mike said he'd wait outside while Lenny took care of his business matters. He wasn't about to leave his bike unattended in that neighborhood. It was the middle of a run-down area that would scare a wild alley cat on the best of days.

Several minutes went by. Then, several more. Finally, Mike stuck his head in the front door.

"What the hell, man? It's getting cold out here."

Lenny was sitting at the table talking to 'the sister'. "Be cool, man." he yelled back at Mike. "The guy isn't here. I have to wait for him. At least a while longer. No big deal. Sit, man." He had smoked some crack; Mike could tell.

He stayed inside, pacing, looking out the door every few seconds to check on his bike. At last his nervous activity got to Lenny so he got up and they left. It looked like Prine was out for the night. The 'business' Lenny needed to conduct would have to wait for some other occasion.

45.

In America they're known as crack houses. In Italy they're called ghetto's. A crack house by any other name is still a crack house. That's where they ended up. At Fronz's ghetto.

They walked right in without knocking. Mike dragged his bike along with him. Lenny opened his mouth to make a bad joke but thought better of it. Mike, he knew, was in no mood.

There was another strange woman sitting in Fronz's house. Her English left a lot to be desired. She had a heavy Nigerian accent. Lenny was able to communicate well enough to find out that Fronz had left a while ago. He hadn't said to where.

Lenny sat and thought for a moment, then told Mike "I think I know where he is, man. You wait here while I go find him. Be back in a few." And he was out the door.

It couldn't have been four more minutes later when the door burst open and two Italian law enforcement persons came into the place guns drawn. It was so *weird*! Mike sat stone still, petrified.

'What the hell....?' He tried to think calmly, telling himself, 'They aren't here for you, man. Be cool.'

He remained silent, hoping they wouldn't even notice him sitting there. The woman cowered in her chair her eyes like enormous black olives protruding from her head. She began to wail in a quiet, primitive way that sent shivers down Mike's backside.

The police had been rummaging here and there, looking under the furniture, opening drawers, eventually reaching a door Mike had not noticed. It was slightly obscured by a large chest of some sort. Sure enough, after a second they pulled a large plastic bundle out onto the floor. It was bound with electrician's tape which they slit, tearing the plastic aside. An enormous pile of money fell out, rolled, came to a stop.

After that, their search became more intense.

Then, Lenny walked through the door. Mike jumped up to warn him off but as he looked toward Lenny, his eye caught movement in the direction of his bike. Before he could open his mouth to protest, the cop was checking out his personal papers which were in the side pocket of his saddlebag. His passport, driver's license, military I.D., money....they were violating his privacy!

He was about to voice his objections when he heard a *click*, realized the other cop had come up behind him and was in the process of handcuffing him. Then it was Lenny's turn. In no uncertain terms, they were informed they were under arrest. One of the cops lifted the phone and called Navy Security. The nightmare had begun.

* * *

Ironically, the very day they were busted, Margo lost her job at the Exchange. The American military system requires foreign job applicants who wish to work for the government in overseas installations to apply for a document known as a sojourner's permit. Margo had lied on her paperwork, stating that she possessed such a document when, in fact, she did not.

And she had never bothered to apply for one. During a routine check of employees, she was forced to admit her subterfuge. She was summarily dismissed, instantly suspecting that somehow Mike had a hand in it. He was the only human being she had told she had no proper permit.

As the saying goes, 'hell hath no fury…' In her mind, he had not only scorned her but now had caused her the loss of her income. She went directly to the NCIS and told them every detail she could recall involving Mike's drug activities. It was the break they'd been waiting for. They were stunned. Both Mike and Lenny were on their list of persons to investigate but they'd been so busy with other aspects of their operation they hadn't gotten around to it yet.

Once Margo had spilled her information, she made a beeline for the Don's house. She told everyone there about Mike's treachery, warned them he wasn't beyond spilling what he knew about the Mafia involvement in several other nefarious enterprises and then confessing she'd said things to him she never should have.

Her objective had been to sic the Mafia onto Mike. It worked. Fronz's house got busted that very evening. A couple of Mafia men were sent to the authorities with enough information, garnered from Margo's memory, to pin-point the location of the ghetto. The Italian law enforcement officers had been assigned to check the place out, gather information, make arrests if they deemed it necessary.

Expecting, at the very least, a long drawn out surveillance, it was considered a stroke of luck by the

M. L. Verne

Italians that Mike and Lenny were there the very night the police made their first raid.

For the two Navy men, it was a bone-crushing misfortune.

46.

Mike was interrogated by Cy Woodall, the Warrant Officer. He recognized the man having met him occasionally at social functions around the area. He'd put the guy down as being a nerd. How wrong he'd been! This man was a true professional who had done an excellent job of acting while he'd been busy doing his undercover work.

They had photo-copied his passport, the ID pages as well as the Turkish visa, the Italian entry and exit stamps. While all of that was going on, Mike sat alone in a small, bare, windowless room, only two straight-back chairs for furniture.

He began to think about the times he'd tried to tell his superiors there were drug deals happening in the command. Fleetingly, he wondered if that was why he'd been taken into custody. Maybe it was some sort of 'sting', using him to identify the real culprits. If it turned out that way, his guilt at having 'used' would know no bounds.

After what felt like an eternity, Cy Woodall returned to ask Mike more questions. He began, "Chief, what was the purpose of your trip to Turkey?"

"My Commander ordered me to take a few days off, go over there and relax, get away from the stress of my job and my personal problems."

"We'd like to search your house and your car. Would you have a problem with that, Chief?"

"On what grounds? Damn right I'd have a problem! Listen, I want an attorney."

He was taken down the hall without another word being spoken. They walked into the office of Lieutenant Hanna Barker, an attractive black woman who, he was told, would be in charge of his case.

His case? Scary! Thoughts of a possible 'sting' vanished.

Woodall left the room, closing the door behind him. Mike and the Lieutenant were alone. She began asking pertinent questions.

Was he involved in drugs? Did he know anyone who was? Had he heard any rumors? What had he been doing at that ghetto? How had he gotten there?

On and on. He denied knowing much of anything, just a little scuttlebutt. He asked her what the hell was going on. Why had he gotten arrested and brought there without an explanation.

She listened to him, watched his body language, told him she was assigned as his defense attorney and that "either they charge you with a crime or they let you go."

"It's that simple, Chief. You are free to tell any or all of them that I have advised you thus. Those are your rights."

Then she took him back to the first room he'd been in and told him to wait. Shortly, a couple of agents showed up and said they'd like to talk to him. He told them, up front, what the Lieutenant had said to tell them. Their faces closed up. They left the room.

Several more hours passed. He paced the floor. Apparently, they had forgotten all about him. Once, he looked out the door to see if anything was happening. He could not see a living soul. It was as quiet as a tomb out there.

He had all the time in the world to review his predicament. He'd never been in such deep shit. He had no idea how to act, what to say. 'Best I simply keep my mouth shut.'

About then, Woodall came back into the room. He told Mike, "We finally got permission to obtain a urine sample from you, Chief. Here's a container. You know the drill. The head is down the hall on the left. Bring it back here when you're done."

There was no choice. If he refused, how would that look? Giving them a sample would cook his goose. He'd smoked just a little and it had been a few hours ago. But the stuff stayed around. It would definitely show up.

His paranoia, always lurking in the background, now hit full force. He *knew* his phone was tapped. His car had some sort of listening device somewhere hidden. There were 'bugs' all over his house. *THEY* were watching his every move.

He peed in the receptacle, left it on one of the chairs in the room and walked out. Hey! No one said he couldn't!

He returned home and called Lenny. As usual, the guy was high and full of himself.

"No sweat, man. Just be cool. They're fishing that's all. They have no bait, man. I took precautions long ago, in the event this was gonna' happen. Bound to. Know what I mean? Just don't let 'em do a number on you. Trust me and we'll do fine."

'Yeah. Right.' Mike knew Lenny had been interrogated too. He'd gone home and gotten high to avoid facing up to reality.

'Besides, he has senior officers he can count on to cover his ass for him. They might not like it, but they'll do it to protect themselves and the Navy image. And who the hell cares about a lowly Chief? Gimme a break!'

The disgust he felt for Lenny almost made him physically ill. '*He* got me into this mess. I hope they hang his black ass from the highest yardarm.'

* * *

His parents returned from Germany. Earlier than Mike had expected or they had led him to believe. He wasn't yet over the shock of his latest situation. He was deep in the throes of guilt, terror and apprehension. Not to mention panic.

He went to the train depot to pick them up. Because he was alone and not very conversant in Italian, he got the directions wrong and almost missed them. Jack and Norma had drifted around hoping Mike would put in an appearance soon, starting to get nervous. What if he didn't show up? They were total strangers and knew they were a long way from the apartment. It was fast becoming a dilemma.

It had gone on long enough and they were at the end of their tolerance when Mike walked into the very door they were about to walk out of. He apologized profusely, explaining what had happened as he led them to the car. It was very late, near midnight, but there was a ragged man in the lot insisting that he was going to wash their windshield.

Mike got rude and angry. He shouted, "You're a friggin' idiot! You better move before I run you down." He rolled up his window and gunned the engine, screeching out of the lot.

Another red flag went up. 'That's not *our* son, acting like that. Something else has happened.'

The ride to Mike's scared both his parents. He was driving erratically, once coming within inches of ramming another car.

Jack finally spoke up. "Mike, what's going on? You know you're scaring your Mother, driving like this. How about telling us what's on your mind?"

"Right, Dad. You know, some days it's just not worth getting out of bed. Today was one of those days for me. Started out at the office with the Brits coming at me with all their crap before I even got inside the door. I went off on them, told them where they could go and what they could do when they got there. Told them if they had any balls they would have said long ago what their problem with me was so we could get it settled. Told them my ancestors had fought a war to free me of the likes of them and they could both kiss my ass. And I went home. Then, damned if there wasn't a message from Lenny on the answering machine telling me he was home, too. So I just went over there and we smoked some crack. Well, there you have it. The big mystery is solved. Now you know what I do when I can't cope. Anyhow, Lenny and I had been over at a friend's place one night after you left and we got busted just for being there. It was all bullshit and I was released right away but it's been a bitch and now they're watching my every move."

Jack and Norma remained silent. Their worst fears became a reality. They'd need to get their thoughts together and see how they might be able to help their son. Hopefully, he would be honest with them.

The remainder of their European 'vacation' was destined to be full of frustrations and feelings of helplessness...

47.

They had not finished their first cup of espresso when Lenny popped into the apartment. Even with guests, he didn't knock. He was hyped.

"We're gonna' take a trip, folks. Did Mike tell you? My in-laws live down in the boot of this country and we're gonna' go down there and visit them for the weekend."

Mike *had* made slight mention of something to that effect. Jack and Norma had considered it sheer nonsense and had promptly forgotten all about it. Stay for a weekend with people they didn't know? Worse, take a long trip with Lenny? Miss spending quality time with their son? Alone? Forget it!

But, they'd never dealt with a personality, an ego, like the one standing in front of them. He cajoled, he wheedled, he coaxed, he manipulated, he enticed them. He told them "This is the *only* way to see Italy. You'll eat handmade pasta to die for. There's nothing like it in the world. The sauces are made from home-grown tomatoes and basil, the smells and tastes straight from the gods. The wines are made right in their small rural town. No preservatives, grapes from the local gardens. I tell you people, you will think you had died and gone to paradise. You won't soon forget it!"

His words were prophetic. As long as they lived, they would not forget that weekend spent with Lenny.

He had finally convinced them. He'd dangled the lures of local family life in front of their noses and they found themselves out- maneuvered. He out-talked their excuses, ignored their insistence that they had made

M. L. Verne

other plans and he had laid down the time schedule for them "so you can all be ready when I come by for you."

They had capitulated, telling themselves that they *were* in a foreign country with one chance to experience something unique.

"We'll leave in the morning. I'll pack a picnic lunch so we can make good time. It's a long drive and we probably won't get there until dinner time."

"Do these people know we're coming, Lenny?" Norma was concerned about popping in on strangers unannounced.

"Not to worry! They're always up for company. They have a large family and someone is forever showing up. The pot is on the stove at all times."

That wasn't the exact answer Norma was looking for but it was all she was going to get.

The troubles started before they got out of Gaeta the next day. They'd needed to stop at a bank to exchange dollars into lira. They were going into a part of the country that was remote from big cities, the people unaccustomed to American money.

Later, they would recall the incident, thinking it had been an omen. They should have paid closer attention.

When Norma and Mike emerged from the bank, they were almost knocked down by sniffing dogs on leashes, their handlers barely able to keep them under control. Jack and Lenny met up with them in the parking lot and told them the dogs had been sniffing around the BMW.

"Forget it, folks. That goes on all the time in this area. Everybody's freaked about drugs and shit. Oops.

CODE NAME: WHITE MUSTANG

Sorry Norma. Anyhow, it's routine. Nothing to worry about."

They had climbed back into the car actually looking forward to a new experience. In reality, it was the start of a trip to hell and back, captives that they were in the car with Lenny.

Lenny was drunk from the time they embarked on their journey. He drove like a crazed man causing his passengers to resign themselves to a fiery death on the highways of southern Italy.

Lenny's in-laws were wonderful hosts. They had been warmly welcomed even though Lenny had not bothered letting them know to expect company until they were within local calling distance.

It was true the pot was on the stove and they ate as if there was no tomorrow. The spaghetti was heaven-on-earth, the sauce the best on the planet. They could not stop drinking the wine which was more than the nectar of the gods and apparently non-intoxicating.

On Saturday, they spent several hours on the coast of the Adriatic Sea, the water as warm as though it had been drawn for a bath. They were enthralled with that because it was late in October and turning cold back home in Minnesota.

The sights were spoiled only by the thick, brown smog that hung over everything in the distance. There were numerous big, expensive homes situated on the hillsides, all appearing abandoned.

They had brought Lenny's mother-in-law with them for a day off. A treat. She explained that the homes were for summer people who were wealthy and lived 'up north' the rest of the year.

She, Caterina, spoke with an enchanting accent that charmed Norma. Lenny treated the old woman abominably, ordering her around as if she were an indentured servant. In reality, she had a sense of humor that caught and held a person's attention and tickled the funny bone.

Norma couldn't help but be amazed at Caterina, so tolerant of a son-in-law who was nasty to her. It had not escaped her notice that Pietro, the father-in-law, did not speak to Lenny. Not one word had been exchanged between them during the visiting at the dinner table the night of their arrival.

They had passed by an ancient castle on their journey and Lenny told them the story went that it had been occupied, centuries past, by a royal family that included a brother and sister. The brother had fallen in love with his sister and after the parents died, he had imprisoned his sister in the castle for her entire life because he could not bear the thought of any other man having her.

While he related the story Norma was thinking, 'This would be the sort of thing this man would know and share. Anything sordid. A tale of incest.' It had taken no time at all for her to sum up the man, to regret having agreed to the trip. But, she honestly had been enjoying everything not connected directly to Lenny. When they had the chance, she and Jack spoke. They agreed the trip had, basically, been worth it. The chance to see parts of Italy they hadn't expected, the opportunity to meet and visit with Caterina and Pietro, the wonderful food and wine, the tour through olive orchards and the information garnered from Pietro about how the fruit was processed. It had been, by and large, a treasure of memories to take home with them.

Their farewell's were warm and friendly. Addresses were traded with promises of corresponding. It would never happen.

Two days after their departure they returned to Gaeta. On the way, they detoured to have a look at Amalfi. Mike had insisted.

"It's my most favorite spot in this country. You *must* experience it. Teea, the boys and I had a weekend here once. It was heavenly."

He'd gotten choked up and couldn't say any more but his parents felt it would be good to go back there so his memories of the place would encompass them as well as his family. It might ease his hurt.

When they left the in-laws Lenny was drunk so Mike decided he would do the driving. A heated argument ensued between the two of them. Jack, relieved at Mike's insistence, got involved. He alone was able to talk Lenny into the passenger seat of the car.

There was very little conversation once they got onto the highway. The drive was comfortable, the short talks subdued. None of them cared to wake Lenny who appeared to be sound asleep. He perked up just as they pulled into Amalfi, slowing to find a parking space alongside the road. When he saw where they were, he began complaining loudly about 'a waste of time.'

They ignored him, got out of the car once they got lucky with a parking spot and wandered about at their leisure.

An ancient cathedral held a special attraction for Jack and Norma. It was situated high on a hill, above

M. L. Verne

the commerce of the town. They climbed, rested and climbed some more. Sixty- six steps up. Entering the dimness of the church, looking at the main altar, several side altars, the statues and relics, they were filled with wonder. Never mind the scaffolds and canvases here and there signifying restoration and some reconstruction. It was stupefying in its antiquity, its holiness, its treasures. They were awestruck. No other word would suffice.

After checking out a few of the shops, they returned to the car where Lenny was leaning against the fender a nasty scowl on his face. No one spoke to him and he spoke to no one. The Steele's were gratified. They all climbed into the beemer and Mike pulled out into the traffic very carefully. It was mind-boggling, the cars passing by in a steady stream.

As they continued down the road they craned their necks to admire the homes built into the tall cliffs on the right, the sea on their left. There were flowers everywhere, hanging from the windows of the houses, seeming to grow right out of the rocks, climbing up and out of nowhere. Every color imaginable was displayed, a rainbow of Mother Nature's touch and imagination.

Then, sadly, they became enshrouded in fog. It required a further slow-down of their vehicle and an inability to further enjoy the scenery.

Once away from the sea, the fog lifted and they resumed speed, tried to relax, recalling as many pleasant things from the weekend as possible. Thankfully, Lenny stayed isolated. It was a blessing.

CODE NAME: WHITE MUSTANG

48.

Mike and his parents had some truly quality time together. They visited several excavation sites in the area, one day going to Naples to tour the home of Nero's wife, Pompeae, a ruin that was being brought to the light of day after centuries of burial following the eruption of Mt.Vesuvius in the first century A.D.

The near-perfect preservation of the artwork on the walls and tiled floors was unbelievable. The tour guide said that Nero had ordered the miniature tiles loosened from their original place and brought from Rome, the workers needing to number each one of them separately so the designs could be recaptured exactly. The colors of the painted art seemed to vibrate in the daylight, as if to make up for the thousands of years of total darkness. The half- exposed swimming pool already looked to be Olympic sized.

Even the fresh water system was still intact, the pipes in place, cleverly arranged to serve the houses. And made of lead. No wonder so many of them had succumbed to lead poisoning so young!

Then, they went on a tour bus to Rome. Mike slept most of the way. Norma knew it was a symptom of withdrawal from narcotics. She was proud of his stamina, his determination.

She was also broken-hearted.

They stopped halfway through their journey for espresso and croissants. The drink was hot, the pastry flaky. It was a pleasant interlude.

St. Peter's was incredible. Huge statues of lesser known saints placed in prominent places, golden domes and artwork to boggle the mind. Sadly, the Pieta was behind heavy glass. Someone had taken a chip out of it! Go figure.

They visited the burial place of St. Peter himself, or so it is said. Many Popes down through the centuries are interred within the walls of St. Peter's Basilica. Dates of births and deaths are inscribed in Latin. Norma had a chance to renew her high school education in the language, remembering that her teacher was so elderly she'd also taught her, Norma's, dad. Norma prided herself in the correct reading of inscriptions.

Perhaps it had been the visit to the basilica. They might never know. But finally, Mike opened up and told them more about his involvement with drugs.

The trend of his narration went in the direction of Lenny being responsible for everything. That he, Mike, had been coerced into using crack.

It was too much for Jack and Norma. Their son, whom they loved, needed to take responsibility for his own actions, his own bad decisions. They sensed he wasn't telling them anything near the enormity of the situation and they felt helpless. If he was going to stay in denial, they could do nothing for him.

When they told Mike they'd changed their minds and were going home sooner than originally planned, he was filled with remorse. He also experienced a sense of relief.

He accompanied them to the terminal on their departure day and waited with them until their flight was called.

For the rest of her life, Norma would retain a picture in her mind of how Mike looked that day. So

CODE NAME: WHITE MUSTANG

thin, so emaciated, so forlorn. Just before rounding the corner and going out of sight, she had turned to throw him one last kiss.

He appeared ghostly, desolate, abandoned. And she sensed he was weeping.

On the plane, she tearfully told Jack she was afraid they would never see him again. Jack was angry. Not at Mike but at himself for feeling so ineffective, so unable to help his son.

If only Mike had trusted them! He had chosen not to and the family, everyone, would be suffering in one way or another before it all came to an end.

49.

Cy Woodall was keeping a log. An undercover log. It contained names of moles and mules uncovered during his long, involved probe. The list was staggering. It covered all branches of the military but primarily the Navy.

There were civilians from Italy, Greece, Turkey, even some south American countries. An international problem of major proportions.

A long time later, after everything that was to happen had happened, Mike would realize there was 'Someone up there' looking out for him after all.

He would also be thankful he'd not known about 'Operation White Mustang' while it was ongoing. His paranoia knew no bounds as it was. If he'd known 'the rest of the story', he might not have found the strength to endure.

Christmas was just around the corner. He was afraid to send a package to his family. '*THEY*' might x-ray it, find the gold chain he'd bought for Teea in Istanbul and arrest him for who knew what reason. He'd bought video games for his sons. Would they be without gifts from their dad?

He couldn't sleep. He was still undergoing cold turkey withdrawal from cocaine. If that wasn't bad enough, his dreams were full of vicious creatures that scared him into staying awake. He'd been shifted around at work again. His job now consisted of shuffling papers, nothing more. In other words, his life was on the skids.

Even so, he had two things he was thankful for, one being Lenny was out of his life. He'd ignored the phone calls, avoided the beer halls and any other places he thought Lenny might be hanging out. There'd been a drunken banging on his door one night, Lenny yelling obscenities at him, Whitey barking loudly.

He remained quiet in his apartment, glad that it was late enough so his lights were all off. The next morning he asked the guards at his gate to 'please don't let him in any more.' They were happy to oblige. They'd never liked Lenny.

The other thing was, since he'd been transferred at the office, he no longer needed to concern himself with the Brits and their infernal harassment of him.

Late one afternoon, as he was returning from work, he went around a corner too fast in a driving rain, skidded on his Harley and hit the street with the bike on top of his knee. He struggled to get out from under, finally managing with the help of a passer- by. As he tried to stand up, he realized his knee was badly injured. The only good news was, he was near the gates to his complex, a block or so away. He limped along, pushing his bike, taking what seemed like forever to get home. The guards were sympathetic, offering their help. He thanked them and said he'd be fine.

By the time he reached his apartment, he was soaked through to his skin and freezing cold. After maneuvering his bike into the living room, he collapsed on the couch, covered up with his afghan and a blanket that happened to be nearby, shivering.

He put a pillow under his leg and lay there trying to figure out what he was going to do. He was afraid to seek medical help. The corpsmen would just prescribe more narcotics for his pain. He couldn't allow that. He'd come so far!

Eventually, he got out of his wet clothes, wrapped his knee in an ace bandage he had available and went to bed. There he remained for two days; Saturday and Sunday.

On Monday, he knew he again had pneumonia. He figured, after all the crack, his immune system was compromised. If he went for help, he'd be put on drugs he didn't want. If he stayed away from the medics, he might die.

'Some dilemma' he told himself while he got ready for work He was weak, shaky and feverish. 'How can a guy be hot and cold all at the same time? If I don't get help and I die, who will take care of my boys for me? Who will be their dad?'

He went for help.

They prescribed the strongest antibiotics available and sent him home with orders not to leave the house until he was well. Then, he was back in hell. Full of pain, unable to breathe properly, refusing to take narcotics, suffering a severe migraine on top of everything else, taking nothing except penicillin.

His phone rang at all hours. He was so glad he'd gotten the answering machine! Inevitably, it was Lenny. He didn't pick up. Would the man ever quit? Why wasn't he getting the message? He was a lot of things, but he was not stupid.

While his parents had visited him, he and his dad had hooked up his TV to the Armed Forces network.

CODE NAME: WHITE MUSTANG

Now he at least had access to a ball game once in a while, a few sitcoms he hadn't seen. It felt grand to listen to the English language coming out of the tube. It helped him keep his teetering sanity on a fairly even keel while he was recuperating.

It took a full week before he could get around without fearing he'd pass out. The one piece of good news was, his knee was feeling better because of his forced bed rest for the pneumonia.

On the very day he returned to work, a man walked into his office and Mike knew at once he was an agent. By that time, he could 'smell' them.

"Chief," he began without introducing himself, "your urine tests turned up positive. I'm sure that comes as no surprise?"

His stomach plummeted. Of course he'd known. He'd been praying the report was lost or something. He looked around at the walls of his office as if trying to find some sort of encouraging message written there.

He hesitated, began stammering and croaked, "I want to see my attorney."

"Absolutely Chief. It's your right. Matter of fact, I was going to suggest that. You go on ahead and see your lawyer. We'll be back in touch with you again soon."

'Oh yeah. I don't doubt that.' In a split second he was out and off to the JAG's offices. There, he found he had a new attorney, Lieutenant Christopher Jaynes. No one offered to tell him what had become of the previous legal officer and he was too shaken up to ask.

Mike had met Lieutenant Jaynes once before, briefly. He couldn't recall the circumstances. As he walked down the hall toward the appointed office, he felt the stares of the personnel in the rooms he passed. 'They all know.' He felt their animosity. Big, bad vibes all around the place. It was a whole new experience for him. 'It's just the beginning, man. Get used to it. At least they allowed you to recuperate from the pneumonia.'

Idly, he grinned, asking himself if he'd end up being the only individual he'd be talking to for the rest of his life, free to say whatever he was thinking.

He thought he was lucky the lieutenant was in his office. He didn't consider the possibility the man was sitting there waiting for him to put in an appearance. He was invited to have a chair and he sank into it gratefully. He was still weak from his illness. His nervous reaction to the situation was making it worse.

"I just had an unannounced visit from an NCIS agent. At least I have to assume that's who he was. He wasn't courteous enough to tell me."

"Chief," Lieutenant Jaynes interrupted him, "do not, I repeat *NOT*, say one word to those men. They haven't a shred of evidence to confront us with. They're digging, sending out barbs, hoping you'll get nervous and spill some important information they can use against you. They'll be watching you like the proverbial hawk so stay out of trouble. Keep your nose clean. So far, I'd say you're doing great. Oh! Don't look surprised. It's part of my job to know what you're up to. If you need anything at all, as we get deeper into this business, you let me know. I'm here for you."

They agreed on certain hours during the following days to meet and to begin their discussions. Mike was reluctant about talking to a stranger concerning his private affairs. He was drowning in paranoia, wishing he could at least get over *that*! If he could, maybe he'd be able to speak frankly with the man.

* * *

Time passed, they met, they talked. Mike withheld pertinent information. His lawyer sensed it. He used his skills, giving Mike plenty of space, gently bringing him around to a less suspicious frame of mind.

As it got closer to Christmas, Mike mentioned his fear of putting anything in the mail to his family, Lieutenant Jaynes suggested they have his yeoman do Mike's mailing for him.

He wrapped Teea's gold and the boys' videos and was pleased he wasn't asked what was in the package. 'Someone trusts me; I still have a bit of freedom,' he thought.

Mike's imagination was in overdrive. His nightmares had become 'daymares'. He was pushing some kind of mental panic button. 'Everyone I meet, even strangers on the street, are out to spy on me, report me to the agents.' His gut was in knots all the time. He was miserable, again making himself sick.

A few days before Christmas, the dam broke. He spilled just about everything. They'd been together and getting closer each day until, finally, Mike was calling him Chris.

"Mike, I am literally stunned. It's a good thing you gave me time to soak up a lot of your story before telling me the rest. I could not have absorbed these incredibly vile things all at once. I am blown away. A senior officer and a senior enlisted man up for commissioning. It's too much!"

Mike thought, 'Who needs a reaction like that from a lawyer. He's young, yeah, but he's not innocent. Maybe I've made a mistake, telling him.'

Chris was still talking. "I have to take this information to the NCIS, you know. You needn't worry, though. We can work out a deal with them and you'll come up smelling like a rose. You have to trust me to do the right thing for you."

"What do you mean, smelling like a rose? I'm guilty. Where do we go from there except to jail?"

"Well, for starters, we'll work on a minimum sentence. Maybe even something better, like full disclosure for immunity to any prosecution or even just forfeiture of a few benefits. Something along those lines. We'll demand *no* confinement. It'll work!"

They agreed to meet the following weekend to begin work on Mike's defense. They spent hours and hours going over and over the facts. They slogged through the ins and outs of drug deals, trips to Istanbul, money, Nigerians, crack houses, other people involved, on and on and on. Two full days sped by. They remained up and working into the wee hours, eating little, doing and redoing the paperwork word for word, making sure every last, minute detail was down correctly.

"There's no room for error, Mike," Chris told him.

Even so, when it was finally done, Mike still had not told Chris all of it. He withheld a few things about Lenny unable to share, even with his attorney, things that would further corrupt Lenny's image. Not because of the man, but because of the rank he carried. Mike still had respect for that in spite of the fact the man who carried it wasn't worth a plugged nickel.

By Monday morning, it was done. They were both satisfied. Chris took everything over to the prosecutors' office. He met with Lieutenant Rodriguez, who had been waiting for the paperwork so he could fill in the gaps for his part of the case. The two of them agreed that Mike shouldn't have to be confined because he had come forward on his own and had been fully cooperative.

Chris confided to his counterpart that the NCIS had come to him several weeks before, told him their investigation of Lieutenant Commander Jones and Chief Steele was going nowhere, had come to a screeching halt, that there was no evidence either one of them was involved in the ongoing 'Operation White Mustang' probe.

Furthermore, there was no trail for them to follow should there be any other illegal activities going on which involved the two of them.

"However," Chris continued, "they did go on to assure me they *knew* there was something afoul of the law and, if the Chief hadn't come forward when he did, they were seriously considering turning the two of them over to the Italian authorities, citing the Status of Forces Agreement (SOFA) by which, as you recall, the Italian government can exercise civil law and jurisdiction over any US military personnel who violate Italian laws."

"In my opinion," Dan Rodriguez said, "they are two damn lucky bastards. Can you imagine life in an Italian prison? They might not survive and even if they

M. L. Verne

did, their people back home would probably never hear from them. Or about them."

During their two long days and nights working together, Chris had told Mike of the SOFA possibility. "I know of at least one American sailor who was incarcerated in an Italian prison a year ago and is still awaiting formal sentencing. You've heard about the notorious penal system in this country. Be proud of yourself, feel very fortunate, that you had the good sense to come in and get this out in the open. In the long run you'll come to realize it was the smartest and *only* thing to do under the circumstances."

50.

Time dragged on. Mike had begun freaking again. He had not found a way to tell Teea what was happening. His parents were a concern too but at least they knew *something* was not right. Bottom line, the boys had to be protected.

Finally, he told her only what she absolutely *had* to know. It was cowardly but he felt it was all either one of them could handle. For the time being.

His parents told him, "Mike, we're aware there's more to this than what you're telling us. It's your choice and we have to respect that. Just don't forget. We are here if and when you need us. We hate what you've done but you know we love you and care about you."

As the days and weeks came and went, he found himself on the brink of a dangerous abyss more than once. During the times of his darkest tribulations, word came that Admiral Kingston had taken his life. It drove Mike into a frenzy. He grieved deeply. Then he was informed his LDO acceptance had been nullified.

At last, Chris called him in and told him, "The Commander has been taken into custody. He's denied everything up to now. It's taken this long to find enough evidence to bring him in. Here's his statement. I want you to read through it and give me your reaction."

Mike did as he was asked, found himself bored with the lies and innuendo's until, suddenly, he yelled, "*SON OF A BITCH!*" He'd jumped up, the veins in his forehead pulsing like a trip- hammer, his face beet red.

M. L. Verne

He'd read "....and the Chief sleeps with his mother..."

Immediately, his memory flashed to the trip they'd taken into the boot of Italy. Mike and his mother had shared a room with twin beds while his dad had slept across the hall, with the door tightly shut, to spare everyone his horrendous snoring. It had been a chance for Mike and Norma to talk privately. They'd shared a couple of laughs and some family gossip. It had been comforting and now the bastard had spilled his vile, evil ideas all over the memory.

"Jesus, Chris, can you believe this? The rotten bastard! Okay. If that's how he wants to play the game, that's how it'll be."

He was set to tell Chris the rest of the story, Lenny's true and total involvement, the information he'd withheld out of respect for the man's rank.

As he opened his mouth, Chris interrupted. "Mike, there's more. When the agents picked him up at his house they found, among other things, a one way airline ticket to the states for a flight leaving Naples tomorrow morning."

Mike's fury knew no bounds. "On top of all his lies, he was going to leave me high and dry to take all the punishment alone? Figures."

He told Chris everything that was left to tell. It tied up the loose ends that had been bugging Chris and it served to purge Mike's soul. Immediately he'd felt at peace, an enormous load lifted from his shoulders.

'I'm gonna' be okay. It will take a while, I'll have to pay for my screw-ups, but I can do that.' He smiled quietly, readying himself for whatever was to come.

51.

Spring arrives early in southern Italy. The days were warmer, the breezes balmier. The sky was a lovely shade of blue, the clouds white and puffy. The countryside was full of bright, blooming flowers. Mike bought a small pot of colorful pansies. Their smiling faces lifted his spirits. He put them on his patio.

On a morning when he'd least expected it, the NCIS came visiting. They had a warrant to search his apartment. For what? He was incensed. He watched helplessly as they dug into every nook and cranny, including his closet. There, they found the incriminating evidence, the leftover airline ticket he'd forgotten.

Stupidity! Irresponsibility! Witless act of recklessness! Even though his boss had *ordered* him to take time off, go to Istanbul, try to relax, because of his confession Mike was sure the ticket was the proof they'd be needing for the courtroom. In black and white.

Chris called his office. "Come over, Mike. We need to review your statement again." While they sat together itemizing, adding, taking out, smoothing grammar, the telephone rang. Answering it, Chris's face had reddened. He'd placed his hand over the mouthpiece and asked Mike if he'd mind stepping out into the corridor for a few minutes.

"It's a private matter," he explained.

Mike had complied, softly closing the door behind him. Something about Chris's demeanor had put his gut feelings on alert. He glanced up and down the hall noting there wasn't another human being to be seen. Shamelessly he'd put his ear against Chris's office door hoping to catch a few words that might tell him his gut reaction was correct.

He heard! It had sent him spinning! "Yes, he was sitting right here when you rang. Yes. Yes, sir. Yes. I understand. Then his sentence will be eight years? Yes, sir…"

Mike raced, as fast as he could, to the head. He was shaking like a leaf. 'My fate is sealed long before the fact. My court martial will be nothing short of a kangaroo court. There's nothing I can do about it.' He vomited again and again.

It would have served no purpose to let Chris know he'd overheard the conversation from Chris's end. Clearly, he was under orders from some source Mike didn't have clue one about. And there was no way to find out.

'This time, it's not paranoia. I know what I heard. Talk about stacked odds.' He vowed he would never forget.

After he'd splashed water over his head and face, combed his hair and taken several deep breaths, he went back to Chris's office, tapped on the door and was told: "Come in."

"It was more information regarding Lenny, Mike. I thought it best you not hear the conversation. But it seems he has reversed the story so that *you* are the culprit and *he* an innocent recruit. Now Mike, it's absolutely necessary that you move onto the base where your safety can be more or less assured. We're going to have to contact the Nigerians and get their input on all of this. They have no loyalties, other than to themselves. It's quite possible they'd want to come after you for misperceptions such as, you've taken away their livelihood because you caused Lenny to be arrested. We can't tell how their minds will twist. So you get moved into Navy quarters. ASAP!"

Mike left the office knowing he'd been railroaded. He would never know it had been Admiral Williams on the other end of that phone call. When the reports on Mike and Lenny had crossed the Admiral's desk, his conscience did a number on his psyche. He began to fear that somehow he would get caught in the undertow of the horrific mess that was about to explode across the planet.

After all, it was he who the Chief had tried to contact about the drug dealings and he had chosen to ignore the man. He felt there was a chance the Chief would mention that long ago decision, inadvertently, during his interrogations. Then where would he, Greg Williams, end up?

He'd wasted no time contacting the judge who would be handling Mike's court martial. The man owed Greg a few favors. It was time to collect. They had a long conversation resulting in the judge agreeing to his 'old friend's' request. Up to a point! He'd go with the eight year sentence, but he refused to even discuss the final results of the proceedings. The favors he owed weren't *that* big.

The Admiral began clearing up odds and ends, thought about his pal Gus, then mentally patted himself on the back for being such a loyal friend.

Two important things; he made a serious attempt at covering up the paperwork which listed his acquisition of expensive new furniture for his villa, compliments of the American taxpayers. Then he laid off the gardeners he'd hired at the expense of the government. It had been his premise that a man of his rank and stature should not be seen pulling weeds in his yard!

The court martial, still to come, was going to be a travesty of justice. It took Mike some time to fully understand what it all meant. He'd spent his entire adult life serving his country, believing and trusting the concepts of a free society.

'Even in such dire circumstances, a man deserves a fair trial. But as I see it, that ain't gonna' happen.'

He went into near-total seclusion. The status of 'protective custody' grated on him. He wasn't a fool. He knew the Nigerians were probably looking for him. Still, living in a barracks-like situation was not to his liking. He slept a lot. Partly from boredom, more-so from his continued withdrawal from crack. The only thing expected of him was that he show up for work.

It was a job designed for a half-way intelligent ape. He was beyond caring. He'd already been degraded to the point of annihilation.

He put a 'For Sale' sign on his car, no big deal, as he couldn't drive anywhere anyhow. He got a buyer immediately. The guy gave him one hundred dollars cash. It was the last money he would have in his pocket for the foreseeable future.

His pride was nowhere to be found. He slept, he ate, he went to the job, he repeated the routine. Once or twice, he called his boys. It was the only bright spot in his otherwise pointless life.

Chris Jaynes had made himself scarce. Mike supposed it was partly because Chris had a guilty conscience. After all, he was going to betray his client.

The last time or two they'd met, Mike had noticed Chris's change in attitude. Even his body language was different. He sat sideways in his chair never looking directly into Mike's eyes. While Mike talked, Chris thumbed a magazine.

Chris advised Mike that a lengthy trial would not be in his best interest. "It would be better for you if the judge does the job. No jury of your peers. They'd be too hard on you. The judge would be impartial."

'Right.' Mike thought. 'Who do you think you're kidding?' But, he kept quiet. Speaking out would not help him. He was in a deep, dark hole and when Chris spoke again, he began to wonder how he was going to get through the coming calamity. In spite of his earlier positive thinking, he was scared.

"Mike, another thing…the trial has to be speedy because I have reservations for a trip I've been planning on ever since coming to Italy. Everything is paid for and is nonrefundable."

Now *there* was a good solid reason to send Mike up the river all by himself! He plodded through the days like a zombie.

He'd long since quit his job at the mart and didn't even have that as a diversion from his personal hell.

Chris called him at work. "Mike, we need to go out to your apartment and pick up your dress uniform for the court martial. You must appear fully decked out, medals and all. I'll pick you up after duty hours today and we'll drive out together,"

It was the one and only time his attorney did a personal favor for him throughout their entire relationship.

52.

On the morning of his court martial, the weather reflected his general frame of mind. Very gloomy. The life he'd lived previously was over. Only God knew what lay ahead for him.

It was as he'd come to expect. A farce. He had never been in a courtroom, never been involved in anything more serious than traffic tickets so everything seemed surreal to him. He gazed around the room in a daze, noting the tacky furniture and the walls that were in need of a paint job. The judge's 'bench' was nothing more than a long, narrow table sitting on four blocks of wood that elevated it slightly above the floor. There were a few chairs scattered around the room in a poor semblance of order, a small table for each attorney. Near Chris's area there was an extra chair where Chris had Mike sit.

There was a total of five persons present; the judge, the two attorney's, Mike and a court reporter, a yeoman. No one spoke. When Mike had allowed himself to think about that day beforehand, he'd envisioned a court room filled with buzzing activity, murmuring, people shifting around in their seats, general pre-trial activity. The reality was the silence of a tomb.

And non-military. Although everyone was in full dress uniform and there was a senior officer present, no one showed anyone else any military courtesy. The judge, a Marine Lieutenant Colonel, didn't *deserve* any respect as far as Mike was concerned. He had heard about this man before his trial but had not believed it could be as bad as it had sounded. In fact, it was worse. The man was slovenly, unkempt, unmilitary and uncaring. He'd been passed over for promotion so many times he was in the process of being shuffled out of the military, forced to retire. Not once during the proceedings did he look Mike's way. At one point, Mike was certain he'd fallen asleep. He asked a few pertinent questions, more that were redundant. It was all Mike could do to keep himself from jumping up with a protest. He wanted to scream at the slob, "This is my LIFE, man! Pay me the COURTESY of your ATTENTION!"

In the end, it took just under two hours to demolish Mike's career, his future, his life as he'd known it.

* * *

The specific charges were:

1. Conspiracy to wrongfully distribute heroin.
   Plea: Guilty,
2. Fraternization with an officer, Lieutenant Commander Lennard D. Jones.
   Plea: Guilty,
3. Wrongful use of cocaine on diverse occasions.
   Plea: Guilty,
4. Wrongful manufacture of some amount of rock cocaine or crack cocaine on diverse occasions.
   Plea: Guilty.
5. Wrongful distribution of $30,000.00 worth of heroin.
   Plea: Guilty.

6. Larceny of $13,000.00.
   Plea: Not Guilty.
7. Solicitation of another to wrongfully distribute heroin.
   Plea: Not Guilty.

The judge asked, for the third and last time, "...these were acts then, you're telling the court, that were done of your own free will...?"

"Yes, sir" Mike affirmed. "No one ever held a gun to my head."

The judge then asked, for the final time, "...they were voluntary on your part...?"

"Yes, sir."

"All right, counsel, you may present arguments."

Lieutenant Rodriguez stood first. From behind his table he began, "What this case is, your honor, is a real shame. The individual sitting here before you, the accused, as you can see by the defense exhibits from his service record book, was an exemplary Chief and an outstanding sailor in every way. Until he came to Italy. When he did come to Italy, he became involved with Lieutenant Commander Jones and a group of drug runners. He reported it to Admiral Williams like a good sailor should and then, instead of doing what his service record would indicate the kind of person he should....he is....he should do, he turned around and got himself involved in it. As he admitted, voluntarily and freely, to the point where it affected his family and has taken his career away, it's endangered everything he holds dear. His testimony, on unsworn, leads us to believe that throughout his career and his adult life, nothing was more important to him than the integrity

CODE NAME: WHITE MUSTANG

and honor of the uniform he wore, yet he sullied it. He destroyed it. And perverted it by using his position to freely move back and forth to Turkey, to distribute drugs, to become part of a ring of distribution, to use drugs. It speaks for itself, your honor. It's a shame, but it was a voluntary act and this accused should be punished severely."

"The government asks that he be confined for ten years, that he be reduced in rank to E-1, that he be adjudged total forfeiture of all pay and allowances and that he receive a dishonorable discharge from the Naval Service."

The judge was scowling. He rubbed his forehead and belched as he reached for a glass of water near his left hand. He emptied the glass, handed it to the yeoman for a refill and once that was accomplished, he said, "Lieutenant Jaynes?"

Chris stood and began by saying "Your honor, this truly is a tragic case. Chief Steele has had a stellar fourteen year career and, as you can see from the exhibits, service record, book entries, it has been flawless. He's made Chief in about eight and a half years, within record time. He was, as of a few short weeks ago, he should have been, accepted for the LDO program. For the past fourteen years, he's devoted his life to his country in serving, which he did honorably. And then he came to Italy and at that point he met Lieutenant Commander Jones. And, as Chief Steele would be…told this court, he was never forced or coerced to commit these offenses; however, he was manipulated, sir, by professionals. Lieutenant Commander Jones and the other Africans in the business of importing heroin are very good at what they do, know how to push buttons. They know how to…how to manipulate people, that's what they do best. They're looking for pack mules to go over to Turkey and they have certain procedures and steps to follow to entice sailors from right here on this base. Chief Steele was first being worked on, approached, his family… by Lieutenant Commander Jones himself, during the day at his job and at his nighttime job. He did what he thought was right, he went to Commander Keef and reported there were some drug activities going on. He was told NCIS would be contacted and at some point in time everything fell through the cracks, and by that time, Lieutenant Commander Jones and his professional group basically engulfed Chief Steele in their organization through drug use, then finally into distribution. And trips into Turkey. It's truly a tragedy, Sir. Chief Steele has taken responsibility for his actions. Since the events, he has tried to do everything right. He fully co- operated with NCIS. He provided statements implicating other folks, including Lieutenant Commander Jones, and several other military members in this area, one retired and since returned to the states. He has also, of more import, identified methods of operation and other local Africans in the community who are preying on our sailors, other sailors who could be here today like Chief Steele."

Chris stopped for a short breather and to gather his thoughts. Mike might have been inclined to feel a bit of pity for him since he was, quite literally, fighting a losing battle. The game was over and Chris was under orders to go with the flow.

On the other hand, it was Mike's life and as far as he was concerned, Chris should have taken his case to some other court, his own career be damned. Or, at least, put into jeopardy until word of the conspiracy could be taken into consideration. Bottom line, Chris was *not* acting for Mike's benefit. So, 'hell no', Mike hadn't found it in his heart to pity the guy. He glanced at Chris, who was standing still, seeming to be dealing with some inner turmoil. 'Too bad,' was all Mike could think. Then Chris went on,

"The information is invaluable, sir. It could well prevent further tragedies. Chief Steele, at this point, has accepted responsibility for his actions and wants to close this chapter of the book and return to his family. To support them. He has a wife and two children now living in Colorado, your honor. We respectfully request that given the….the situation, that Chief Steele did take responsibility for his actions, did cooperate, benefited current investigations and also future investigations, which will prevent other sailors from becoming entrapped in this web, that his confinement be limited to one year so that he can return to his family as soon as practically possible. Until then, his family has no means of support. Respectfully request your honor take into consideration that he does have a wife and two children back in Colorado and that fines and forfeitures be limited, within the discretion of the court. Thank You."

His defense was far short of brilliant. In fact, it was as redundant as the judge's questions had been. Now Mike knew what 'hopeless situation' was all about. He struggled mightily to remain militarily straight in his chair, to not fall to pieces. Only his badly wounded pride kept him from slumping, from sliding down and sitting on his tail bone with his head bent low.

The judge closed the court, rose and left the room. Even then he didn't favor Mike with so much as a glance. Chris leaned over and whispered to Mike that his honor was going to his chambers to deliberate.

'I wonder why?' Mike pondered. 'Everything has already been decided. Has to put on a show, I guess. But who for?'

Almost in the blink of an eye, 'His Honor' was back. To a man, the participants were thankful. The room was stifling. Lieutenant Rodriguez had tried to open a window without success. They'd been painted shut years before. By the time the judge returned, all of their uniforms were as wilted and wrinkled as his had been from the beginning.

Custom required they all stand as he entered the room. He told them they could sit and he said, "Chief Steele, it is my duty as military judge to inform you that this court sentences you to the following:

1. To be discharged from the United States Navy dishonorably.
2. To be confined for eight years.
3. To total forfeiture of pay and allowances.
4. To be reduced in rank to E-1.

"Now may I please have the Sentence Appendix of the pretrial agreement? As I understand it now, the dishonorable discharge may be approved as judged. Do you agree?"

Mike answered, "Yes, sir."

The judge continued, "As to confinement, the court adjudged a confinement period of eight years. It is my understanding that they...that that might be approved..."

The hair on Mike's arms quivered. 'Was that a Freudian slip?' he asked himself. '*THEY*? Who did he refer to?'

"...however" he was continuing, "the agreement goes on to state that any and all confinement and/or any other form of restraint in excess of twenty four months will be suspended for a period of twenty four months from the date of the convening authority's action, at which time, unless sooner vacated, will be remitted without further action. This agreement constitutes a request by the accused for, and approved by, the convening authority..." Mike began to squirm. 'What is this? Some sort of legalese? I don't understand one word this guy is spouting.'

The judge droned on, as bored with his decree as was everyone else in the room. Mike supposed Chris understood what was being said. He looked at his lawyer out of the corner of his eye only to discover Chris staring at the ceiling, his thoughts obviously some place else.

'Probably thinking about his vacation that's more important to him than my *LIFE*.' Mike was steeped in self pity again.

Finally, 'His Honor' took a deep breath and emptied his water glass another time. The yeoman stood to get him another refill but he was waved off.

"Again" the judge stated, "the bottom line here is, if you do not violate the Uniform Code of Military Justice, you will not have to serve the additional six years that the court adjudged. Do you understand that?"

Mike had timed it. It took exactly one hour and fifteen minutes to destroy him, his career, his family life and his income. To top it off, he was humiliated. Oh, he'd known how it was programmed to go down but the reality of it was an enormous shock, nevertheless.

What was worse, he still had to face Lenny at *his* court martial. That would rub salt into his open wounds. He'd been told he was going to be 'the most important prosecution witness' in the upcoming, loathsome litigation starring Lenny, and using him, Mike, to pull the plug. There was no joyful anticipation on his part, only grave concern for his own well being and his safety.

53.

Ironically, he was now 'free' to come and go at will. He had boundaries but they weren't excessive. He was certain everyone in charge of him knew he wasn't about to break and run. Where would he go? How would he get there? He no longer had a passport. That alone made him their prisoner. He had no job, his time was his own. He wandered around for a few days and, along the way, met several 'pals'. They shunned him. The word was out. Once, he caught a glimpse of Margo in the distance. He could have called out to her but didn't. He'd heard she had reunited with the father of her child. They were to be married. In his heart, he wished her well. He had used her and was ashamed of himself.

After realizing that he was anathema to everyone who'd cared about him in his 'previous life', he stayed away from the populated areas. He lazed about on the beach acquiring a splendid suntan. He went to the gym and worked out. He was appalled at how out of shape he'd gotten. It felt good, though painful, to use the major muscles again for something other than routine activities. He hadn't had adequate time to read for pleasure in years. Now he could indulge himself, catching up on some good, true mysteries, which were his favorite.

He did go to one party. It was painful. All the people there were sympathetic and caring. He couldn't help the tears that kept blurring his vision. He didn't stay long. There was alcohol in great abundance and part of his agreement with the court was, he would not only not do drugs but also would not drink booze. It was very difficult so he made excuses and left. If he stayed and took one drink, he'd be back on crack by morning.

He may have been a 'man of leisure' but his thoughts were constantly with Teea and the boys. He was helpless to do a thing for them, worried how they would make it without him.

Then he would chide himself. 'You should have thought about that before you screwed yourself into this hole.'

He'd talked to them several times. Teea was handling the twins in her own way. She was also handling him. She was cold, had no problem telling him exactly what her opinion was of him and what he'd done. Her words and attitude only served to darken his days. He shed tears in private. He was on the verge of finding some crack 'just to ease the pain a bit', enough 'to get through the next few days.' It would be easy to reach one of the Nigerians without getting caught. In fact, on his worst day, he thought he really should find them and maybe they'd kill him. Then he'd have no more worries!

He was alerted, on the last day of his 'hold out', that he was to report to the flight line within the hour. He was going to Germany. Many months later he'd recall how close he'd come to ending up serving the full eight years of his sentence. If that call hadn't come when it did, he'd have been out on the street calling Prine or Fronz.

Since his trial, he'd been packed to leave. He had only to put his toilet articles in his bag. He wasn't *allowed* much of anything else. He was at the terminal in twenty minutes. He could not wait to get out of Italy! His personal business had been taken care of, what little there was. The rest of the furniture had been sent to Teea, along with his clothes.

They had trusted him enough to get to the terminal on his own but there was an escort there to accompany him on the flight. Wasn't that just like the military? Where would he go by himself in Germany where he knew no one and had no money? Never mind he'd be on an airplane with the escort, too. Did they think there'd be a way for him to escape from the plane in mid- air? He shook his head in disgust.

"Hurry up and wait." The old adage was in place. The flight was three hours late taking off. Mike again got antsy. He lectured himself. 'See? Good thing this guy is here. You might yet take a notion to run.'

They finally left only to land and take off twice more before arriving in Germany. By then it was the middle of the night. Not the best time to be assigned a bed in a barracks with other felons who had been sound asleep and were awakened by his arrival. He prayed they would understand and forgive him. He had enough on his plate without 'the guys' getting pissed.

Some thoughtful person had given him the best news yet. Lenny was already 'locked up' somewhere in the area. Although Mike had been taken there to testify at the court- martial, he hadn't thought about the possibility of accidentally running into Lenny. But, 'locked up' meant exactly that for Lenny. That had eased Mike's apprehensions. He was to be given a fair amount of 'freedom', in the sense that he would *not* be locked up and would be able to roam the grounds.

M. L. Verne

The more time that evolved and the more Mike thought about it, the more he realized how important it was for him that he'd been fully honest about everything. He'd come to the conclusion, in his mind, that Lenny was going to be the real loser because he'd been so devious. At least that's what he'd heard via the military grapevine. Still, he couldn't help feeling a sense of pity for the guy. He'd lost so much! And for what?

* * *

The waiting was long, tedious and often boring. That was the bad news. The good news was he'd been getting in shape, working hard on his physical condition. And, in the process, he'd been elated to discover his craving for cocaine was beginning to wane. Oh, it was still there and probably would be for a long time to come. It was the nature of the beast. He was eating three squares a day, substantial if not gourmet. And, he was playing ball. It caused him to think a lot about Teea and her athletic prowess. They were good thoughts, reminders of how he'd always admired her for staying in shape. It gave him added incentive to keep at it.

The ball games were the highlight of his days. Most of the team members were black and they had tagged Mike with a nickname....FLWG....'Flug'... 'funny little white guy'. Truly, *they* were the funny ones! Mike laughed with them until his sides ached. It was a great boon for his morale.

Even in the brig, rank has its privileges. Mike was the senior non-commissioned officer in the enlisted compound and he was respected. He had an idea that his gray hair had something to do with it. Also, his air of authority. As the days passed, his pride returned little by little, his determination to pay the price and get on with his life solidifying.

Occasionally, a phone call would come through from Teea or his parents. He couldn't call them so it was always a treat. He didn't know what Teea had told the boys. When they asked questions, he tried to evade straight answers, saying as little as possible without lying to them.

Then, without any warning, he felt Teea backing away. Nothing said specifically, just a gut feeling on his part. His sensitivity was at an all time high. He simply *knew*. Again, he got depressed.

His nefarious activities had affected many lives and he was only beginning to realize it. He'd been too wrapped up in the 'oh, pity poor me' syndrome. He was so contrite, too ashamed to answer letters. Eventually, Teea stopped calling. Her family and his siblings no longer wrote. That left his parents. They saw him through, loving him unconditionally, supporting him, being there.

54.

Breakfast was almost over when a runner stopped at his table to tell him he'd be expected to appear in court by o-eight thirty hours. He was to get into the basic seaman uniform which was complete degradation. White jumper, neckerchief, a get-up he hadn't worn in many, many years. No rank, no insignia, none of his hard and well-earned citations.

One thing he'd been thankful for ever since his troubles began. He'd never been handcuffed. Now, even though he'd been roaming the entire compound by himself, they cuffed him. To walk four blocks to the legal building. And if the basic uniform and handcuffs weren't enough humiliation, they made him wear an orange arm band with bold black letters which announced to the world 'BRIG'.

He'd thought angrily, 'If I live to be the thousand-year-old man, I'll not understand why they must kick a guy when he's down and almost out.'

His escort had led him into the courtroom and he was told to sit down in the rear row of seats. He glanced around at the surroundings and thought 'Lenny's getting better furniture. This *looks* like a court room.'

The judge's bench was elevated, built of dark wood and polished to a bright sheen. The American flag and the flag of the U.S. Navy stood at opposite sides and behind the chair the judge would occupy. The requisite tables were in place with an adequate number of chairs all around and there sat Lenny with his counsel.

'Wouldn't you know,' Mike smirked to himself. 'Way to go, man.' A gorgeous blonde Lieutenant, tall and willowy, attentive to her client and seriously business-like.

Lenny didn't know Mike was present which gave Mike an opportunity to study him. They hadn't met in quite a long while. Mike thought Lenny looked thinner. He also looked resplendent in his full dress summer whites, a stark and eye catching contrast to his gleaming black skin. A small lump of pity had formed in Mike's throat for an instant.

'This man was once my friend, on his way to a future filled with unlimited possibilities. We are neither one of us yet forty years old. What an enormous, odious, grotesque waste.'

His thoughts roamed, touching on past events. The night of the ill-fated dinner with their wives, the trip for Lenny and Cate that had been such a disaster, Lonzo's abuse at the hands of his father, the vile things he had put into his statement regarding himself, Mike, and his mother, that Lenny had purchased a ticket to run and leave him behind to carry the onus of their illegal activities….his short spurt of pity had turned to inner rage.

The judge entered, everyone stood, the court was called to order and the proceedings began. They were destined to go on and on. No short-lived, pre-fixed trial for the Lieutenant Commander! His attorney had obviously worked diligently on her client's case, commanding everyone's full attention with her presentation.

Lenny sat very straight, eyes front and glued on the judge. They held the same rank, both were black and both were militarily sharp looking.

Mike had gotten so absorbed in his thoughts he almost missed the calling of his name. He stood and walked slowly forward to the witness stand, studiously avoiding eye contact with Lenny and, quite out of the blue wondering, 'Where's Whitey?' He was never to know.

The lovely blonde Lieutenant wiped the floor with him. It took every last scrap of his inner strength to avoid bolting out of the building. He was being tried all over again! She accused him of everything he'd done and all of Lenny's activities too. She blatantly told the court that it was he, Mike, who had begun the operation, had recruited Lenny, had gotten the Nigerians to work for him, had made all of the arrangements for the trips in and out of Turkey.

"Your honor," she continued, "this man has built himself a large offshore bank account which he intends using for making more drug money, once he is out of custody and back into society. Not only did he deal drugs, a bad enough offense, but he also stole money from his drug partners. There is not a salvageable trace of goodness in this person, Your Honor!"

At one point she asked Mike a bizarre question, referring to the Nigerians. Mike couldn't help himself. He looked at Lenny with disbelief. Lenny had the balls to stare back at him with a sarcastic smirk on his face. Mike wanted to jump at the bastard and smack him in his lying mouth.

When it was all said and done, Mike was stand-up proud of his self control. He'd managed to remain totally cool, composed, credible. He'd told the absolute truth, beginning to end. He'd spoken promptly, respectfully, firmly and up front to the judge. The court had listened carefully, appreciating Mike's forthrightness, his military bearing and demeanor.

When he was finally dismissed, the judge thanked him! Better yet, he'd referred to him as 'Chief.' Unprecedented!

Sitting through Lenny's testimony was the most difficult thing Mike had ever done. From start to finish it was all lies. It was obvious he was out to try and save his skin any way he could. He swore under oath that he'd done nothing illegal, that it was all Mike's gig, that he, Lenny, was an innocent bystander who had been sucked into an undertow against his will.

He had sounded like a fool but was fooling no one.

The court bought none of it. Lenny was sentenced to twelve years in a federal penitentiary. He was stripped of his rank, all pay and benefits, dishonorably discharged and fined a huge sum.

He began to weep. Mike was horrified. Phlegm ran in thick globs from his nostrils, long strands of spittle dripped from his mouth, all of it congealing on the front of his once immaculate, spiffy dress uniform. Some of the slime caught in his ribbons and hung further down. It was a disgusting spectacle. Mike was certain he'd seen the judge rolling his eyes with contempt.

Lenny was asked if he had anything to say. Lenny had nodded 'yes' and turned to look at Mike. Actually, he stared straight through Mike. His face was a study in contempt. He then turned back to the judge and said,

M. L. Verne

"Your Honor, I want to apologize to Chief Steele for all of the trouble I've caused him and his family."

Briefly, Mike wished he could believe in the sincerity of the words. He knew better. There would *never* be any remorse from the man. Mike would have staked his life on it.

Abruptly, as everyone stood while the judge left the room, Mike was filled with an enormous sense of relief. It had been so unexpected he'd reeled with it. 'It's over!'

His escort led him back to his area and he knew, as he walked, he'd do what he had to do and would, in due time, re-enter the free world a better man for having had the experience.

He walked tall, pride surging back into his soul, his silver braced smile shining in the sunlight.

* * *

They were destined to meet one more time. It was unexpected. Both of them were in the departure area at the flight line, accompanied by their escorts, awaiting their boarding calls. They were on their way back home to begin serving their sentences.

Mike's escort suggested they shake hands. Mike extended his hand in a friendly gesture, an offering of forgiveness.

Lenny gave Mike a look so filled with hatred it was scary. Then he growled, "Fuck you, man," and walked away.

It was enough to make Mike's blood boil.

EPILOGUE

As expected, Teea divorced Mike. Initially, he'd been devastated. She'd been his wife for almost thirteen years. As time passed, both of them settled in; she in Colorado, he in the brig and looking forward to an early release. Eventually, they were able to establish a different kind of relationship; cool in nature, civilized, manageable.

It took a while for the twins to understand that their lives were changed forever. They had been very angry at their dad. For a while, they even refused to speak to him on the phone. But, as the months rolled by, they came to terms with all of it, showing uncommon maturity in their final acceptance of the inevitable. Mike and his boys re-built a loving and satisfying rapport. It was enough.

When Teea was finally able to tell Mike she had left him alone in Italy because of Lenny's torturous behavior, his harassment of her, it was the cathartic release she'd needed As for Mike, he'd been through so much by then he wasn't surprised, shocked or enraged. It was just more of Lenny's treachery and it was history. Nothing could be done to change it. For him, it was sufficient that she'd trusted him enough to tell him. He respected her for that.

Both Admiral Williams and Commander Keef retired with full honors. They agreed not to communicate with each other. Neither one of them spoke very often of their Naval careers. Each of them retained a personal measure of paranoia, a fitting legacy. One lived in Florida, the other in Oregon.

Gus Keef had a heavy burden to carry. The events he had shared with Admiral Kingston on the day of his death would haunt Gus forever.

He'd been called into the admiral's office where the admiral had handed him a copy of the latest report just received from the NCIS 'Operation White Mustang' in Italy. His own name, Commander Gus Keef, jumped out at him off the page as did Admiral Gregory Williams'. What he read was…"both are suspected of involvement in drug activities at some level yet to be determined."

There it was, in black and white, just what Gus had feared. When he glanced at Admiral Kingston, the look in the man's eyes was empty, bottomless, lifeless. Neither one of them spoke. They stared at each other for a brief moment, then Gus turned and left the room. He never again saw Admiral Kingston alive.

Later that day, when he was informed of the admiral's apparent suicide, he went into shock, then quickly realized it would be his responsibility to meet with the press.

But first, he found a secure phone and called his pal Greg for advice.

"Destroy that report and all copies. The information will come to light eventually but meanwhile, let me see what I can do to suppress it. Tell the reporters the admiral was despondent over personal criticism of him in the media as well as the on-going problems the Navy is having. That should hold them until I can put a lid on it."

Gus Keef never knew, nor did he ever ask, if the admiral really had that much clout or if it was a simple case of his 'having the goods' on someone holding more rank than he did. In any case, time went by and nothing came of it.

As with all sensational events, something else came along to take the attention of the public away from the Navy and its loss of a fine leader. World affairs replaced even the most sensational rumors surrounding Admiral Kingston's death.

Of all the personnel who had served with the admiral during his long and distinguished career, no one would remember him with more respect and genuine sorrow than Chief Petty Officer Mikel J. Steele, United States Navy.

M. L. Verne

CODE NAME: WHITE MUSTANG

Excerpts from

PANORAMA

NATO Community, Naples, Italy
Friday, May 17th, 1996

"…NCIS arrest thirteen on charges of drug smuggling
in a pre-dawn raid…sailors suspected of conspiring
with area non-Italian civilians to smuggle
heroin and cocaine into Italy from Turkey
and other European countries…
seized in excess of four-and-one-half kilograms
of heroin and several thousands of
dollars…arrested several third-world
country nationals living in the area
who were enticing military
members with promises of cash…
task force code named
Operation White Stallion
represents the largest counter-drug
operation ever, in Europe…

M. L. Verne

CODE NAME: WHITE MUSTANG

Excerpts from

The Associated Press
June 1998

TOO LATE, ADMIRAL AWARDED HIS V'S

Admiral Jeremy "Mike" Boorda was entitled to wear
combat decorations on his uniform,
the challenged Viet Nam awards that
led to his suicide…
…when his right to wear the decorations was
about to be questioned,
…the first enlisted man to become
the Chief of Naval Operations in the service's
198-year history went home,
wrote a note to 'my sailors' stepped into
his garden and shot himself.…

M. L. Verne

ABOUT THE AUTHOR

This novel is the first of several more books the author is working on. After raising a family of eight and returning to college to complete a nursing degree, she is now retired and spends her time writing and traveling. She lives with her husband in Washington state in the summer and in Arizona in the winter.

Printed in the United States
824100001B